Suicide

squeeze

Robert Miles Novels
Recount
Rebound
Rematch
A Capital Killing

Suicide squeeze

David Everson

ST. MARTIN'S PRESS   NEW YORK

Fantasy camps are real. And Illinois has riverboat gambling. But Major
League Dream Game Camp, Inc., Casinos for Kids, and all else between
these pages is fiction about fantasy.

Design by Dawn Niles

Library of Congress Cataloging-in-Publication Data
Everson, David.
    Suicide squeeze.
        p.   cm.
    "A Thomas Dunne book."
    ISBN 0-312-05520-X
    I. Title.
    PS3555.V385S85   1991   813'.54—dc20   90-15558

First Edition: March 1991

10   9   8   7   6   5   4   3   2   1

For the '69 Cubs, the best team never to win the National League Pennant.

And for Judith, sine qua non.

Suicide

squeeze

It was midafternoon of the last day of May as I left the capitol by the automatic doors at the east exit. A stunned House had just adjourned for the day. The Speaker had struck without warning, catching the Guv and the House Republicans with their pin stripes down.

I strolled past the statues of Stephen Douglas and Abe Lincoln, paired for eternity. Both were covered with clear plastic—for cleaning. Over time, they had taken on that moldy green characteristic of outdoor statuary.

At Lincoln's foot, I spied a bright new penny.

I picked it up. Ex-ballplayers aren't any less attuned to omens than Nancy Reagan.

It was a warm day as I headed up Capitol Street. On my left, I passed the construction site of the new state library. The names of thirty Illinois writers—including Oak Park's Ernest Hemingway—were already carved in stone in a frieze around the building, which was evidently carefully designed to look thirty years old the day it opened.

I walked under the railroad overpass to Fourth Street where I could look south and see the Guv's mansion. The odds were better that I would win the Illinois lottery—without buying a ticket—than that he would spend the night in Springpatch. The Guv had made Chicago the unofficial state capital, and he was out of the country more often than Secretary of State Jim Baker.

As I walked, I pondered the Speaker's latest coup—"Casinos for Kids." My leader—the Speaker of the Illinois House of Representatives—had taken a sudden tack in the wind, abandoning a long-held position against extending games of chance in Illinois, and passed riverboat gambling in less than four hours. He had totally short-circuited the normal legislative process.

Being Speaker means you get to create your own norms.

His plan had targeted all the money from the floating casinos for elementary and secondary ed and had cut the Guv out of the action completely, adding to the Speaker's already considerable reputation as the Silk Razor of Illinois politics.

He cuts your throat and you don't even notice until the blood drips onto your shirt collar.

I fingered the penny in my pocket. I could have increased it a thousandfold that day if I had bet that in less than a month I would be playing shortstop under the lights in Wrigley Field, the Chicago Cubs would be in the hunt for the National League East title, and I would be up to my batting helmet in a murder investigation.

"I were you," Mitch Norris, peering at me over his reading glasses, said, "I'd pay the ransom."

I paused, awaiting the punch line.

"Your barber's been kidnapped."

I grinned and touched the back of my mane. "Hey, I'm not due for my semiannual clipping until July. I got a whole month left on the warranty on this one."

I had just stuck my head inside the office door of Midcontinental Op—that's me—and Associate—that's Mitch. I'm Robert Miles, central Illinois's premier—and practically only—sleuth.

The office had some new furnishings. Mitch's old war club, a 38-ounce Louisville Slugger with his name on the trademark, was propped up against the desk next to a pine tar rag. I rested a hip on the corner of the desk and gripped the bat.

Mitch took off his reading glasses and lowered a slick tab-loid to his lap.

Each morning, Mitch asks himself: What would the late baseball maverick Bill Veeck wear today? The answer is *never* a three-piece suit. Today Mitch sported a bright orange tropical shirt and yellow- and green-checked Bermuda shorts. He was leaning back in the swivel chair, resting legs garbed in lemon socks and feet in black, size 13 tennis shoes on the desk.

"You look like the golf pro at Putt-Putt," I said. "What're you reading?"

"*American Spectator*," he said. "Kind of a hoot. The editor thinks he's H. L. Mencken," he said. "Makes William F. Buckley look centrist. It's mildly diverting. I especially like the inside of the back page where they highlight the latest ravings of the loony left." He grinned. "Bobby, I think the only true Marxists left in the world are in American universities."

Thinking about some of the faculty at Lincoln Heritage University, where Lisa teaches, I said, "Tell me about it." I touched the tip of one of his tennies. "When did you break the skis off these?"

He removed his feet from the desk, sat up, dumped the *American Spectator* into the wastebasket, and reached for some papers on the desk.

I picked up the bat and rested it on my right shoulder. "What's with the lumber? Going to cut it up and sell it for firewood?"

He grunted, "Nah," and took a stub of a cigar out of his shirt pocket and stuck it in the corner of his mouth. Deliberately, he picked up a box of kitchen matches, pulled one out, scratched it on the box, and lit the stub. He took a long drag and exhaled smoke. "Check this out," he said. He handed me a brochure and a letter.

The brochure was glossy—cream-colored paper with dark blue print. A picture on the front showed a locker room with white Chicago Cubs and gray New York Mets uniforms hanging from opposite racks. There was a blue logo—a triangle of a ball, bat, and glove—in the upper left-hand corner. Under it was a blue imprint: "P&D Productions." The heading announced: "Major League Dream Game Camp, Inc."

The text read: "Always dreamed of playing alongside real big leaguers? Now you can. A limited number of spaces are available in the week-long Dream Game Camp to be held in beautiful Wrigley Field. The highlight of the camp will be a night game in Wrigley Field pitting the '69 Cubs versus the '69 Mets. You will suit up and play with the real Cubs or Mets. For information, call 312— . . ."

I put down the brochure and glanced at the letter. It invited Mitch Norris to be a player/coach in the camp. For two weeks. At a substantial salary. The starting date was two weeks from today. The letter was signed by Joseph "Pork" Barelli.

I turned my palms up. "So?"

"I'd really like to do it," Mitch said. "If you don't need me. It's a two-week deal." He rotated his right hand. "A chance to strap it on one last time. My comeback."

"Comeback implies you were somewhere." I laid the bat back against the desk.

He laced his battered fingers behind his head and leaned back in the swivel chair. "Bobby," he said deliberately, "I'm the one drawing a big-league pension."

He had me there. I shrugged. "Fill me in."

"Sports nostalgia is hot right now. You got the Seniors Tour in golf. Old timers' games in baseball and basketball. And the various fantasy camps. This particular version is Pork Barelli's brainchild," he said.

"Barelli?" I closed my eyes and retrieved an image of a left-handed batter peeking over his right shoulder and spraying line drives all over National League parks. "The old Cub and Cardinal pinch hitter?"

He nodded. "Played for the Reds and Angels too."

"I thought Randy Hundley invented these fantasy camps."

"He did." Mitch leaned forward, picked up his bat, and started rubbing it with the pine tar rag. "Barelli used to work with him. Now Barelli's a competitor. Supposedly, he's got some well-heeled Chicago backers. I just talked to him on the phone. According to the Porker, this is the crème de la crème of camps. One full week in Wrigley. Only a limited number of campers for each team. Lots of personal attention. At a normal camp, there's about forty to fifty guys. The traditional thing is that on the last day, the campers play the ex–big leaguers. Get their ass stomped."

I frowned. "If the camp is one week, why do you need two?"

"Barelli thinks that the coaches need the extra time to get ready to play. He's serious about trying to win this game. He flat hates the Mets."

"I'll bet."

"The dream game plays on the fact that this is the twentieth anniversary of 1969."

I covered my eyes. "Bad karma," I said slowly, "still coming 'round."

"Right. Cubs blew it big time in September. Remember the black cat game in Shea?"

"Thanks for the memory. Mitch, I suffered through the whole collapse at a distance. I was playing in Double A in Texas. After a while, I stopped looking at the box scores. Even so, it put me in a slump."

"How could anyone tell?" He put down the bat and picked up the brochure. "In this game, Cub campers will play on the same team with ex-Cubs against Met campers and ex-Mets."

"Met campers will come all the way to Wrigley for a week?"

"Hey, guys pay big bucks to fly from all over the country to the Arizona and Florida fantasy camps. This fantasy kick—it's part of feeling good about America."

"Don't worry, be happy?"

He nodded.

I scratched my head. "You didn't play for the Cubs in sixty-nine."

He nodded. "True. Sixty-five and part of sixty-six. The rules are a little loose about the coaches. Hundley has a lot of the sixty-nine Cubs tied up. Anyway, Barelli hurt his knee a week ago in a camp in St. Louis. Can play, but doesn't want to catch. So he called me. Whatta you say, Bobby?"

I shrugged. "We're not that busy." I paused. "But you know the Speaker. He's unpredictable."

Mitch nodded. "Casinos for Kids."

"You heard?"

He inclined his head toward the transistor radio on the window ledge.

"What if I said no?"

He shrugged. "I'd probably go anyway."

I grinned. "Okay. Just make sure you kick a little Met ass," I said.

"Want to tag along?"

"No can do," I said. "I promised to take Lisa to Mad City."

2

The next morning, I went for a long run, stopped at McDonald's on the Old State Capitol Plaza for a power breakfast, and it was nearly 10:00 when I moseyed down the hallway toward the office. I spotted a slender woman standing in front of the office door, smoking. She noticed me, took a last puff, and stamped out her cigarette on the floor.

As I approached, key in hand, she looked at me expectantly. She wore a drab brown suit, white blouse, no hose, and flats. Her hair was dull blonde with a slight trace of gray and tucked up in a bun. She wore thick glasses and no makeup.

The mouse in the brown paper wrapper.

"Mr. Miles?" she said timidly.

"Yes."

"Perhaps I should have made an appointment. But I was down for the day. With my husband, Arthur. Your message service said . . ."

I spread my hands. "No problem. I'm running a little late this morning."

"Nathan Wood suggested I see you."

I frowned, involuntarily.

She reacted to it. "Is that a problem?"

I shook my head. Wood was a downstate Democratic Rep from Urbana/Champaign, a criminal defense attorney, and a low-life sleaze. His constituency included the University of

Illinois. He never saw an appropriation for higher ed or a trendy liberal cause he couldn't support. But around the General Assembly, his word was worth as much as last week's Mexican peso. His firm defended the scum of central Illinois.

Thanks to me, the Speaker had joint custody of Wood's family jewels, and as a result, Wood threw some routine investigative work my way now and then. Business was slow. I could not afford to be squeamish about where my cases came from. "Probably not."

I opened the office door and said, "Why don't you come in and tell me what it's all about?" I went around my desk and sat in the swivel chair and tried to look professional.

Her eyes inspected the small office. She narrowed them at the dusty desk, the single gray filing cabinet, drawer half open, and the small bookcase crammed to overflowing with *Illinois Blue Books* and several other out-of-date reference works. Her lips pursed. I wished I had at least emptied the wastebasket.

This month.

A red Classic Coke can peeked out of the top of the pile.

Waste is such a terrible thing to mind, I thought.

She made an almost imperceptible shrug and then glanced over my right shoulder. Her eyes lit up for a moment. "What a nice view," she said.

I nodded. Midcon's office is in an alcove on the second floor of the old Leland Hotel, three blocks east of the statehouse. Through the dust streaks, my window afforded a variety of impressionist views of the capitol dome, depending on the time of day and the weather. Today, it gleamed in the bright June sun.

"My name is Kennedy, Mrs. Anne P. Kennedy," she said. "Anne with an e." She sat down in the straight-backed chair, adjusting her skirt, so that no glimpse of knee would show.

I made a note of the name on a scratch pad and underlined the e. "Down from where?" I asked.

"Winnetka."

Chicago. North Shore. I frowned again.

Again she visibly reacted to my expression. She started to stand. "Maybe I've come at a bad time, . . ." she said uncertainly.

I put up my right hand in a stop sign and smiled. "I don't get much business from the Chicago suburbs," I said. "Especially the North Shore."

She nodded and sat back down. She reached into a small, brown, leather purse and pulled out a spotless white handkerchief and unnecessarily wiped her oval face. "My husband," she said with pride, "is Arthur J. Kennedy."

"White Shoes" Kennedy, I thought. Not just a lobbyist. *The* lobbyist of choice. Former colleague and good friend of the Speaker. A flashy dresser who drove in the legislative fast lane. A key player in the Casinos for Kids coup. I couldn't fit White Shoes with the mouse in front of me. I suppressed another frown. "The hired gun?"

She narrowed her gray-green eyes. "We prefer Legislative Affairs Consultant."

"Contract lobbyist," I said, seeking terminological middle ground.

"Arthur's a close friend of Nathan Wood," she said. "They served together in the House. So when this problem came up, . . ." She paused, gulped, and dabbed her eyes with the handkerchief. But I saw no sign of tears.

I looked more closely at her. Good skin. From what I could tell, all the parts in the right places. With a minimum amount of attention, she could have been quite attractive.

I had half a mind that this was a carefully contrived performance. "What is the problem?" I asked.

She gulped again. "My daughter, Kris . . . Kristin . . . she's . . . missing. Well, not exactly missing. We just don't know *precisely* where she is. We're terribly worried. She's in Florida, we think."

"That narrows the search," I said. "How old is Kris?"

"Kristin. Nineteen. I prefer Kristin. Kris sounds so juvenile. She, naturally, prefers Kris." She shook her head at the perversity of teenage daughters.

"How long has she been 'not exactly missing'?"

"About three weeks. Almost a month, actually."

I widened my eyes. "You haven't heard anything from her?"

She shook her head in response.

"She normally lives at home?"

She shook her head again. "Only in the summer. And not much of the time then. She's often up in Wisconsin at the lake. She was at school. Southern Illinois University—Carbondale. She left in early May before taking finals. She usually keeps in touch every week. We hadn't heard from her. We tried calling her. She was gone. The school had no idea . . ."

"Roommate?"

"She has her own apartment."

"Have you tried the police?"

She almost gasped. "Heavens, no. This is not a police matter. And the negative publicity. Arthur . . ." She shook her head at the mere thought of it.

"Why do you think she's in Florida?"

"We don't know."

"Let me rephrase that. What makes you think she's there as opposed to, say, North Dakota?"

"She has a gold VISA card that Arthur gave her. And a telephone credit card. We have obtained some charge receipts from an airline, a car rental agency, a gasoline station, two motels, a restaurant . . ."

I frowned. "So quickly?"

"Arthur has some influence at the National Bank of Illinois. That's where he got the card. The calls were charged to our home phone."

"I see. Where in Florida?"

"She seems to have flown from St. Louis to Gainesville. Through Atlanta. Rented a car in Gainesville."

I leaned back in my chair. "Do you have any family in Florida?"

She shook her head.

"Friends?"

"No. But we own a condo in Sarasota."

"Think she could be there?"

"It's possible. But we've tried to call. No answer."

The job sounded like a laugher to me. Follow the paper trail. Work on my tan. I told her the rate. "Two-fifty a day, five hundred retainer, expenses."

She nodded. "That's fine. Will a check do?"

I nodded. "Do you have a picture of Kris . . . tin?"

She nodded again. "Yes, I do." She dug into her brown purse and pulled out her checkbook and what I assumed would be a standard graduation portrait. She handed it to me. I did a double take. Kristin had posed hipshot in an azure bikini. She was standing on a white sand beach with a skinny, long-haired young man in bright red trunks. Deep blue water of a lake in the background. Her long blonde hair had that artfully tangled look. Her eyes appeared to be seawater blue-green. Her smile had more than a trace of pout. Her figure was sensational. I raised my eyebrows.

A faint tinge of red rose from Mrs. Kennedy's cheeks. "I know," she said. "I was in a hurry. This was the only picture I could lay my hands on."

Somehow, I doubted that. "Who's the boy?"

Her lip curled a fraction. "Her half brother, Kevin." She shook her head wearily. "He's such a bad influence on Kristin."

"Your stepson?"

"Absolutely not," she said quickly. "Peter's . . ." She paused and shook her head.

"Any idea why she skipped out?"

She frowned. "Her motivation is not an issue."

"Boyfriend?"

She shook her head, looking annoyed.

"Family problems?"

She took out a gold fountain pen and started to fill in the check. "No."

"I see," I said.

I didn't. I didn't get any of this. Inwardly, I shrugged.

She handed me the check, some credit card receipts and a phone bill. "Find her," she said curtly, all tentativeness gone. "Tell us where she is. Do not, under any circumstances, attempt to contact her."

"Contact" as a verb. Nero Wolfe would have had Archie Goodwin toss her out of the office for such a linguistic faux pas.

Wonder what old Nero would have thought of "hopefully"?

She nodded significantly at the picture. "Do I make myself clear?"

This is not a hands-on job, I thought. I nodded.

"Call me immediately. Arthur and Nathan will handle the rest."

After she left, I called Mitch down in Auburn. "Can you watch the office for a couple of days?"

"Sure thing. All I'm doing is scouting high school tournament games. You going out of town?"

"Yes."

"Just be back before I go to camp."

"No problem."

"Where you going?"

"Florida."

"In June? Be sure to get out-of-season rates."

Then I called Lisa. She's my wife, but we have a no-fault separation. Hey, it works for us. And we get to file a joint tax return. "Lisa, I'm outta here for a few days. Can you stop by the apartment and feed Clockie?"

My fierce, orange watchcat, Clockwork.

"Sure. We still on for Madison?"

"Absolutely."

"Where you going?"

"Florida."

"In June. Be sure to use a sunscreen."

3

My working vacation lasted two full days, a large part of which was spent in airports, on airplanes, in motels and cars. I logged zip beach time. I didn't need a sunscreen—it rained both days.

Airline deregulation has long since driven all the major airlines out of Springfield. I hate small commuter flights. The ones where they ask you how much you weigh before you board. So—like many Springpatchers—I drove to St. Louis and parked my red '81 Toyota Tercel in the long-term lot and flew out of there on Eastern to Gainesville through Atlanta.

General Sherman had to change at Atlanta on his march to the sea.

It was late morning when we landed in a drizzle in Gainesville, a north-central Florida city of about 80,000, home of the University of Florida Gators.

The girl at the car rental counter in the ultramodern Gainesville airport could not positively identify Kristin Kennedy as the young woman who had rented a Pontiac Sunbird convertible on May 4. She gave me a cute shrug. "She wore these huge purple sunglasses and a big straw hat." She frowned. "I had the impression she was somewhat older than nineteen. More like midtwenties." She looked at the forms and said, "The car was returned here on the twenty-fourth."

"Thanks." I rented a black Dodge Omni from her. It had a cracked window and tended to die at traffic lights. It was raining hard as I drove into Gainesville.

My first stop was a multistory yellow and green Holiday Inn at the corner of 13th and University, close to the campus of the university. I slipped on my light tan jacket and hustled into the lobby. I killed time in the coffee shop reading the baseball stats in USA Today and waiting for the afternoon clerk to come on duty.

Shortly after 1:00 P.M., he arrived and told me he thought the blonde in the picture might be the woman who registered as Kris Kennedy and spent one night there on May 4. He also mentioned the big sunglasses and hat. After I slipped him a twenty, he showed me a copy of her bill. She had made a long-distance call from the room. Within the 904 area code. North Florida, I thought. A clue. I made a note of the number and slipped it into my jacket.

It was still raining as I drove out University past the campus. The most prominent sight was the large white dome of the sports arena. My next stop on the old paper trail was the Oaks Mall at the edge of Gainesville, just off I-75.

From sea to shining sea, the main strips of every American town now look the same. Burger King, Taco Bell, Pizza Hut, Wendy's, the Golden Arches. Except for the palm trees and the names of the grocery stores—Publix and Winn Dixie— Gainesville was no different.

Across from the mall was the large North Florida Hospital with a small duck pond and attractive grounds. Traffic around the mall—which could have been plunked down anywhere from Bangor, Maine, to El Paso, Texas—was heavy. I parked as close as I could, dodged the raindrops, and went in through Sears.

Kris Kennedy had purchased $345 worth of sports clothes at a dress shop for young women in the mall. But the clerk who had waited on her was a student who had gone home for the summer.

I was hungry when I left the mall, so I drove to a Perkins Restaurant up the way, and ordered the chicken-fried steak. As I ate, I looked at the three remaining receipts. In late May, Kris had filled her car with gas at a station in Micanopy, about fifteen miles south of Gainesville. I got a creampuff for dessert and left feeling bloated.

I got on I-75 south and presently rolled through a large marshy area called Paynes Prairie. I turned off the interstate at Micanopy. It was now late afternoon.

Micanopy could have been the locale for a southern gothic set in the 1930s. Muddy side streets. Moss-covered trees. Old multistory mansions. The main drag was nothing but antique stores. You could get aspirin only in an apothecary jar.

At the edge of town, I found the Payless gas station and waited at the full-service pump for what seemed like five minutes. I tapped the horn. No one came. I got out in the rain and ran into the station. A wiry attendant in a grease-stained uniform ambled out of the garage. "Sorry," he said. His name patch said "Billy Jack."

Billy Jack?

I showed him Kris's picture and described the car. "Billy Jack," I said, "have you ever seen this girl before?"

"Damned straight," he said. "I remember *her.*" He grinned and cupped his hands in front of his chest. "Yeah. Who could forget? Little gal—big sunglasses—big knockers."

"She say anything about where she might be headed?"

"*She* didn't." He grinned some more. I could see black rot in his back teeth.

"Someone did?"

"The yo-yo with her."

I handed him a twenty. "Do you remember what he said?"

"Damned straight. Guess he didn't think I was moving fast

enough. Told me to 'haul ass, meat.' Said he didn't want to be late for the race."

"What race?"

He shrugged. "Might'a been a drag race in Gainesville or a dog race down in Tampa."

"What'd he look like?"

"Dark hair, mustache, skinny bastard. A real jerk."

On 75 between Micanopy and Ocala, I passed numerous large horse farms and orange groves. At Ocala, I drove through a McDonald's to get a Coke. Then I continued on down 75 past Wildwood to the Tampa Bay area for my next stop, a Red Lobster. It was close to 8:00. The Latin-looking waiter remembered the blonde with the sunglasses and straw hat and the "skinny bastard."

The waiter tugged at his handlebar mustache and said, "I *never* forget a bad tip. We were really busy. I had to give them a table in the No Smoking section and *then* take flak about it. Before I turned around, she lit up. I had to ask her not to smoke. The guy got all bent out of shape about it. Then to top everything, *they* had one hell of an argument. Screaming and yelling. Ended up, she threw a drink in his face. Gin and tonic." He shook his head. "Guy deserved it. A real asshole."

I went out to the car and thought about my next move. Mr. Magoo could have followed the track this far. I could head on down to Sarasota or go back to Gainesville and check out the Hilton Inn.

Sometimes I am not the most efficient investigator. I took I-75 back to Gainesville. At 11:25 I checked into the Hilton where Kris had stayed on the twenty-third of May. No one remembered her.

I went to my room and turned on the TV to "Headline News" hoping to catch the Cub score. I learned that the Baby Bruins had lost to the Astros. I shook my head in resignation and pulled the piece of paper out of my jacket and punched out the number that appeared on Kris's bill from the Holiday Inn. The line was busy. I'd try again later. I slipped the number back into my jacket pocket. I called Mitch in Auburn.

He said, "Mrs. Anne—with an e—Kennedy wants you to call." He gave me the number. The area code was 414.

Not Chicago.

I punched it out. When I got her on the line, she said, "You can stop looking for Kristin."

"Why?"

"She's home."

I flew back the next morning. About twenty miles out of St. Louis on I-55, there's a smart-ass billboard put up by the airport authority that never fails to piss me off. It says smugly, "If you had flown, you'd be in Springfield by now."

4

A week later, I stood at the Speaker's third-floor window looking at the east grounds of the capitol. Both north and south fountains spewed small blue geysers of water. Beyond the lawn, I saw a well-tanned, bare-chested jogger running south on Second. A blue and yellow cab spewing sooty exhaust started up from the light.

The Speaker sat behind his immaculate desk making red check marks on a yellow legal pad next to tasks completed. His suit jacket was hung neatly on a rack in the corner, and he wore a crisp white shirt and a yellow tie with blue triangles.

I was the next check mark on his agenda.

I had just returned from Lake County—one of the suburban "collar" counties—just north of Cook. It had not been my favorite kind of work—taking depositions from witnesses to a hit-and-run. The accused was the son of Republican state rep, Peter Duke. I had figured I was just adding ammo to the Speaker's opposition research files.

I soon found out I was wrong.

"Fast Freddy" Martin slithered into the room from the outer office. He gave me a sour glance. He wore a light blue shirt with white stripes and an almost clerical white collar. His sleeves were rolled up precisely below the elbow. His tie was loosened exactly to the first button on his shirt. Black and gold suspenders held up his baggy gray slacks just a quarter-inch over his gray loafers. He wore no belt and he smoked a cigarillo. "Miles," he said out of the corner of his mouth. "What's the good word?" He stood with his back against the wall, ready to make notes on his yellow legal pad.

"Yes, Robert," the Speaker said folding his hands. "What did you learn about Peter's son?"

Peter? "Kevin Duke is in deep doo-doo."

There I go again. George Bush is my role model.

The Speaker's poker face betrayed no immediate reaction. Then his pale blue eyes frosted. "Oh," he said softly.

He's pissed, I thought.

Fast Freddy scowled. "Based on what?" he challenged. He bounced off the wall a step. "I heard he has a strong defense. The guy was lying in the road, for Christ's sake. Probably drunk."

"Bullshit," I said.

"Miles," Fast said. "Get with the program."

The Speaker shot a laser-blue bolt at him. "Let Robert continue."

Fast flushed.

I blinked. This was not going the way I had anticipated. Fast was acting like the kid's defense attorney. "Based on the facts," I said.

"Totally circumstantial," Fast snapped.

"But," I said, "consider the totality of the circumstances."

"Summarize," the Speaker said.

I shrugged. "Not much to tell. The press accounts are basically accurate."

"'Basically,'" Fast Freddy sneered. "The only resemblance between what gets in the media and what actually happened is purely incidental."

I rubbed my eyes. I tried for a Joe Friday matter of factness. "Kevin Duke was clocked at sixty-three miles an hour in a school zone." I held up one finger. "Speeding."

"School's not in session," Fast countered.

"The speed limit is forty-five when school is *not* in session." I held up a second finger. "He ran a red light, *incidentally* smashing into an upright pedestrian in a crosswalk. Instant brussel sprout. If they pull the plug on the life-support system, Kevin Duke is looking at a vehicular homicide charge." I held up the third finger. "Then he fled the scene of the accident. Hit-and-run." I held up the fourth. "Finally he tried to avoid the police in a high-speed chase and crashed into a police car. Fleeing to avoid arrest, damage to public property." I held up the thumb. "And one for the thumb," I added. "He failed the breath test. They got him on tape trying to crawl a white line. DUI."

"The test was given two hours after the accident," Fast said.

I snickered. "Because he fled the scene. You want to argue that he smashed the guy, then got smashed himself? You think that *helps* the case? You should see his priors."

"Prejudicial," Fast said.

"You bet. Get this. The vanity plate on his $25,000 fire-engine-red Porsche says 'Bigbang2.' Think how that will play with a jury."

The Speaker's face was impassive. He made a temple of his hands. "I see. Are there any mitigating circumstances?"

I shook my head. "Not that I'm aware of."

"Loopholes?"

"There are always loopholes," Fast said.

His credo.

I nodded. "One. Maybe."

"Spill it," Fast snapped.

I shrugged. "One detail. The eyewitnesses disagree on how many people were in Kevin's car. Three say just one. Two say two."

"That's a hell of a detail," Fast said. "I'd call it a massive contraction."

"I was glad to see that Fast Freddy had not lost his ability to mangle the English language.

The Speaker frowned. "But when the car finally was stopped by the police?"

I shrugged. "Just Kev."

"Look into it," the Speaker said. "You talked to Kevin Duke?"

I shook my head. "He's been incommunicado."

"I see. That's unfortunate, Robert. Leaves a gap."

I rolled my hand over. "I could try again."

"Do that. I'll speak to Peter about it. Turn your preliminary report over to Nathan."

"Who?"

"Wood," Fast Freddy said.

"Nathan Wood?"

"Close-captioned for the hearing impaired," Fast cracked.

"Wood's defending him?" I asked.

The Speaker nodded. "It would, of course, be unwise for Pomper and Duke to take the case. Nathan is good at what he does."

"Defending the indefensible," I said.

He sighed. "Alfred, give me your take on the short-term political consequences."

Fast perked up. His field of expertise. "Duke's Senate race?" He shook his head. "Minimal. It's a Republican district. Our candidate is a sacramental lamb."

The Speaker nodded. "What about the longer term?"

Fast pulled on his suspenders and thought for a few seconds. "If he goes for statewide office—especially governor—it could come back to haunt him. The level of media scrutiny goes up geologically. What your family does becomes your responsibility."

"So a favorable verdict is highly desirable? In the long run?"

Fast nodded.

Favorable for Peter Duke, a Republican, I thought. But what about the Illinois *Democratic* Party? What was the Speaker's game?

The Speaker picked up his silver gavel and toyed with it. "Maybe we need more time to build a credible defense for Kevin. Maybe we should try to get the trial postponed until after the special Senate election."

Fast Freddy nodded. "By that time, the whole issue could be mute."

5

"That's the ugliest tie since the Iran-Iraq stalemate," I said as I collapsed into a canvas-backed chair in Ben Gerald's cubicle at the *Springfield Journal Review*. Ben's their top political columnist. "What can you tell me about Peter Duke?"

Ben squinted at me through his thick horn-rimmed glasses. He fingered his wide hand-painted tie. He picked a rubber band off his desk and faked snapping it at me. Then he tossed it to me. "Don't say I never gave you anything."

I caught it. "Huh?"

"Tie that ponytail down."

I grinned. "Duke?"

"Didn't you read my profile?"

"I must of been out of town," I said.

"You missed a journalistic classic." He dug around on his desk. "Got a copy here somewhere. What's your interest?"

"Just curious."

He stared at me skeptically. "Miles, you have the normal curiosity of a tree stump." He pushed glasses back on his forehead. "Except when you're working for the Man." He frowned in concentration. "Peter Duke . . . one of the senior Republican members of the House . . . always a maverick . . . now running for the state Senate to fill the open seat caused by an unexpected resignation. Partner in a hotshot Chicago law firm with Harold Pomper. World-class blowhard. Mr. Windy City. Pomper, that is. Ladies' man. Duke, I mean. Harold's own true love is the sound of his baritone. You know he's heading up the commission."

"Ben, could we confine ourselves to Duke?"

"Sure. Progressive Republican. Pro-choice, pro-environment. Pro–civil rights. Almost a liberal—except for one small defect—he's the point man for the gun lobby in the General Assembly. Thinks there's a constitutional right to bear a bazooka. I heard something about him recently." He closed his eyes. Nodded. "His kid's in the shit?"

I shrugged.

"You're working for Mach-2?"

That was Ben's pet name for the Speaker since Casinos for Kids. Machiavelli's *The Prince,* the sequel. I shrugged again.

He frowned in concentration. "'Course you are." He grinned. "One of our reporters picked up some scuttlebutt that Nate 'the Skate' Wood was defending Kevin Duke. Lots of luck there—unless the little slug bribes the jury." He picked up a pencil and tapped it against his teeth. "Wood wouldn't take a crap unless the Speaker approved. You're the Speaker's gumshoe." He nodded. "I believe I have a scoop. The Speaker is helping one of his political opponents defend his son in a hit-and-run case. Interesting."

I nodded. "You didn't get this from me."

"How are you involved?"

"Interviewing witnesses."

"To the hit-and-run?"

I nodded.

"Learning anything?"

I shrugged. "Depends on your point of view. I thought I was gathering ammunition for the Senate campaign against Duke. The punk's guilty six ways from Sunday. So I came back and gave my report. Thought I'd get a standing O. Instead, I got the big chill." I paused. "We never had this conversation."

He nodded back. "You made that point. I can get confirmation that Wood is defending the kid. The rest is," he wiggled his eyebrows, "pure political speculation."

"Help me, Ben. Why is the Speaker on Duke's side?"

His turn to shrug. "I don't know. I can make some guesses. Mach-2 has his own logic. Your leader and Duke have always been close." He rubbed his eyes. "Still, friendship . . ."

I frowned. "Refresh me. Why are they so close?"

"Goes back to seventy-three. Before you hit town. They were both rookies in the House. The Repubs had an eighty-nine to eighty-eight edge—this was before the size of the House was cut back to one-eighteen. Duke voted 'present' on the speakership. That created an eighty-eight to eighty-eight tie. Forced the game into overtime."

"Why?"

"Duke was trying to leverage a Republican leadership spot."

"As a freshman?"

"Duke's always been a man in a hurry. Anyhow, after a hundred and one ballots, Duke voted for Tree Courtney, the Democratic candidate. That's not unprecedented in Illinois. Your leader brokered the deal. Duke was persona non grata in his party for a while. Your guy got a leadership post and the rest is history. Here." He fumbled around on his desk and handed me some clippings. "The whole story's in the profile."

I glanced at it. The headline said: "Duke Shoots for Higher Office?" On one side of the story was a full-face color picture of Peter Duke. Distinguished gray hair perfectly in place. His pro pol's practiced-perfect smile. On the other, a shot of Duke in a dark blue jacket, prone, aiming a rifle at a target.

"It doesn't compute," Gerald said. "Here's a chance to steal a Republican Senate seat and add one more vote for a Democratic map in ninety-one. The Speaker's top priority is remaining Speaker, and the key to that is redistricting. You know the game. Chicago's losing population. Suburbs gaining. How do you keep seats for the Demos in the city? Answer—draw bowling alley districts out into Cook County. Rig the numbers so that they are safely Democratic and waste Republican votes." Ben rocked back in his chair. "The Speaker's too tricky sometimes." He reversed field on me. "I'm hearing the Guv may step down."

"And lose his travel budget?"

"Rumor is he's expecting a cushy federal job from Bush." He grinned. "Duke would love to run for governor." He switched back. "I love the end of a decade. Census. Reapportionment. Pure politics of self-interest and revenge. Remember eighty-one when Fast Freddy and his wonder computer drew that special district for Senator Alvin 'Bud' Light?"

I frowned. "Bud Light?"

"Yeah. You know. The dork from Bloomington who made such a stink about the legislative pay raise and returned his part of it? He was always ranking on his colleagues."

I nodded and started chuckling. "His new district stretched a hundred miles from LaSalle-Peru to Decatur."

Gerald grinned. "And was about as wide as U.S. fifty-one."

At the office, I had two messages on my answering machine. One was from Mitch. "Bobby," he said, "I'm at the camp and—guess what—I need a private detective."

He left a number for me to call.

The second message was from Lisa. "Good and bad news," she said. "The good news is that I got the NEH grant to spend next year studying Faulkner. The bad news is that I have to go to Mississippi to do it."

The next morning, I trudged the six blocks from my apartment on North Sixth to the AMTRAK station. I travel light. I carried only my small red and blue Nike gym bag. In it there were a change of shirts, a pair of old jeans, a running outfit, and my toiletries.

Thanks to the Speaker, I had an appointment with Kevin Duke in front of the Chicago Art Institute at 3:00. And I was to see Mitch at Wrigley Field at 4:30. He had been coy about his need for a detective. "Tell you when you get here. Gives you an incentive."

"Terrific," I had said.

Just in case, I had made a reservation for the night at the Bismarck Hotel, state Democratic headquarters. In my billfold was a VISA card issued by the state Democratic Party.

The waiting room was crowded with state bureaucrats in their mandatory navy blazers and beige slacks and tourists in regulation shorts, with 2.5 kids and cameras.

I bought the Chicago *Herald-Star* from a machine for thirty-five cents and sat on the hard wooden benches to read it. The headline screamed: "Nazi Resurgence in Germany." What else is new, I thought. And not limited to the Fatherland. Hell, we elect the Klan to the legislature in Louisiana.

I turned to "Wink," a political and entertainment gossip

column, heavy on the constant infighting in Chicago politics. Above the column was a closed eye. No byline. In the capitol, there was constant speculation about who "Wink" really was. Today the lead item said:

Harold Pomper, chairman of the Illinois Commission on Waste and Mismanagement in State Government, is scheduled to testify before a special legislative joint hearing to be held at the State of Illinois building tomorrow. The report prepared by the commission is said to be longer than the U.S. income tax code. Harold Pomper—partner in the law firm of Pomper & Duke—is known as the man who uses three words to say what ordinary mortals can say in one. Look for him to unleash a blizzard of verbiage about the pork in the governor's "Rebuild Illinois" program. In addition, the commission is expected to criticize "giveaway" tax incentives to foreign investors. Sources close to the commission say that Pomper has "smoke coming out of all his orifices" over what the commission staff has uncovered.

The next several items concerned the upcoming mayor's race in '91. Then a final item said: "What former Cub pitcher from the 1984 team is seeking a tryout with the current squad? Hint: He left baseball under a dark cloud."

I turned to the back page. In sports, the Cubs were scheduled to open that night in St. Louis with Rick Sutcliffe pitching. I love the Red Baron's bulldog competitiveness, but I can't stand to watch him pitch. The Cards would put their roadrunners Vince Coleman, Ozzie Smith, and Willie McGee on base, and the stalling would begin. With Rick's all-deliberate-speed approach to his work—marked by endless attempts to pick off runners—I figured the game would end well after my usual bedtime.

Ten P.M.

The Cubs had fooled everyone by not folding before the All-Star break. I hoped Ryne Sandberg would snap his batting slump—so far he was zero for the month. Andre Dawson's knees were still hurting, and he wasn't supplying the power. Yet the Cubs were still in the hunt.

For now.

Chet Hagan's "Toy Department" column ran on the inside of the back sports page. Hagan was a cynical Chicago sports writer—if that's not redundant. The theme of his column was that "the surprising Cubs cannot compete with the Mets, Cards, and especially the Expos without additional help in the starting rotation."

No news there, Chet.

I took note of the fact that the first Mike Ditka–Jim McMahon story of the summer also appeared. Soon the Bears' intersquad games would drive baseball out of the headlines.

Yawn.

In the upset of the century, the train pulled out virtually on time.

In my seat, I finished the paper and then stared out the blurry window. I like taking the train to Chicago. But it's not for the scenery. If you want a view of the backside of Illinois, AMTRAK's the ticket. Flat *can* be beautiful—consider Audrey Hepburn in *Breakfast at Tiffany's*. But there is an unending monotony to central Illinois's landscape.

The roadbed was as rough as the Atlanta Braves infield after a Falcons exhibition football game. We rocked by the endless rows of corn and rolled by the soybean fields and silos. When the train slowed for small towns, we saw nearly empty town squares, run-down trailer courts, fertilizer tanks, and the accumulated junk of backyards.

Near Bloomington, I staggered like a sailor on a rolling deck to the club car for a Coke. Back in my seat, I reread the paper. In about thirty minutes, the train passed Pontiac State

Prison. Prisons rank just below insurance, corn, soybeans, and herbicides as downstate industries. Near Joliet, we passed the stockyards and oil refineries and under so many power lines I expected to glow in the dark.

I thought about Lisa. I had called her back, congratulated her on the NEH grant, told her we had to postpone the Madison trip, and asked her to look after Clockie.

I had that hollow feeling about her good and bad news. Politically, I'm a mainstream Democrat. I still use the L word. I believe in labor unions, social security, the minimum wage, civil rights, the New Deal, the New Frontier, and the Great Society. And *big government.* I think FDR, HST, JFK, and LBJ were all great presidents, especially Truman.

But personally, I'm conservative. No sudden changes in my life. I hang on to things. I won't buy a new car until my 1981 Toyota is certified DOA. My no-fault separation from Lisa has become an institution. I like living apart—no one goes around closing my windows when it rains or throwing out the Sunday paper before I've read the sports a second time. Lisa and I have finessed our incompatibility by living apart.

But not that far.

I shifted my thoughts to Mitch's mystery call. After talking to him the night before, I had phoned the Speaker's office. As I suspected, Fast Freddy was still working. I told him that Mitch wanted me to work on something to do with a fantasy baseball camp in Chicago.

"Fan-damn-tastic," he had said. "I can tell where your priorities lie."

"Hey, Fast, I'm not even sure I want the job. Just see if the Speaker has any problem with it," I had said. I figured he would, and I would be off the hook with Mitch.

"Get back to you."

In fifteen minutes, he had called back. There was a trace of surprise in his voice. "As long as it doesn't interfere with the Kevin Duke business," he had said.

I shrugged. Well, I could still tell Mitch, "no way."
Sure I could.

I pulled my copy of Ben Gerald's profile of Peter Duke out
and started to read:

> Peter Duke has lived the American dream. He was
> born on Chicago's northwest side, the son of poor
> immigrant parents. He was a track athlete—in the
> mile and cross-country—and an honors student in
> high school. He won an academic scholarship to
> the University of Illinois where he graduated Phi
> Beta Kappa. He enlisted in the Army. In 1968—
> after returning a decorated hero from Vietnam
> where he earned a Silver Star—he married Anne
> Pomper, the youngest daughter of Harold Pomper,
> a well-known Chicago attorney. Anne Pomper had
> been a model and actress and had appeared in
> many local television commercials. In 1968, he
> entered the Loyola Law School. He graduated with
> honors in 1970. In 1972, he was elected to the
> Illinois General Assembly as a Republican, and he
> has represented his North Shore district ever since.
> He has earned numerous "Best Legislator" awards.
> He had one child, Kristin, by his first marriage. In
> 1970, he divorced his first wife, Anne. Since then,
> Anne has carved out her own career dealing in ex-
> pensive antiques. In 1971, he married Julie Farr, a
> member of a prominent DuPage County Republi-
> can family. They had one son, Kevin, born in
> 1972. They divorced in 1982. Duke is a partner in
> the law firm of Pomper & Duke on LaSalle Street,
> specializing in entertainment and sports contract
> negotiations. Recently, Pomper & Duke have
> formed P&D Productions, a sports promotion en-
> terprise. Duke, a progressive Republican, has often
> figured in rumors about statewide office, but it is
> said that the state party is too conservative to nomi-

nate him. As one statehouse insider has said, "The Duke is too damned independent for his own good." Some feel that Duke, like John Anderson or John Lindsay, might be more at home in the Democratic Party. Duke is an avid outdoorsman—hunter and fisherman. He lives in Zion but has a summer home in Lake Geneva, Wisconsin. A prime spokesman for the gun lobby in the General Assembly, he is a superb marksman and has trained his family—including his wives and both of his children—in the safe use of firearms.

By the time we pulled into Union Station, it was nearly 2:00. The crowded station smelled like mold, sweat, and popcorn. I took an escalator up to Adams Street. I crossed the bridge over the Chicago River to Wacker and walked down to Randolph where I turned east.

I saw lots of brisk men and women in dark suits, carrying briefcases, striding along purposefully like schools of eager fish. The women usually wore white hose and running shoes. The men tried to look like Pat Riley.

At one of the stoplights, a black man in a long coat tried to sell me a "five-hundred-dollar watch" for fifty dollars.

"Ten," I offered.

"What do you think I am, man," he said scornfully, "an Iranian rug merchant?"

I reached the Bismarck, now past its glory days. It's just west of city hall. On the other side of the street is that slanted glass monster, the new State of Illinois Building. Down the block, I could hear some sort of demonstration going on. Par for the course in this city of racial, ethnic, and neighborhood divisions.

I registered at state rates and checked my bag at the desk.

It was 3:30. The sky overhead had clouded up. I stood in front of the lions at the Chicago Art Institute watching the world go by. Out of the corner of my eye, I thought I caught a glimpse of Elvis. Behind me were numerous banners announcing an Andy Warhol exhibit. I couldn't imagine anything more tedious, unless someone published his diary. Kevin Duke was late, and I was starting to burn.

A skinny street person with long, dirty hair approached me. He wore baggy shorts with holes and a torn black tee shirt. The shirt touted *Guns 'N' Roses*. The derelict had what looked like a paper clip stuck in his left ear. On his feet, black high-top Nikes, untied.

Panhandling, I thought. I put on my "get out of my face" face.

"Mr. Mills?" he said.

"Miles."

"Kevin Duke. Okay?"

7

"I'm really bummed out about this, okay?"

We were seated at a park bench in Grant Park. A city park employee inched toward us, stabbing randomly at trash with a spear. Over toward the lake, I could see Buckingham Fountain and hear the rush-hour traffic on Lake Shore Drive. I glanced at my watch. It was 3:45. I was probably not going to make the appointment with Mitch on time. I looked around. To the west, the gray skyline almost obscured the Sears Tower. To the north, I couldn't even see the John Hancock Building.

I turned to Kevin. His face was pale and boyish. His beard was light. His eyes were greenish gray. He fidgeted as if he were on speed. He closed his eyes and sighed. "I don't know what this *person* was doing in the street anyway." He drummed his fingers on the bench. He hooked his right leg over his left knee and swung it restlessly. "You know?"

"Can we go back to the beginning?" I asked.

He brushed greasy hair out of his eyes. "Okay."

"You were driving on a suspended license," I said.

Kevin made a sour face. "Yeah, okay. The cops have it in for me." He sighed. "I can't just *quit* driving. The old man expects me to work at a crummy job. He wanted me to be a secretary. Lucky for me, I can't type. I run messages for *his* law firm. How am I supposed to get down here"—he inclined his head toward Michigan Avenue—"and home?"

"Train?"

"No way, man. That's too . . ." He couldn't find the words.

I glanced at his outfit. "Tacky?"

"Really."

"Tell me what you remember about the accident."

He tapped his right foot on the sidewalk. "I was at the No Problem with Kris."

"No problem?"

"A student hangout in Lake Forest."

I nodded. "A bar."

He shrugged. "Right. Happy hour. Had a few G-and-Ts."

"Gin and tonic?"

"Right."

"How few?"

"Man, I don't know, you know." He shrugged. "Who's counting? Let's just say I was feeling no pain. Six . . . maybe."

"Drugs?"

He stared at me. "No way. I don't *do* drugs. They mess up your mind. I stick to booze." He grinned. "Like First Lady said, just say no."

"What about the Valium?"

I had gotten that question from a "Wink" item in the *Herald-Star*.

He shook his head. "The Vitamin Vs don't count. I got them on prescription. From my doctor." He brushed hair out of his eyes again. "Yeah, I probably popped a Valium. Or three. Nerves, man."

"What time did you leave the No Problem?"

He sighed. "I don't know. About six. Give or take fifteen minutes. I don't wear a watch, man."

"Alone?"

He looked at the ground. "Yeah."

"You sure?"

"It's not real clear." He brushed hair out of his eyes once more. "I don't really remember. But yeah, I was by myself."

"This is important, Kevin. At least two of the witnesses said there was someone else in the car. Was there?"

"No way, man."

"What about this Kris?"

He drummed his fingers on the bench again and then reached up and brushed his hair back. "Must of stayed at the bar."

"Who's he?"

He sighed. "She."

"Who is *she*?"

"My sister. Sort of."

"She came with you to the bar?"

He nodded.

"In your car?"

"Yeah."

"But she stayed?"

He shrugged. "Probably. With some of her *friends*."

"You were driving where?"

"Home."

"What do you remember about the accident?"

He looked up at the sky. "It's pretty fuzzy. I wasn't . . . you know . . . tracking too well. I came up to this traffic light. Man, I *had* the green. Okay? Just as I reached the intersection, it turned yellow. I went through. Okay? Guy stepped out of nowhere. Okay?" He looked down at the ground. "I'm real sorry it happened."

"Five witnesses say you ran the light."

He glared at me. "They lie. If my old man weren't a politician." He said it like most Illinoisians do—with contempt. "The *only* reason this is a big deal is because he might run for governor."

"Who gave you the Valium prescription?"

"My doc."

"Family doctor?"

He shook his head. "My psychiatrist. You see, when I was thirteen . . ."

He kept talking. I half-listened to him ramble, wishing I were somewhere else. Or here, with someone else.

"Man, my best friend . . . Donnie . . . committed suicide. Right in front of me. Up at the lake. Okay? Stuck a shotgun in his mouth and pulled the fuckin' trigger, man. Blew the back of his head off. I freaked out. I've been in treatment ever since. I know I have a problem. I'm dependent. I'm going into AA or something. Soon. You know. Okay, man?"

I sighed and shook my head. I tried to imagine him in court. "Got a tip for you before you go to trial," I said.

"What's that?" he said, indifferently.

I pointed at his head. "Get a haircut." I pointed at his clothes. "Get cleaned up. Some decent threads. Okay?"

He stared at me and muttered something.

"I didn't quite catch that."

He gave me the once-over. "You're one to talk, man."

8

I flagged a Yellow Cab going north on Michigan. As I slipped into the back seat, the driver looked over his shoulder at me. He had dark, thinning hair in front, and it was tied in a pigtail in the back, like Danny DeVito in *Twins*. He was sucking an orange Popsicle. "What'll it be, ace?"

"Wrigley Field," I said.

"No game tonight, ace."

I nodded. "I know."

He shrugged. "No skin off my ass. Want a Popsicle, ace?"

"No thanks."

He shrugged as if insulted and barged into the heavy traffic without a backward glance. Brakes squealed and horns sounded. He removed the Popsicle stick from his mouth and chortled.

Somehow, he got the cab up to fifty in just half a block before slamming to a stop at the next red light. A half second before the light changed, he honked at the car in front. He repeated this sequence all the way out to Lake Shore Drive. I rode braced against the front seat.

I took a few deep breaths, but it was hard to kick back and enjoy the view of the lake. Like a good hitter who uses the whole field, Popsicle used all the lanes, frequently crossing three lines of traffic for a momentary advantage. He tailgated so close to other cars that I could read expiration dates on the license stickers. All the time, he was turning his head to share his bellicose views on foreign policy, especially dealing with terrorists. "Scorched earth policy, you know what I'm saying? We ain't heard too much out of Ka-Daffy lately, you know what I'm saying?"

He turned off the drive at Belmont and fought his way west through the late afternoon traffic to Clark and turned north. When we arrived at Addison and Clark, the entrance to Wrigley Field, he said, "Nine seventy-five."

I handed him a ten. "Keep the change," I said.

"Screw you, ace," he said.

I got out and stretched. The cab tore off, peeling rubber. I looked up at the old ballpark, thinking that from the outside it looked like a white warehouse with lights. I showed a pass to a park employee to enter by a small gate.

"You remember Jess 'The Mule' Farmer?" Mitch said. He nodded in the direction of two middle-age men in dark blue Cub sweat shirts who sat across from each other in a booth in the Wrigley Field stadium club. Four empty bottles of Old Style in front of each of them. One got up to shake my hand. He had a craggy, grim face and looked as though he had stepped out of a Depression-era photo album. His chin was covered with blue-black stubble, and his hair was jet black flecked with pepper gray.

"Do I ever?" I said. "Spring training, 1965. Ninth inning. Two outs. Bases loaded." I shook my head. "You threw me one hell of a sinker—bottom just dropped out. 'See you later, Miles.'"

Farmer allowed a small grin to soften his look for a second. "Sounds right," he said.

Mitch playfully punched Farmer in the arm. "You loaded one up on a rookie in spring training?"

Farmer just shrugged and motioned for me to sit next to him. "Natural sinker," he said.

Mitch sat down next to the other man who had a fringe of

gray hair, a round crimson face, and dirty gray eyes. A cigarette dangled from his lips. A silver cigarette lighter, a pack of cigarettes, and a full ashtray were carefully arranged in front of him. He reached a hand across the table to me. "Joe Barelli. Most folks call me 'Pork.'" He grinned. "Or somethin' worse."

"You could flat hit," I said.

"Still can," he said with conviction.

Farmer nodded. "This man could get out of bed on Christmas morning and hit with a wet *Sporting News.*"

Mitch cleared his throat. "As I said, Bobby worked with me in the commissioner's office as an investigator."

"We'll forgive that," Barelli said.

"Now," Mitch added, "he's a private detective in Springfield. I'm his . . . associate."

"Well, we damned sure need somethin' like a detective," Barelli said.

I spread my hands. "So what's the deal?"

Mitch nodded at Barelli, who crushed out his cigarette and then took a deep breath. "This dream camp of mine could be in big trouble. You have to understand—I bet the ranch on it. I got everything I own—and a lot I don't—in this baby. If the sucker works, . . ." he paused, grinned and patted his middle, "fat city." His look turned serious. "I can't afford any bad publicity. My backers are skittish about that. They have political concerns."

Political? I glanced at Mitch. He shrugged.

"It took a lot of negotiations," Barelli said, "to put this thing together. Now this Dewey tryout thing might screw everything up." He trailed off and looked over at Mitch. "You tell him, Professor." He reached down, grabbed another cigarette and used the lighter to light it.

"Dewey tryout thing?" I said.

Mitch nodded. "Dewey Farmer."

"I thought . . ."

Mitch held up his right hand. "I'll explain. The dream

camp has use of Wrigley Field for a week. Team's on the road, park is vacant. But the Cubs don't let just anyone in. As you might imagine, getting it for a week was difficult to swing. Especially the night game. Pork also scouts for the Cubs. So one hand washes the other. As part of the agreement to use the field, Dewey Farmer," he paused and nodded at Jess, "Jess's younger brother is coming in tonight to coach in the camp, maybe even pitch briefly in the dream game."

"I don't. . . ," I started to say.

"Patience, Bobby. The real purpose of having Dewey in camp, of course, is so the Cubs can take a close look at him. Put the radar gun on him. Check his work ethic. See how he performs in a game-like situation."

I frowned. "But wasn't he suspended for life?"

Mitch grunted impatiently and cut me short again. "Yeah. 'For life' means until the commissioner says otherwise. This is an unofficial tryout. The Cubs want no advance publicity."

"Tell that to 'Wink,'" I said.

Barelli nodded grimly. "I saw that. I'd like to know where that leak came from." He glanced at the Mule. "I bet I know."

"I can tell you," Farmer said. "Dewey. He's been talking to Chet Hagan about something."

Barelli nodded. "Figures."

"Cubs didn't expect to be in the hunt this year. They need pitching help," Mitch said.

"Perpetually," I said.

"Yeah, well, they're desperate," Barelli said. "That's why they're willing to roll the dice with Dewey." He shook his head. "Not the best way to put that. But they don't want the spotlight on Dewey, at least until the night of the game. They could take a lot of heat for this."

I nodded. "Dewey was on the eighty-four team, as I

recall. He sure as hell didn't play with the sixty-nine Cubs."

"Would you look at that?" Barelli said, pointing his cigarette over my right shoulder. I looked back and saw a television monitor mounted over our heads. It was tuned to ESPN. Sound down. They were showing professional women's volleyball. On a California beach. On the large screen, we saw a close-up of a blonde Amazon digging a shot out of the sand. "I'd like to spike *that*," Barelli said.

Mitch cleared his throat.

Barelli glanced at him, grinned and rolled his head back and forth. "Sorry. Back to the subject. So we bend the rules a little. Mets will have some ringers, too. I heard Gene Garland. Count on it."

"The camp is really a cover for the tryout for Dewey?" I asked.

"That's not the way I'd put it," Barelli said. "Not at all. It's part of the price of *having* the camp. Had my way— sorry, Jess—Dewey would never cross those white lines again. I don't trust him."

Farmer nodded a fraction.

I shrugged. "I guess I still don't see the problem."

Mitch nodded at Farmer. "Your turn."

Farmer took a deep breath. "My shithead brother," he started, "had all the God-given talent you could want. He threw it all away. He was suspended from baseball for gambling right after the eighty-four season. He's been out of the game for 'most five years. He has to be certified by the league office as clean for the lifetime suspension to be lifted." He wrinkled his nose as if he had smelled a skunk. "But he's gone and got himself in trouble again."

"Gambling?"

Farmer just stared at me. Finally, he said, "Who knows the reason? It could be money trouble or it could be woman trouble, knowing the kid. Long ago, I figured out that I can't be my brother's keeper."

I shook my head. "I guess I'm slow, fellows. I still don't see the problem."

"He's been getting some threats, Bobby," Mitch said.

"What kind?"

"Notes. Phone calls. They say pay fifty grand, or he won't live long enough to pitch again."

I thought about that. "This tryout doesn't seem to be a very well kept secret. Sounds to me like he has some gambling debts. Sounds to me like he's *not* clean. Sounds to me like the Cubs should take a pass."

Mitch shook his head. "Maybe. Maybe not. He denies it. And if he owed a shark, they wouldn't fool around. They'd just come in and slam a drawer shut on his fingers or something. Not try to waste him."

"Huh?"

Farmer nodded. "Dumbass got in a fight in a bar in Wildwood the other night. Guy tried to ream his guts with a knife. Lucky the cops showed up when they did."

"Is Dewey a hothead?" I asked.

Farmer grinned. "Does the bear shit?"

"So this incident could have nothing to do with the threats?"

"Granted," Mitch said.

"'Nother question: Can he still pitch?"

Farmer held up his left hand. There was a large dark bruise on it. "That's a good question. He's rusty, no doubt. All I know is that the dumb shit can still bring it, at least for a few pitches. Before I came up here from Florida, I was working out with him." Then he reached over and shook one of Barelli's cigarettes out of the pack and took his time lighting it with Barelli's lighter. He let smoke dribble out his nostrils. He shrugged. "Five years is a long layoff for a pitcher."

I looked at Barelli. "What do you want me to do?"

Barelli coughed. "Join the camp coaching staff." He

looked at me skeptically. "We can always use another body."

"Especially with the Professor around," Farmer said, grinning at Mitch. "He don't do much of anything but lecture."

"Tell me about it," I said.

"Mule," Mitch said, "I'm hurt. You were my boyhood idol."

Farmer chuckled.

"And?" I asked.

"Keep a close eye on Dewey," Barelli said.

I shook my head. "Mitch, you know I don't do protection. Too much like baby-sitting."

"With my brother, I'm afraid that's what it would be," Farmer said.

I nodded. "For long stretches, it's too damned monotonous and then, suddenly, it's too damned exciting."

Mitch shook his head. "Your main job will be to find out if he's clean. We can make other arrangements for the baby-sitting."

"Such as?"

"The House."

"Big House" Bellamy. Springfield's Budget Rent-a-Muscle. I had used him often enough before. Mitch and Big House got along like Newt Gingrich and Jim Wright. Mitch's suggesting the House showed me how seriously he was taking this. "Maybe. Who's going to pay the freight?" I asked.

"The Cubs," Barelli said. "Through me."

I fell back on a practical argument. "I haven't played in twenty years."

"It's like . . ." Mitch started to say.

". . . *falling* off a bicycle," I finished. "I don't have any equipment."

Mitch rolled his eyes. "Bobby, they sell sporting goods in Chicago. Let's take a hike."

"Yeah," Barelli said. "I need to gas up."

"Me, too," Jess said.

*   *   *

Mitch and I stood outside the Stadium Club under the grandstand. He held an unlit cigar stub and a box of kitchen matches. He was humming something from an opera to himself.

"I don't like it," I said.

He poked the stub at me. "Forget all the pros and cons," he said. "Did you see those names on the wall in the club?"

I nodded.

"Frank Chance, Hack Wilson, Stan Hack, Phil Caveretta, Ernie Banks . . ."

"Let's play two," I said, voicing Ernie's preference for doubleheaders.

". . . and all the rest of the Cub greats. Forget the money. Think of it this way. This is a chance to play in a baseball shrine." He pointed the stub around the tunnel. "This window of opportunity will never open again. You get to strap it on one last time." He paused and lit up.

The cigar smell blended with the damp odor of hotdogs, beer, piss, and sweat. I inhaled deeply. I loved it.

My baseball skills had always been marginal. I was not, in the vernacular, a natural. No power. No speed. Weak arm. I had a good eye at the plate, the ability to make contact with the pitch on the hit-and-run, and I could bunt. With a runner on second and nobody out, I could get the man to third more often than not. I would give up my body for the team. I had led three leagues in getting hit by pitches. On defense, I depended on anticipation and knowing where the hitter tended to hit the ball. On which pitch. My game, such as it was, depended on street smarts and practice, practice, practice.

I had played a little slow-pitch softball in the '70s. Hated it. A game for guys with beer bellies, big arms, and small IQs.

If I put on a uniform again, I ran the risk of serious embarrassment. Then there was the whole matter of the Cub-Met fantasy game. The curse of '69, which still weighed on Barelli, might linger.

And I loathed personal security work. Especially with a jerk like Dewey Farmer.

All of that was against doing it.

On the other side was Mitch's argument.

He knew me well. I couldn't take a pass on this chance to help rewrite baseball history.

"Where do I sign?" I said.

Dewey Farmer sauntered out of the boarding area, bantering with two stews. He was tall, slim, and had a handlebar mustache like Rollie Fingers. He wore stone-washed jeans slung low on his hips, a jet-black cowboy shirt open to the navel, tan Stetson hat, and dark brown cowboy boots. He had three gold chains around his neck, plenty of dark chest hair, and a plug of tobacco in his left jaw. He patted one of the stews on the back, just below the hip, leaned close to her, and said, "I'm staying at the Hotel Easton, babe. I'll be in the bar."

I stepped into his path. "Dewey Farmer?"

He got an annoyed look. "Meat," he said dismissing me, "I don't do unpaid autographs." He started to step around me to rejoin the stews. They kept walking briskly, tails switching. "Wait up," Dewey hollered. They kept moving.

I grabbed his arm.

He faced me, face white with anger, and removed my hand. "You didn't get the message, sport." He started to push by me.

"Pork sent me," I said. "To pick you up."

He paused. "The Pork-butt? You got the limo?"

"Yes," I lied.

"Stretch?"

"For sure."

He glanced ahead. "Maybe we can offer them a ride. Let's haul ass," he said, and he started walking quickly after the stews.

As we hurried down the long corridor past the boarding areas, I said, "Tell me about the bar fight. And the threats."

He stopped dead. "Who told you about that?"

"Pork. I'm in charge of security."

He looked at me in disbelief. "You? Tell that fat ass I don't need a baby-sitter."

Exactly my sentiments, I thought. "Talk to Pork about it. What can you tell me about the fight?"

He shrugged elaborately. "No big deal. Just a barroom brawl till the nig . . . until this guy pulled a knife. I woulda made him eat it if the cops hadn't gotten there."

"The threats?"

Matter of factly, he said, "A couple of notes. One phone call."

We resumed walking. "You still got the notes?"

"Pitched 'em."

"The call. Recognize the voice?"

"Nah."

"Male?"

He nodded, distractedly.

"Did you go to the police?"

"What could they do?"

"Trace the calls."

He stopped again and stared at me. His eyes were dark brown and had the vacant look I associate with someone more than a little around the bend. "You know they called from a public phone. There's one at every minimart." Ahead of us, Farmer spotted a small cocktail lounge. "Let's change oil, meat," he said.

He ordered a gin and tonic from a cocktail waitress in a very short skirt. He gave her the eye.

I had a Coke.

"Some drink for a tough guy," he said.

I shrugged. "What did the letters say?"

"Pay fifty K or I wouldn't live through the camp." He shook his head. "Hell, I told the guy on the phone the only way I'd ever see fifty K again is *if* I live through the camp. He told me to go fuck myself and just get the dough."

"Who do you think it is?"

"Beats me." He drained his glass and signaled for another. "Probably some small-time hustler."

"Gambling debts?"

He narrowed his eyes. "That's ancient history. I rehabilitated myself. I don't think about it." He stopped and signaled again. "If I get my yakker back, I can win the division for the Cubs. Nobody can hit my good yakker."

A yakker is a curve ball. Dewey had had one of the best.

The waitress was behind the bar, profile to Dewey, talking to the bartender. "Bitch," he said. He held up his glass and waved it for her to see. "Babe!" She turned and nodded, a trace of annoyance in her face. He shrugged. "If I hang the sucker, it's dial eight—long distance."

She brought him another drink. He tossed it down. "I lost five fuckin' years from my career. I could of had Hall of Fame stats by now. I was screwed over by the baseball establishment."

"How so?"

He shrugged again. "Some low-life geeks supposedly got immunity to testify against me. It was all bullshit. The Feds had them cold. Drugs and stuff. They lied to save themselves. But the Feds never charged me with nothin'. Not one damned thing. But baseball banned me without due process." He rubbed his mustache. "Anyway, what's wrong with a little friendly wager? Gambling's legal now in most states. They got a lottery in Florida. Horse racing. Dog racing. I heard they're going to have riverboat gambling here in Illinois, too. I never got my due process. Sons of bitches blackballed me right out of the league. Just like old Shoeless Jack Johnson."

"Joe Jackson."

"Whatever. You seen that flick?"

"Field of Dreams?"

"Yeah." He signaled for another drink. "Slow, man. Real slow. You dig those funky old gloves? With the short fingers. How'd they ever catch the ball?" He stared out at the stream of passengers. His eyes lit up. He pointed at a tanned girl in tight pink shorts with a frill of lace at the bottom and a matching tube top. "Like to lick the honey off her melons," he said.

She looked about fourteen to me. "A little young," I said.

He looked at me in disbelief. "You're shittin' me."

"Let's split," I said.

"I could use another quart of oil."

"Hotels have bars."

"Where's the limo?"

I pointed to the row of cabs. "That yellow one there."

"Oh, man." He gave me a pained look.

We got in the back seat. "Easton Hotel, make it snappy," he said.

I shook my head. "Bismarck. Take your time."

The driver shifted his look between us.

"Bismarck," I said.

The driver lifted his shoulders and turned to business. Dewey glared at me. I shrugged. "Pork's orders. It's a discreet little out-of-the-way place. Elegant."

He sighed. "I'm going to climb all over his lard butt. How come we don't stay where the action is?"

"Because that's where the action is."

He leaned back in his seat and closed his eyes. "You play the game?" he asked indifferently.

"Yes."

"It's a great life. The Show?"

"One at bat."

He shook his head. That didn't count. "When?"

"Nineteen sixty-seven."

He opened his eyes and looked at me as if I were an extraterrestrial. "So Meat, what was it like trying to field with those funky, old black gloves with the short fingers?"

After I got Dewey checked in, I called the Right Stuff from my room. It's an eastside Springfield saloon owned by B. J. "Bull Jive" Johnson. The Right Stuff is the unofficial home of the Springfield blues, a spot where blacks and whites mingle to listen to jazz. "Maximum Security Face" Johnson—Bull Jive's brother—answered the phone in the courteous manner he had trained in the joint to achieve. "Yo?"

"Big," I said.

"Big who?"

"Top Peewee," I said sarcastically. "Don't jerk me around, Max. Put the House on."

I could almost feel his glare. I expected him to slam the phone down, but in a few seconds a laconic voice said, "Whatta you want?"

"It's Miles. Got a job for you."

"Bodyguard?"

"Right."

"You know the fee."

"Right."

"Where and when?"

"Chicago. Now. I'm feeling a certain sense of desperation."

"I need a day to take care of business. Who'm I babysitting?"

"Dewey Farmer."

There was a pause. "The ex-ballplayer?"

"Yeah."

"Set down for gambling?"

"Yeah, . . . Big?"

"What?"

"Somebody's made an attempt on his life. Bring some firepower."

"Don't leave home without it."

IO

The scene behind me was unique and familiar to anyone who follows America's real team—the Cubs—on WGN on cable. (So far as I can tell from the empty seats, the Braves aren't even *Atlanta's* team.) I was standing between first and home on the foul line, half-turned so I could see the outfield walls covered with lush green ivy. Over the yellow 400-foot sign in dead center field were the bleachers—slightly off center—extending in a terrace to the old-fashioned, slate-gray scoreboard. Fans used to sit in the lower center-field bleachers, but after several serious beanings, it was closed off to provide a better hitting background. Above the scoreboard the hands on the clock said quarter to 10:00. On either side, flags gave the league standings. The Cubs were still second in the National League East.

About halfway between center field and the left-field line, there was a bend in the wall. There was a similar bend between center and right. Called the wells. The short distances in left and right center make Wrigley a hitter's park if the wind is from the southwest. With the wind blowing out, any routine fly is a threat to reach the bleachers, and well-hit balls leave the park completely. With the wind blowing in, however, a cruise missile will be caught on the warning track. The wind saved a Ken Holtzman no-hitter once by blowing a ball hit by the Hammer—Hank Aaron—back into the park.

Along the top of the wall was a wire net called the basket. The basket was intended to prevent fans from obstructing a ball hit near the top of the wall. Lots of hitters—most on opposing teams in recent years—had hit line drives that just made the basket.

Behind the left-field bleachers, across Waveland Avenue, I could see the dirty-yellow brick building whose roof served as seating for tenants and friends. Over the right-field wall, there was a large black *Torco* sign with a white oval border, and several more apartment buildings. On the right-field flagpole, the flag had a blue number twenty-six for Hall of Famer Billy Williams. The left-field pole had a blue number fourteen for Ernie Banks. The flags showed the wind was blowing out today.

Hot dog.

Too bad the wind couldn't help my ground balls.

This was a real baseball park—not some indoor amusement park with cement grass and the air-conditioning blowing out at five miles an hour. Not designed for football, with baseball a summer frill.

And real fans like the bleacher bums. They throw the ball back if the opponents hit a homer, and they throw the fan back who tries to start the wave.

I wore white baseball shoes with plastic cleats. My blue Cub uniform top with white stripes had a red number two on the back. Underneath, I had on a blue sweatshirt. I wore my white pants just above the knee. My blue and white stirrup socks were carefully in place. My blue Cub cap was set at a jaunty angle. I even wore red and white Rawlings batting gloves. I held on my shoulder a silver aluminum bat with red and blue trademark.

Color-damn-coordinated.

Pork Barelli stood directly in front of the ten campers, swaying slightly. He was bareheaded and held a bat at his left side for support. I was standing to his left with the other coaches. Most of the campers looked a little uneasy in their new uniforms with that smaller red C inserted in the larger blue circle over the left breast. And the cute little blue Cub patch in the red circle on the left shoulder.

As I looked them over, I did a double take. An unexpected bonus—one of them was a young woman with dark hair tucked under her cap. She stood in the back, nervously tapping her blue glove.

"This is a week-long boot camp, troops," Pork said, "and I'm the drill instructor. You've all seen the movie starring Clint Eastwood or some other macho man." He pointed his bat at me and the other coaches. "These are my drill sergeants. Before this week is over, you'll hate me, you'll love me. But no one will say they didn't get their money's worth. I tell you what, folks—I generally don't like the Mets too good."

A fat camper clapped and whistled.

Pork grinned. "I'll never forget sixty-nine. I intend to win that game on Saturday. Today we work on fundamentals. Later on, we'll play some games. I kid you not. I want to win as much as I wanted my wife on my wedding night." He paused and wiggled his eyebrows. "Maybe more. The only way to have fun in this game is to do things the right way. And win. I don't like good losers. Losing is . . . for losers. You'll be divided into four groups and rotate. Hitting, infield, pitching, and outfield. I'll handle the hitters. Let me introduce the other coaches." He pointed his bat directly at Mitch. "If they ever open a wing in the Hall of Fame for bull pen catchers, this man is a cinch. Meet Mitch 'The Professor' Norris. Talk your ear off. To loosen up, just take a lap around him."

Mitch grinned and doffed his hat. "Pork, you're the guy who showers in a car wash," he said.

Barelli put up an imaginary score for Mitch. "The Professor will help with the pitchers." He pointed the bat at me. I was looking good except for a small grass stain on my left knee that I had picked up while playing catch with Mitch. And the hair peeking out of the back of my cap.

"Next, Robert Miles." He pointed the bat at my knee. "We call him 'The Human Napkin.' Nappy, for short. He'll take care of your laundry and work with the infield."

I tipped my hat. I read the lips of the fat camper as he mouthed to the young woman with the dark hair, "Who's he?"

She shrugged.

Pork pointed to Jess Farmer. "The other pitching coach will be Jess 'The Mule' Farmer, star relief pitcher for the sixty-nine Cubs."

Jess stepped forward, expressionless. Nodded.

"Also involved with the camp will be Jess's brother, former Cub, Dewey Farmer. Glad you made it through customs, Dewey."

Dewey made a pistol with his right forefinger and thumb and shot Pork. "Thanks, Pork-o." He nodded at the campers. "Fair warning—I'm not some old broken-down hoss like these guys. I belong in the Show." He seemed to rest his eyes on the girl for a few seconds. He turned back to Pork. "When do I get my shot at the fresh meat?"

Pork flushed a little redder and dug his finger into his right ear. "Later," he said. Then he pointed his bat behind the campers to a video camera set up in the stands behind the plate. "You may notice that they are videotaping the whole camp. That's for a documentary we are shooting. You will have your own copy of the game on Saturday. Any questions?"

The portly camper said, "When do we break for beer?"

The field was busy with activity. Standing off to the side of the batting cage, I hit grounders to several campers in the infield. Another group was down the right-field line taking batting practice off the machine, under Pork's critical eye. The hitters were enclosed in a long net to keep the balls from flying every where. The outfielders were in center field, catching balls launched from another pitching machine, which was angled upward. And the pitchers were down in the left-field bull pen throwing to Mitch. Jess Farmer stood beside the pitchers, often taking the ball and demonstrating something. He wore a white number thirteen on his blue back.

The infielders lobbed the balls back in to Dewey Farmer, who grudgingly retrieved them for me. He also wore number thirteen. Pretty soon, I got into the flow of hitting sharp three- and four-bouncers to them. I felt a warm moistness start to spread on my back. I kept up a steady stream of advice saying all the things coaches have said since Abner Doubleday. "Charge the ball. . . . Play it, don't let it play you. . . . Hands in front . . . soft hands. . . . Get the good hop. . . . Get down . . . keep your butt low and your hands relaxed. . . . You can move back up, but you can't get back down . . . don't back up on the ball."

The young woman with the blue glove was a little stiff and mechanical, but she handled anything hit at her.

After twenty minutes, I handed the bat to Dewey. "Hit some to me," I said.

"Yes, sir," he snapped.

I trotted out to short. "Watch," I said. I showed them how to stand on the balls of their feet, how to anticipate, and how to use the crossover step. I nodded at Dewey. He deliberately pulled a hard ground ball into the hole, out of my reach. Foolishly, I dove but missed it. And banged my left knee into the infield dirt. The ball rolled into left field. I got up and limped back to my position.

Dewey grinned at me and said, "Nice range, Meat."

Then he hit some routine balls that I fielded flawlessly. "One more," I said. He hit a smash up the middle. I moved quickly, but if the ball stayed down, it was by me. Luckily, I got a charity hop. I snagged it with one hand.

The young woman grinned at me.

"Muscle memory," I said. "What do I call you?"

"Pat," she said.

After half an hour, the groups changed stations. When everybody had gone to every station, the campers took batting practice off the machine, which catapulted the ball at the hitter. Pork Barelli stood behind the cage and dissected everyone's swing.

"Don't let him in there," he said repeatedly. "Don't let him into your kitchen. Don't get jammed. Don't jam yourself. Get that bat moving."

When Pat stepped in, with a determined look on her face, he said, "Let's see what you can do, player."

She hit the ball consistently but not hard. Barelli motioned for her to come behind the cage. He put his arm around her and demonstrated how to cock the bat. "Player, you got to get that thing started," he said.

Near the end of practice, the coaches took some batting practice off the machine. Then Pork looked at Dewey and said, "Let's see what you've got, rookie."

Dewey said, "All right!" and sprinted to the mound. He threw half a dozen warm-ups to Mitch. His pitches smacked into the glove.

Pork took his familiar corkscrew stance, peeking at Dewey over his right shoulder. Dewey delivered in a distinctive submarine motion, his fingers almost brushing the ground as he released the ball. It streaked toward the plate. Pork swung hard and missed. And almost tipped over from the force of the swing.

Mitch snapped the ball back to Dewey.

Dewey laughed. "Nice swing, gutbucket."

Pork settled back in. "Bring that shit in here," he said. On the next delivery, he drove a hard-liner that made Dewey duck. I could hear Mule laughing from the dugout. For the next couple of minutes, Pork whistled line drive after line drive into the outfield. I could see frustration start to build in Dewey's face.

Then Mitch took off the catching gear and stepped in and

put the first pitch in the left-field seats. With his deceptively easy swing, he hit several more ropes to all corners of the outfield. "Just a stroll in the park," he said as he left the cage.

Dewey had started to sweat heavily. Pork said, "Nappy, get in there."

I stepped in. Dewey fired a fast ball under my chin. A message. Don't dig in. Then he bent a breaking ball over the outside corner. I hit a weak pop-up to second. The girl backed up a step and caught it.

"Want to move up to the ladies' tee?" Dewey called in.

I got furious and tried to take the ball deep. I topped rollers, squibbed balls off the end of the bat, and jammed myself repeatedly. Finally, I stepped out. "Shit." I stepped around behind the cage.

"You're gripping the bat too hard," Pork said. "You got to relax up there. Chill out. But be ready to strike like a cobra." He cupped his hands at his mouth. "That's it for today! Let's pound some brewski!"

As I dragged off the field, Pat ran up beside me. She grinned and said, "We both need to work on our hitting."

I nodded. "My muscle memory got amnesia."

"Fuckin' son of a bitch!"

I looked over my left shoulder. The locker room was empty except for Dewey Farmer—wearing only a white towel around his slim waist.

The campers, excited by the practice, had all eaten, showered, dressed, and departed. Pat had had to use the women's restroom. Baseball was not *that* liberated yet.

He was staring at something in his locker.

"What's the problem?" I said. I was seated on a folding chair, still in my uniform and sock feet, sipping a Coke and killing time. Pork had called a meeting for the coaches in his office in ten minutes.

Dewey gestured impatiently for me to come see. I did. A blue-clad toy Cubby Bear—one you could buy at a concession stand for a couple of dollars—dangled by a cord from a hook. The head was twisted around, and the neck was partly broken. There was a piece of paper pinned to the doll. I reached in and took the doll off the hook and removed the piece of paper. The number thirteen was written in blue ink on it. Below it was scrawled: "Pay up or die, sucker."

Farmer snatched the doll from me and fired it over the table and across the room. It struck the wall and fell to the floor. "I won't be intimidated," he said to me. "No-damn-body can intimidate the Dewster." He reached into his locker for his black bikini shorts and started dressing. "What are you going to do about this?" he asked.

"I'll look into it," I said.

He slipped on his jeans. "Do that, sport."

"I'll raise it at the meeting," I said. "You coming?"

"I'm not going to any bullshit meeting. I got to gas up," he said. "See you in the Stadium Club."

I picked up the doll and took it into the manager's office. Behind the desk, Pork was in his sweatshirt and jockstrap, smoking a cigarette. Mitch leaned against the wall, puffing on a cigar. Jess Farmer was perched on the edge of the desk in his jockey shorts, also smoking a cigarette.

There was enough passive smoke in the room to make me think I was back in the General Assembly.

I showed them the doll, keeping the note in the other hand.

Pork held the doll up and grinned. "Asshole got excited by *this*?"

I nodded. "You see anything unusual around the camp?" I asked.

"Aside from your hitting?" he said. Then he shook his head. "Nah. It's probably just a clubhouse prank." He handed the doll to Jess.

I shook my head. "I don't think so."

"Nappy's right, Pork," Jess drawled, as he examined the doll. "This is pure meanness."

"Looks like another warning to me," Mitch said.

Pork frowned. He turned to me. "You see it that way?"

I shrugged and read them the note. "I don't think there's any doubt about it. I think we have to play it as if we have a real problem. How secure is the locker room?"

"Tight," Barelli said. "One of the conditions the Cubs put on us. No one allowed in but campers or coaches. They have a guard on duty at all times. No friends. No lovers. No visitors. No nobody."

"Which means . . ." Mitch said.

"That it's one of the campers . . ." I continued.

"Or one of the coaches," Pork finished.

"That changes everything," I said.

"Why?" Pork asked.

"Whoever it is, they got somebody on the inside of this camp."

Pork shook his head. "Can't be one of the coaches." He looked up. "We're all here."

"Except Dewey," Mitch said.

I picked Dewey up at the Stadium Club. He had three empty shot glasses in front of him. We cabbed it back to the Bismarck. "Why do we have to stay in that hole?" he complained. "The rooms are like closets. Nothing to do. I went down to the bar last night—thought I'd wandered into a retirement home. Just sit around and watch the old farts die."

12

When I got up to my room on the sixth floor at the Bismarck, my red message light was blinking. "Call Alfred Martin," was the message.

Truly excellent. All I wanted to do was collapse on the bed.

"What's happening?" Fast Freddy asked.

"I talked to Kevin Duke."

"I know. Peter Duke called the Speaker. He's pretty pissed off about it."

Oh, oh. "The Speaker?"

"Nah. Duke. He wants to talk to you."

"Why?"

"Seems you didn't show the proper degree of sympathy."

"Next time I'll send a card. Look, I don't . . ."

Fast cut in. "Duke's at the Marquette Club till four. Wants you to stop over this afternoon. This is not negotiable."

"Okay. But . . ."

"Yeah?"

"Tell the Speaker he should cut his losses on this one. I don't know how or why he got involved . . ."

"That's none of your business."

". . . but this kid has loser written all over him."

"Don't take that attitude into your talk with Duke."

*   *   *

I left Dewey in his room—with the command to stay put—and walked to the Marquette Club, just off Michigan Avenue near the Art Institute. The sky had developed a few high clouds, but it was almost a perfect summer afternoon. Most of the businessmen on the streets had shucked their jackets and rolled up their sleeves. They seemed to bounce along, but I felt like I had gone ten rounds with Sugar Ray Leonard.

My left knee was sore, my right arm ached, and I had blisters on both feet and hands.

But just before I got to the club, I found another shiny new penny in the middle of the sidewalk.

Luck?

When I entered the club, a doorman in a scarlet and gold uniform directed me to the elevator. A similarly dressed attendant pushed the buttons for me on the elevator. When I got off, a woman in a blue blazer escorted me to the library, which had high ceilings, large wooden fans, medieval banners, stained glass windows, and a billion-dollar—taking inflation into account—view of the lake. The walls were lined with shelves of books with dark leather covers.

I was shown to a corner table near the windows, where Peter Duke was sitting with two other men. One was Arthur J. "White Shoes" Kennedy, Chicago's top hired gun. The other—older—man had a florid face and also seemed familiar. In front of him and Duke were snifters of what I would have bet the franchise was brandy. Kennedy had a tall glass of beer with a nice head of foam.

Duke and the older man each wore a variation of the LaSalle Street regulation dress—gray, pinstriped three-piece suits and conservative dark ties. Kennedy made his own fashion statement in a lavender suit, red bow tie with white dots, and red suspenders. White shoes, of course.

Duke stood and shook my hand. His gray hair was as carefully crafted as Ted Koppel's. "Care for a drink?"

I shook my head.

He nodded at Kennedy, who was smoking a thin filter-tipped cigar. Kennedy remained seated. "My good friend, Art Kennedy."

Kennedy nodded at me as if to say, I'm slightly bored with it all.

The other man stood. He was a good ten years older than either of his companions. His face was florid, and he had pale gray, watchful eyes.

"My law partner and trusted advisor, Harold Pomper," Duke said.

"I didn't know this was a conference of the bar," I said. I shook Pomper's hand. It was warm and fleshy. "How's the waste and mismanagement game?"

"Flourishing, I can assure you," he said in a deep voice. "The stories I could tell you about squandered money would raise the hair on your head." He glanced at my mane and involuntarily raised his bushy gray eyebrows a fraction.

Duke smiled. "Art and Harold are advising me on this problem. That's why I asked them to sit in. Nate Wood may join us later. His plane was delayed."

I can live with that, I thought.

Duke motioned for me to sit. "I've heard good things about your work."

"All a man has is his reputation," I said.

Kennedy seemed to smile to himself.

"To be sure," Pomper said. "And that's what . . ."

Duke cleared his throat. "Let's get down to business. You're doing the background investigation for Nate on my son's case?"

I nodded.

"What's your assessment?"

"Have you seen my preliminary report?"

Duke shook his head. "No. I'm deliberately leaving the legal details to Nate. The old maxim applies. You should never be the attorney in your own or your son's case. I'm just not objective. But an overview?"

"Well, . . ."

"No man could be," Pomper interjected. "Objective. In my judgment," he said, in his well-practiced baritone, "— and this is from my years of experience in the law—the prosecutor has way overstepped his bounds. Making this a criminal matter. If Peter were not such a prominent attorney and public figure, I doubt whether these charges would ever have been filed. This person was lying in the road, possibly, quite probably inebriated, wearing dark clothing. It was night. He was practically invisible. Almost asking to be run over. An unfortunate accident, to be sure. Kevin was wrong to flee. Quite wrong. We concede that. We stipulate that. He's young. A mistake of immaturity. He was confused and frightened." He paused. "What do you think, Mr. Miles?"

"Well, . . ." I paused to search for the diplomatic way to say, "You're full of shit." I was too slow.

Pomper didn't wait for my reply. "I believe we have to seize the initiative in this matter," he said. He looked toward the ceiling. "Grab the high ground. Play offense, not defense. Be proactive, not reactive. Have you. . . ?"

Peter Duke cleared his throat again. "Ah, Harold, why don't we hear what Mr. Miles has to say?"

"Quite right," Pomper said. "Just what I was about to suggest and recommend."

I looked at Kennedy. He wore that secret smile again.

"Sorry," Pomper said. "It's just that I get so worked up." He smiled and stopped. Then he cleared his throat. "I'll make just one more comment. This case should never have been filed."

"We might as well face facts," I said.

"One man's facts are another man's fiction," Pomper said. "Context is everything in matters factual. That's why, as an attorney, I . . ." Pomper paused and seemed to notice the look of clear annoyance that crossed Duke's normally impassive face.

"My point exactly," I said. I turned to Duke. "It's going to be difficult to build a credible defense for your son. Given the context. The man was *not* lying in the road. It was still daylight. It doesn't matter what he was wearing. He was not drunk. He was crossing with the green light. In the crosswalk."

Pomper looked affronted. "That's not the way Kevin tells it."

Duke fingered the knot on his tie. "Are you certain?"

"There are five witnesses."

He looked sobered. "I doubt that Kevin can get a fair hearing. He's already been tried and convicted in the media. Because he's my son. Harold's right about that."

"Of course, he can't," Pomper said. He looked up at the ceiling again. "If the libel laws hadn't been emasculated by the Warren Court . . ."

"Bull puckey," I said.

Kennedy laughed.

"I beg your pardon," Pomper said, looking indignant.

"Let's skip the sugarcoating," I said. "He's guilty."

Kennedy winked at me.

Duke just stared at me.

The folds of fat around Pomper's eyes seemed to inflate. His cheeks puffed. "Really."

"I suggest," I said directly to Duke, "that you talk to Wood. And read my report. And figure out a way to help Kevin deal with his problems."

"What do you know about *his* problems?" Pomper demanded.

I shrugged. "Not a lot. But you don't have to be a brain surgeon to see he's a very troubled young man."

Duke nodded. "The truth often hurts. Though I must tell you," he said, "that in all candor I didn't think you were very tactful in your interview with my son."

I shrugged. "As you said."

"You've prejudged his guilt," Pomper said.

"I'm not on the jury," I sighed. "Look," I said, "here are the facts as I know them. You be the judge." I summarized the report.

Duke listened intently. His face gradually paled. What kind of a cock-and-bull story had he heard to this point? Kennedy nodded at each major conclusion.

After I finished, there was dead silence. Then Pomper patted Duke's arm. "This man has gone through hell over that kid. Remember the . . ."

Duke shook his head slightly at Pomper.

Kennedy cleared his throat and spoke for the first time. "Gentlemen," he said, "Mr. Miles has done us a service by giving us a large dose of reality therapy. We need to decide what to do—pragmatically—to make the best of a very bad situation. Peter's political future, P&D Productions, and a lot else are riding on how we handle this."

"I still think," Pomper said, "that we should look into this so-called victim's background. I heard from reliable sources that he was drunk—maybe lying in the street."

"Nonsense, Harold," Kennedy said. "We're not going to get anywhere if we continue to believe in fairy tales." He pointed his cigar at me. "He's on a life-support system?"

I nodded. "So I understand."

"All we need is for someone to show a videotape in court. Has anyone approached the family about a settlement?"

Duke said, "No. I wanted to avoid the appearance of a . . . bribe."

"Still, we should explore that option," Kennedy said. "Very delicately. I can handle that. The potential for a messy trial that would have a negative impact on your state Senate race is not inconsequential. Not to speak of the," he glanced at me, "possibility of a statewide race. Every step up the ladder is fraught with greater peril. I'm talking about media scrutiny."

"M-e-d-i-a," Pomper said, using the word like a curse. "The balance of power in our society has gotten completely out of whack."

Kennedy narrowed his eyes in thought and puffed the cigar. "The best we may be able to do is contain this by delaying the trial until after the special election. Let things die down a little." He turned to Peter Duke. "Have you considered getting Kevin into treatment?"

Kennedy accompanied me to the elevator, rode down with me, and walked me along the street to Wabash where we stood under the el. On the corner opposite, a black man was playing a trumpet for a small crowd. Kennedy lit a new cigar.

I inclined my head at the entrance to the club. "How does a Democrat like you get tied up with two fat-cat Republicans?"

He laughed. "Lobbying is nonpartisan."

"Sure it is."

He shrugged elaborately. "P&D is a client."

"P&D?"

"Pomper . . ."

". . . and Duke. I get it. What's the Speaker's interest in Peter Duke?" I asked.

He rolled his right hand back and forth. "An old friendship."

"Oh." A train rumbled overhead. "How's your daughter?" I said, just to make conversation.

He looked puzzled.

"Kris."

Comprehension dawned. He nodded. "Oh." He shook his head. "Kristin. She's not *my* daughter. I have no children of my own. She's my stepdaughter—Anne's child by her first marriage." He nodded back toward the entrance to the club. At that moment, I realized that Peter Duke's former wife, Anne Pomper, was my client of May, Anne Kennedy. "She's fine." Then he snapped his fingers. "Oh, you mean that Florida fiasco. That's right—you were the detective who went to Gainesville looking for her. I'm afraid Anne overreacted. Kris was just taking a delayed spring break. Needed to get away by herself. She was in Sarasota all the time. Just forgot to tell us."

A likely story. I decided not to tell White Shoes something else she evidently forgot to mention.

Airmailing her drink at her dinner companion.

As I walked back to the Bismarck, I tried to figure out how long I was going to be able to coach in the camp, keep an eye on Dewey, and still do the Kevin Duke job for the Speaker.

I decided to let it ride for a while.

When I got back, Dewey was nowhere to be found.

I fingered the penny in my pocket.

I couldn't decide whether it was lucky or not.

13

"How's Dewey?" Mitch asked.

"Young and restless," I said. "And AWOL. He cut out on me while I was mingling with the elite at the Marquette Club."

Mitch raised his eyebrows. "The Marquette Club?"

I explained about the call from Fast Freddy and the meeting with the Pomper & Duke legal brain trust.

"Harold Pomper," he mused. "I've heard him on talk radio. Even his bullshit is bullshit."

"You said it."

It was early evening. We were in the bar at the top of the John Hancock Center—above the restaurant—on the ninety-fifth floor. The hostess had shown us to a window table with a breathtaking view. I looked out into the clear night. Well below, I spotted the Prudential Building, which had been one of Chicago's tallest buildings when I first came up to Chicago from Terre Haute in 1962. Somewhere over the lake, I noticed the blinking red and white signal of a small plane. Beyond, the lights of a ship. "I can't wait for the bugle to sound and the House to ride in and save the day," I said.

"Me either," Mitch said sarcastically.

"The House was your idea."

"Good point. He doesn't get here soon, I may do Dewey

myself. If the Pork man doesn't beat me to it." He punched my arm lightly. "How you feeling?" he asked.

I touched my right elbow. "Terrific. I've got blisters on both hands and feet. And my knee is banged up. Thanks to the Dewster."

He nodded. "I warmed Jess and Dewey up today. Then caught batting practice. My knees are killing me. Not to speak of this." He held up a huge left hand, badly bruised.

"What kind of stuff did the scuzzball have?"

"In the pen, nasty. His sinker ball is *heavy*." Mitch paused for a sip of beer. "His control is uncanny. When he wants to, he can paint the black. In warm-ups, the son of a bitch threw some pitches in the dirt to make me scramble around back there. I had to tell him to cut that shit out."

"So you think he can help the Cubs?"

"Didn't say that." Mitch rubbed the side of his face. "This is the scout in me talking. Did you see him sweating and puffing after throwing about five minutes of b.p.? I don't know how long he can hold his stuff." He shook his head. "Five years is a long time. Hitting off him, his heater seemed straight as a string. I didn't have a gun on him, but I think he's lost about a yard off his fastball."

"I didn't notice."

"Hard to when you're on your back. Bobby, the margin for error for getting out big league hitters is very, very small." He shook his bald head. "Dewey's going to have to trick 'em, and I'm not sure he's smart enough."

"He doesn't have to be a rocket scientist to pitch for the Cubs."

"True. What do you make of this voodoo doll thing?"

"One of the coaches or one of the campers has it in for Dewey."

"Bobby, we already figured that out. It couldn't be Pork— he hired us. Unlikely to be Jess—his own brother. Can't be Dewey unless he's nuts."

"Don't rule that out."

"Really. We're the other two coaches. Must be a camper. I have an idea."

"Shoot."

"I'll get Pork to give me their camp applications tonight. Look them over. See if anything jumps out at me."

"Good idea. One more point."

"Yeah."

"Are you are sure we can eliminate the Porker? Dewey rides him pretty good."

"Let's ask him," Mitch said, nodding at the elevator. "Here he comes."

"Beer," Pork said to the cocktail waitress. "Michelob. Not light. Draft."

She turned away.

"Wait."

She turned back.

He held up two fingers. "Make that two beers, actually. And a round of whatever for these guys." He turned to us. "I wanted to talk away from the campers," he said. "Give you some more background on the asshole situation."

We both nodded. "Dewey?" I said.

"You seen any other buttheads around the camp?" He carefully laid out his pack of cigarettes, his silver lighter, a pile of crisp new dollar bills, and an ashtray in front of himself.

In a couple of minutes, the waitress brought him the beers. One for Mitch. A Coke for me. "Keep 'em coming, honey," he said with a grin. He handed her a couple of ones for a tip. "Run me a tab." He took a long swallow. His throat bobbed. "Ah," he said. "Cold beer makes life worth living."

"Along with fine guitars and firm-feeling women," I said, quoting my cultural hero, Waylon Jennings. "What's the word, Pork?"

He drew a deep breath. "All this is classified. You know

I'm kind of a superscout and troubleshooter for the ball club. They think they got a serious shot at the Eastern Division. I have my doubts, but stranger things have happened. Dewey could give them the lift they need. As a spot starter and long reliever. Just like he did in eighty-four. But," he paused to light a cigarette with the silver lighter and then snapped it shut, ". . . you saw him today." He shook his head. "He didn't show me much. He definitely needs an attitude adjustment. And his stuff didn't impress me."

"What Mitch just said," I said. "I had a different perspective."

Pork nodded. "The club is depending on me for a judgment. I'm biased against the asshole. But if he can still pitch . . ." He shrugged. "I would recommend that the Cubs sign Lefty Charles Manson if he could get Strawberry out with the bases loaded." He tapped ash into his ashtray. "It seems as if the jerk may still be in hock to gamblers. I have to make my recommendation to the ball club at the end of the week so they can petition the league office." He looked at me through small, dirty gray eyes. "A mistake here and I'm history with the Cubs. I'm relying on you, Nappy, to give me your best judgment. Is he straight?"

"I can answer that right now. He's as about as straight as Fernando Valenzuela's best scroogie."

Pork nodded. "I agree. By the way, where is asshole now?"

I shrugged. "I know where he's not. In his room."

Pork grinned. "I should have guessed."

I took a long swallow of Coke. "Pork, I'd give him a thumbs down right now," I said.

Pork shook his head. "Let's reserve judgment. A lot is riding on this." He paused to stab out his cigarette. "The pennant. My job. Not to speak of the camp." He started on his second beer. "What do you think of the campers?"

"There are some players," I said. "And some others . . ."

He nodded. "What about *my* player?"

When I got back to my room, I called Lisa.

"Are you back?" she asked.

"Negative." I told her about the camp and the dream game. "Looks as if I'm going to be here the rest of the week. How's La Grande Orange?"

"As regular as . . . Clockwork. I'm going to have to get another large sack of litter. It goes on your tab. Rob, I feel sorry for the little guy. He's getting lonely in your apartment with only unwashed socks to play with. I think I'll drive over this morning and take him to my place."

"That's not necessary."

"He's company. Besides I'm having a few people from the department over Friday night."

"Oh, he'll love that." Clockie likes Lisa, tolerates me, and is terrified of most other humans.

"He will, Rob. He's a purr-fect party animal."

"Cute. Lisa?"

"Yes?"

"Why don't you drive up on Saturday?" I said. "Catch the beauty of central and northern Illinois. The Joliet refineries, the stockyards, the power lines, the prisons. I'll spring for the gas. You can get in some serious shopping during the day. Michigan Avenue. Water Tower Place. See me play at night in Wrigley. After the game, we're talking peak experiences. Late dinner at the Top of the Hancock and god knows what else. You can drive me and Mitch home on Sunday."

"Food is mediocre at the Hancock."

"View is not. What do you say?"

"Rob—to put it in your parlance—I think I'll take an intentional walk."

"Oh."

"Why should I come two hundred miles to see the Cubs lose to the Mets again?"

The next morning, I forced myself out of bed at 6:30 and ran down Randolph toward the lake. The traffic north on Lake Shore Drive was already heavy. At considerable peril, I dodged across Lake Shore Drive and then jogged south toward the Field Museum. The museum, with its massive stone wings, sits at the south end of Grant Park and divides the north-south traffic on Lake Shore Drive. As I ran past the yachts at anchor, I heard the jingle of the masts and sails in the slight breeze. To my right, homeless men were stretched out on blankets on the wet grass, all their worldly possessions alongside.

Many other runners were out. Most of them passed me, running effortlessly. As did one black guy on pink roller skates with bright yellow—almost green—laces.

When I reached the Shedd Aquarium, I turned left to run out the finger of land to the Adler Planetarium. There was so much haze that as I looked out on the lake I could not tell where water ended and sky began.

To my right stood antiquated Soldier Field where Mike Ditka does his thing. To my left, Meigs, a landing field for small planes. It was always a thrill to descend on that wedge of land surrounded by lake. Especially on a windy day. Dead ahead was McCormick Place, Chicago's huge exposition center and the object of much political infighting in Chicago, where the line between public works and private greed is—to say the least—blurred.

I reached McCormick Place, turned around, and headed back to the hotel. When I got to the north end of Grant Park, I walked.

All the time I was trying to figure out the asshole situation. As far as I knew, Dewey hadn't returned to his room at the Bismarck last night. My only conclusion was that I would be damned glad when the House arrived.

Back at the hotel, I ordered the continental breakfast with a large fresh orange juice and read the *Herald-Star*. The front page headline said: "Bush to introduce flag amendment: People for the American Way and ACLU to Lead Opposition." And you thought the '88 election was over, I mused as I turned to the back page.

The Cubs had squeaked out a three-to-two victory over the Cards in St. Louis to move ten games over .500 in July!

Vatican—trot out the old devil's advocate—Chicago is about to canonize Don Zimmer.

"Wink" reported that "State rep Peter Duke denied yesterday that he has any plans to run for statewide office in 1990. 'I'm concentrating all my efforts on the special senatorial election,' he said. The Duke declined to comment on the legal problems of his son, Kevin, alleged to have been involved in a hit-and-run accident in early July."

"Wink" also teased "that an important announcement is due out of the governor's office soon."

I thought about Kevin Duke. To me, he was the classic case of an overprivileged kid run amok. I would bet that his room at home was a totally self-sufficient environment: CD player, private phone, TV and VCR, fridge, and microwave. True, he had an alcohol problem, which had started in his early teens. Possibly triggered by trauma and neglect. I knew it was tough being a legislator's kid. Pols trade home life for working the crowd. And Duke had been divorced, remarried, and divorced again. Pols' marriages have the life expectancy of those of street cops. And Kevin had witnessed a tragedy, the suicide of a friend. None of which—to my mind—came close to excusing his irresponsibility.

I decided to call the Speaker and tell him I had done all I could. No matter what Nate Wood and White Shoes Kennedy cooked up, the kid was going down for the hit-and-run.

"Meat, they shoot sentries for this."

I started and looked up. I had dozed off in the lobby of the Bismarck, waiting for Dewey to show. He stood over me, grinning. He wore a Tampa Bay Bucs jersey, number thirteen, jeans, tennis shoes—untied—and no socks. He looked as wired as the vote for Casinos for Kids in the Illinois House had been. He winked at me.

"You missed bed check," I said.

He shook his head. "You didn't check the right bed." He sighed with pleasure. "Chicago broads can suck an olive through a straw."

I tried to explain to him that we couldn't provide security if we didn't know where he was. He just shrugged. "That's not my problem. I always know where I am."

We went down to the street to grab a cab. After we got in, I said, "Dewey, what have you been doing since you were suspended?"

As I waited for his response, I looked at the photo over the driver's license. Our cab driver bore no earthly resemblance to the picture. He drove like a Domino's Pizza delivery boy with a bounty on pedestrians.

Dewey thought about my question. He shrugged. "Chilling out. Going to the track. Pounding down some brew. Chasing pussy. What else is there?"

"Tell me about Dewey," I said to Jess Farmer, as we strolled in the outfield on the warning track next to the ivy.

He shrugged. "He's an asshole. He's my brother. What's to tell?"

"Can he make it back?"

He shook his head. "I don't know. He had it all and pissed it away. I don't know if his head's on straight. I don't know if he's got the stuff."

"As a pitcher?"

"As a man."

"Who wants to hurt him?"

He stopped, turned, and faced me. "Most ever' woman he ever met."

"Oh?"

He spit tobacco juice to his right. "Dumbass thinks with his dick. Likes the young stuff. Middle-aged stuff." He shrugged. "Even the good old stuff."

"How young does it go?"

"How young does it get?"

"How old does it go?"

He grinned. "For Dewey, there's no limit as long as it's still in the same place."

I worked with the infielders again. "Let's work on the double play." I motioned to the girl. "Pat, we need to work on your pivot."

She pounded her blue glove. "Yes, sir."

I showed her how to take the throw, glide over the bag with a phantom touch, and get the throw off sidearm. "Make that runner get down," I said. "Let's try it together. See if we can get the timing right. Rhythm is everything . . . in baseball."

She winked. "In all sports," she said, with an impish grin.

I took a few grounders at short and fed her the ball, which she relayed to first. Her throws were awkward but true. She started to get the hang of it. "Good," I said. "Consider me your personal tutor."

"I do."

After the stations, we divided the campers into two groups to play a simulated game. Jess Farmer, wearing blue number thirteen, pitched. He warmed up with Mitch. He threw easily, using a distinctive submarine motion that was nearly identical to Dewey's. To give the campers more at-bats, the coaches played in the field all the time. Pork looked at Dewey. "Play right field, thirteen."

As Pork explained the rules, Dewey stood capless, his arms folded across his chest, looking pissed. When Pork finished, Dewey shook his head and said, "I ain't pitching, I ain't playing. Too much of a chance of getting hurt." He turned and sauntered over to the dugout and sat down.

"Asshole," I heard Jess mutter.

Pork just stared at Dewey. "Fine," he said. "You can keep score."

We took the field. I played short, Pork played first, and Mitch caught. Five campers joined us in the field. After three outs, the campers switched.

We played five innings. Pat went hitless but handled two balls in the field flawlessly.

I handled half a dozen routine chances and felt good about it. My arm was still sore; however, I could make rainbow throws to first, given the speed of most of the campers.

Afterward, the coaches took b.p.

Pork motioned to Dewey. "Let's see what you got today, stud."

Dewey took his warm-ups, throwing to Mitch. He was popping the glove. Pork stepped into the cage and took his corkscrew stance. He sent the first pitch off the ivy in right. The slight wind blowing in had held the ball up, and a camper staggered and caught it on the warning track.

Mitch looked up through his mask and said, "Pork, you were into your home-run trot. You thought it was out of here."

Pork stepped out, grinning. "It was in the Lake if the wind hadn't held it up."

"Just another routine fly, Porker."

"You are a sick man, Professor. I can hit any asshole that ever lived."

Behind the batting cage, Jess leaned over to me. "If you
can hit, you can hit."

"Yogi Berra?"

"Mike Tyson."

On the way off the field, I noticed Dewey cutting Pat out
of the herd. He put his arm around her shoulder, talking
intently. To my dismay, she grinned up at him and nodded
her head affirmatively. I didn't think he was asking her what
she thought of the trade deficit or Third World debt.

Damn it, Dewey, I thought. She's too old—ancient—in
her midthirties at least.

But to all intents, she still had it in the right place.

When Dewey and I got back to the Bismarck lobby, an
extremely large black gentleman was sitting in a chair, peering at a *Wall Street Journal*. He was wearing a Los Angeles
Laker warm-up outfit, purple trimmed in gold. Purple shades
pushed up on his forehead. He glanced up at me. "Miles,
my man." He stood and towered over us. His bullet head
gleamed in the light from the multicolored chandeliers.

Dewey took one look and stage-whispered to me, "Ar-
nold Schwarze-nigger?"

I shut my eyes.

"Say what?" Big House said.

"Nothing," I said quickly. "Big House Bellamy, this is
Dewey Farmer."

Dewey looked at Big as if he expected a reaction.

But Big merely nodded a fraction. Pushed down the
shades. No visible expression on his face. "Farmer," he
said.

"Yo, blood," Dewey said, doing a little shuffle. He tried
to give Big a high five. Big turned it into a regular white-
bread handshake. Except for the muscle. Dewey visibly
winced. "You dig rap music, bro?"

"No."

"Big House? That your address or your name, bro?"

Big stared at Dewey as if he had just farted in church. Finally, he said, "Name. It was Muhammad Muhammad, but I changed it."

"Dewey," I said, "Go to your room."

"Cracker," Big said. He sighed dramatically. "You always give me crackers."

I nodded ruefully. "This one's an animal," I said. I gave Big the big picture.

When I finished, he said, "So you think they already made one try in Florida?"

I shrugged. "Maybe. Maybe not. Anyone who met him even casually might like to take a piece out of him."

Big nodded. "Clown's so jumpy, he'd make coffee nervous. Let's go up to his room and make sure this bozo understands the House rules."

When we got to the room on the sixth floor, however, there was no answer to my knock.

Big flipped his glasses up and stared at me. "Hotel elevator run all the way down to the ground floor?" he asked.

"Yeah. It does."

"Miles," he said in a long-suffering tone, "I'm thinking your elevator doesn't go all the way to the top."

The next morning after a short run along the lake I called the Speaker's office. It was just after 7:15. I knew he would be in and Fast Freddy would not. I gave my leader a blow-by-blow of my meeting with Kevin Duke and the conference with Peter Duke, Art Kennedy, and Harold Pomper. "Harold," he said with disgust. "A one-man filibuster."

"For certain." I took a deep breath. "I want to close down my end of the Kevin Duke matter," I said.

"Oh?"

"I've done all I can do. Nate Wood has his work cut out for him. He should try to plea bargain."

Silence.

"I'm curious about something. Let me see if I have it straight. Harold Pomper's daughter married Peter Duke?"

"Yes."

"And then Duke and Pomper formed a law partnership?"

"That's correct. Very successful."

"Then the daughter and Peter got divorced, but the law partnership survived?"

"Of course," the Speaker said. "That was business."

Ever the consummate pro, I thought.

"Anyway, I've played out the string on Kevin Duke."

"Robert, I'm surprised at you."

The Speaker is a completist. Passionate about details. Closing loops.

"What do you mean?" I said.

"I seem to recall . . ."

In photographic detail, I thought. The *second person in the car,* I thought.

". . . your report indicated there was conflicting testimony about how many persons were in the car at the time of the . . . accident."

"Yes. Two witnesses thought there was another person, but Kevin doesn't claim that."

Silence. Then, "If he were intoxicated . . ."

"I see your point."

"Do some more checking. You said that Kevin was at this bar with someone."

"Yeah. Before the accident. His sister. Kris."

"She might have a better sense of whether anybody left with Kevin. Don't you think you'd better talk with her, too?"

He had me, as usual. Why don't you be the detective, I thought. I'll play Speaker. "Right," I said.

"How's this fantasy whatever going?" The Speaker spoke the word "fantasy" as though it was not in his working vocabulary.

"Camp. Fine."

"Good. Robert . . ."

"Yes?"

"Get me something I can use to help Peter."

Big and I sat in the Bismarck lobby, waiting for Dewey. Big wore a dark navy Nike jogging suit, a light blue beret, bright yellow Ray•Ban sunglasses and white Reebok basketball shoes. After he finished the *Wall Street Journal,* he said, "I've been studying this threat bullshit."

"Oh?"

"Nobody but the cracker saw the notes or heard the calls? He wouldn't go to the coppers? And it's his word about the bar fight?"

I nodded. "Partially true. Supposedly, the police were called to the bar fight."

"But you don't know that for sure?"

I shrugged. "But I have the doll. And that note."

"He could have planted them." He took off his sunglasses and polished them on the sleeve of his running suit. "Sucker's catting around all night. Doesn't seem to be taking this danger bit very seriously. He's either reckless or . . ." He paused.

I bounced that around in my head for a few seconds. ". . . he *knows* it's a hoax?"

Big nodded.

"But why?"

"Dude's making a comeback?"

I nodded.

"Out of baseball for five years?"

I nodded again.

"*Five fuckin' years.* Could you of stayed out five years and come back?"

"Big, I couldn't play when I played."

"Five years out of football, I'd of been killed, I tried to play. He might'a lost it. But if it looks like someone's trying to hurt him, the publicity might make him a . . ."

"Martyr?"

He nodded.

I shrugged. "I don't know. This whole deal just made Pork more nervous about recommending him to the Cubs. That's why we're here. And I don't think Dewey's that imaginative."

Big sighed. "Who says he working alone?"

Dewey showed up in the lobby about 9:15, as jumpy as a cat around a power lawnmower. "Let's haul ass," he said, motioning impatiently, as if Big and I were late.

"How was your date?" I asked.

"Don't ask," he snapped.

I grinned.

When we got to the ground floor, we left by the revolving door. The sounds and smells of the city hit us. Horns, the rumble of cars and construction, the clatter of a train on the el, exhaust. A spotless white Lincoln Continental was parked at the curb. The Illinois vanity plates said: "Big 1." Big took the keys from the attendant and gave him a major tip.

Dewey tapped my arm. He leaned into me. He nodded at the car. "Fancy wheels." His breath was sour. "The big spook's a coke dealer, am I right?"

I shook my head.

"Pimp?"

"Nah. Mechanic."

"Works on cars?"

"Contract hitman," I said. "He's a stone killer."

Dewey nodded, impressed.

Big motioned for Dewey to join him in front. I sat in back. Big started the car. Flipped down his sunglasses. Then he turned, reached his left arm across Dewey's body and grabbed Dewey's right arm and jerked him around so that Big was literally in his face.

Dewey struggled. "Hey, you're messing with my career, bro," Dewey whined.

Big put his right forearm under Dewey's chin and pushed him back against the side window so that his head bounced off it with a dull clunk. Dewey turned white. "*Don't* call me, bro," Big said. "And if you pull any more of that disappearing shit, I'll tear off your arm and piss down the stump." He released him. "Do you read me?"

Dewey nodded and looked back at me as if to say, do you believe this?

"Stone killer," I mouthed.

Big negotiated the Chicago downtown traffic as effortlessly as Sinatra crooning "My Kind of Town."

As he blended with the traffic on Lake Shore Drive, I said, "Ever thought of a second career, Big? As a chauffeur?"

He glared at me in the rear view window.

"Guess not," I said.

Pork was seated behind his desk in the manager's office, smoking a cigarette. He wore a blue Cub undershirt with long sleeves. He looked up and his eyes widened.

"Pork," I said, "This is Big House Bellamy, Farmer's baby-sitter."

"Some baby," he said slowly. "Some sitter. Big? Good name. You're big enough to go to work . . . big enough . . ."

"To go bear hunting with a switch," Big said. "I've heard every 'big' joke. Pork? The other white meat?"

Barelli chuckled and then asked, "Play any ball?"

"Foot," Big said. He pretended to catch a pass. "Tight end."

"Speaking of the pigskin," Barelli said, nodding at me, "Nappy here oughta wear his glove on his feet."

"Nappy?" Big said.

"The Human Napkin."

Big nodded. "He *is* a mess." He touched the back of my head. "Needs a trim, too." He pretended to punt a ball. "Glove on his feet?" He smiled. "'Cause he kicks so many?"

Pork grinned. "'Nother thing. Nappy should never leave his glove out in the rain."

"'Cause it'll rust."

"Eddie Murphy and Nick Nolte," I said.

We had settled into a practice routine. Stretching. Running in the outfield. Fielding practice for the campers. Batting practice for the campers. Intrasquad game. B.p. for the coaches as the campers showered and dressed. Lunch. Coaches' meeting.

Big had roamed the stands like a restless panther during the practice.

"Rainbow coalition," Big muttered to me.

We were outside the park, approaching Big's white Lincoln parked in the lot on Waveland that was usually reserved for Cub players.

Three street toughs were leaning up against the car. One black, one Hispanic, and one white. Each wore a yellow bandanna on his forehead, a checked work shirt with long sleeves buttoned to the top, and black pants cut off at the knees. Black tennis shoes. White socks. Hair cut down to the skull.

They gave us stony looks. The black made some hand signals to his companions.

"Assholes," Dewey said.

We stopped about fifty feet from them.

"Want me to get security?" I said to Big.

"Good idea," Big said. "No sense looking for trouble."

"Thought you were security," Dewey responded. "Jesus, come on." He glared at the three.

The Hispanic pulled out a screwdriver and pretended to run it along the gleaming finish of the Lincoln.

"That tears it," Big said softly. He took a long step toward the car. "Hey!" he yelled. "Don't be hurting my wheels." Big took another step forward.

"You a big dude," the black said laconically to Big. He was no minnow himself—about six feet but weighing at least 250. Weight lifter's arms. Slightly crossed eyes. He grinned. "This here is, like, a people's parking lot. We liberated it. The parking fee is . . ."

"This is the Cubs lot," Dewey snarled. "I'm Dewey Farmer."

"And I'm Malcolm X," the black said.

"Get lost, scumbags," Dewey said.

The black shook his head sadly. "Price just went up, man." He reached for his back pocket and pulled out his own large screwdriver. Wickedly sharpened. He came off the car in a fighting stance.

Dewey started to move forward. Big reached out and pushed Dewey back. Hard. He turned to the black. "No trouble, homes. I'm a man of peace." He sauntered up to the black, grinning easily. The black backed up a step. Big pointed to the screwdriver. "No need for that, man," he said in a soothing tone. "We pay." He moved in closer and put his arm around the punk in a fatherly manner, turning him slightly away from his friends. He reached into the pocket of the top of his running outfit and pulled out a full billfold. I could see it was crammed with green. The punk's eyes widened. He started to reach for it.

Big tried to flip it open with one hand, but it dropped to the pavement. The punk bent down for it. Big hit him quick like Ali dropped Sonny Liston. His punch traveled no more than six inches, and the punk collapsed like a punctured tire. Big drop-kicked the screwdriver away and faced the other two. The Hispanic grinned crazily and slapped his screwdriver into the palm of his hand; the white pulled a chain from his back pocket and started to twirl it. Big unzipped his top and showed them something. They backed off. "Homeboys," he said calmly, "get him the fuck out of here."

They dragged the black guy away, giving nervous glances back every few seconds.

The whole thing had not taken more than a minute.

"Way to go, blood," Dewey said. He tried to give Big a high five.

Big slapped his hand away. Hard. "*Don't* call me blood. Next time, keep your mouth shut."

"Man, I could'a . . ."

Big silenced him with a look.

When we reached Lake Shore Drive, I said, "About time we moved over to the Easton."

"Fuckin' A," Dewey said. "Let's go pound some brew." He turned to Big. "What'd you show those guys?"

Big looked at me in the rearview mirror. He winked. "It wasn't," he said, "my American Express Card."

"What's the greatest baseball record?" I asked.

Mitch, Pork, and I were in the darkened bar at the Easton. The walls around us were decorated by red signs advertising foreign beers. Over the dark wood bar was a row of glasses, upside down.

"DiMaggio's hitting streak," Mitch said. "No question about it."

"Why?" I challenged.

He gave me an impatient look. "Hitting a baseball is the hardest thing in sports. The Clipper hit safely in fifty-six straight games. Consistency. Mark of greatness."

"I was great at not hitting the breaking ball," I observed, leaning back in my chair. At that moment, Pat Anderson entered the bar. She paused to adjust to the dim, looked around, saw us, gave a shy wave, and then strolled over to the bar. She wore a yellow sweater over a blue blouse and off-white jeans. She looked as cute as Whitey Ford's pick-off move.

She ordered something and then turned to face the room. I motioned for her to join us. She nodded and came over. "Can I join the party?" she asked. "Or is this a men's only club?"

"For *players* only," Pork said. "You're a player."

She grinned. "Be right back." She sauntered back to the bar.

Pork leered. *"That's* what I call affirmative action."

Pat returned with her beer and sat next to me, brushing my arm with hers. "Let's play a game," I said.

Mitch gave me a sour look.

"Sure," Pat said.

"Baseball Jeopardy. Category: Numerology. The answer is fifty-six."

Pat shook her glossy head, gray eyes twinkling. "Too easy. DiMaggio's hitting streak," she said. She patted the back of her short hair.

"Buzz!" I said. "You didn't answer in the form of a question."

She grinned. "Oh, Alex. Don't be such a stickler. Did you know he hit sixty-one straight in the Pacific Coast League?"

"Everyone knows that," Mitch said.

She stuck out her tongue at him.

"Your turn," I said to Pat.

She frowned. Then she grinned and said, "Thirty-six."

"Thirty-six?" Mitch narrowed his eyes in concentration. "Denny McLain won thirty-one."

Pork looked squarely at the front of Pat's sweater and shook his head. "Any other numbers go with that? Like twenty-two and thirty-six?"

She blushed. "Give you a hint. Chief Wilson," she said slowly. "Give up?"

"You mean Earl Wilson," Mitch said. "Lifetime homers for a pitcher?"

She shook her head. "Wes Farrell holds that."

"Chief Bender?" I said.

"Chief Wilson. Thirty-six triples in nineteen-eleven. No one is even close. Change the subject?"

"Definitely," I said.

She turned to Pork and said, "Why'd you guys blow it in sixty-nine?"

"The lady knows how to get to the heart of the matter," Mitch said.

Pork got a faraway look in his eye. "I always thought one game killed us."

"The black cat game?" Pat asked. "In Shea?"

"Nah. Earlier. At Wrigley in early September. Against the Pirates. We had a one-run lead with two out in the bottom of the ninth. Jim Hickman had just hit one out to give us the lead. Willie Stargell up. The Mule was pitching. The wind was blowin' in a gale from right field. King-fuckin'-Kong couldn't have hit one out." He glanced at Pat. "Sorry."

She grinned. "Pork, I'm a coach—I've actually *used* the *eff* word."

He grinned back. "Mule kept throwing Pops spitter after spitter. Pops fouled 'em off. I'm halfway in the tunnel, reaching for a cold one on each pitch. Finally, one of them suckers didn't drop. Stargell crushed it, clean onto Sheffield Avenue. Tied the game. We lost in extra innings. Things seemed to fall apart from there."

"You know what I think," Pat said.

"What, player?" Pork said.

"Nine guys don't win a pennant."

Mitch nodded. "Mets had the pitching."

She nodded back. "And bull pen and bench. The Cubs had the best starting lineup, but the Mets won because they were the better team."

17

"I've got some batting tips for you," I said to Pat.

She grinned. "I could use some."

Pork put his elbows on the table. "Player," he said, "that's like going to the Pope to learn safe sex." He tapped himself on the chest. "There's only one real heavy hitter at this table."

"I'll buy the 'heavy' part," I said. I took her arm. "Let's get out of all this smoke."

She nodded. "Let's." She picked up her half-consumed beer and stood.

I dropped a dollar on the table. Mitch gave me a dirty look. I walked her over to an empty table in the corner. She sat down. I said, "Watch." I pretended to tap a bat on an imaginary plate. I wiggled my butt. "You got to do something to time the pitch," I said.

"Rhythm," she said.

I nodded.

She looked at my rear end. "So that's what Pork means by getting *it* moving," she said.

"Distracts the catcher, too," I added. "You married?" I sat down and looked into her pale gray eyes.

She shook her head. Shrugged. "Divorced. I'm a tennis coach. Indiana State University. Bruce couldn't take the long practices, the road trips, and the recruiting." She looked at my left hand. "You?"

I held it up. No ring. Never had one. In my mind, men and jewelry don't fit. Big's an exception to the rule. "Gray area."

She frowned. "You either are or are not. It's like being a little—"

"Pregnant?"

"Dead."

I explained about Lisa and the concept of no-fault separation.

"Convenient," she said. "For you."

"I just hope I don't mess up Saturday night," Pat said. "I don't want to be the Donna Young of the game."

I chuckled. Don Young was the unfortunate outfielder who messed up a couple of plays in Shea in July of '69. Lots of Cub fans felt that those misplays turned the season around. Ron Santo made some critical comments in the heat of the moment after the game that didn't help either.

"You'll be fine," I said. "You watch much baseball in Philly?"

She nodded. "My sister and I. We were almost groupies at the Vet. We loved Mike Schmidt. Talk about your basic wiggle." She paused and some sadness crept into her eyes. "Sis adored him."

"Ever boo him?"

She blushed. "Once. Sis almost killed me." She paused. Her gray eyes got remote. Then she said, "You didn't play with the sixty-nine Cubs."

"Right. Sixty-seven. One at bat."

"What'd you do?"

I touched my left elbow. "My specialty. Hit by a pitch."

"Another Ron Hunt," she said. "What do you do now?"

"Research."

She frowned. "College?"

I nodded. "In a way. The school for scandal."

She frowned.

"Just kidding. The Illinois General Assembly."

"What kind of research?"

"Political. I'm sort of a consultant. Whatever it takes."

"You seem to know Mitch Norris pretty well."

I nodded. "We work together. Can I ask you a personal question?"

She shrugged.

"Why'd you go out with that asshole?"

"Who?"

"Dewey Farmer."

Her gray eyes hardened. She gave me a cool appraising look. "That's none of your business." She moved around in her chair as if getting ready to get up. She reached for her purse. "Getting late," she said. "Don't want to break training."

I nodded. "Listen, don't go away mad."

She shook her head and smiled. It seemed strained to me. "No problem. I just want to get my rest." She paused. "I like Mitch." She frowned. "Say, who was that big black guy around the park today?"

I frowned as if trying to remember such a fellow.

"The one with the yellow shades, the blue beret, and the attitude. Always roaming the stands."

"Oh," I said, feigning an effort to recall. "Maybe I did see him. Must work for the Cubs," I offered.

She shook her head and gave me a disbelieving look. "I saw you talking with him after practice. Then you left with him and Asshole."

I nodded. "I think I know who you mean. He kind of looks like Willie McCovey?"

She nodded.

I decided to change the subject. "See *Bull Durham*?"

She shook her head. "Yes, I love Kevin . . ." Then she paused and her eyes widened. She was looking over my shoulder. "Company," she said. "Old number forty-four."

I frowned.

"Willie McCovey."

"What's the story?" the very annoyed—make that honked off—man in the rumpled brown suit asked. He sat slumped in a chair at a table for four in the Easton Taproom. It was after midnight.

I yawned.

"Somebody took a little bite out of the cracker," Big said.

"Cracker?" the man said.

"Dewey Farmer," I said.

The man rubbed his chin stubble. "*The* Dewey Farmer?"

"Only cracker named Dewey Farmer I know," Big said.

The man in brown pinched his nose. "I lost a bundle on him in eighty-four. Where is he?"

"Hospital emergency room." Big shook his head. "He ain't hurt bad. Just a few scrapes."

Brown suit's name was Al Podolak. He was a Chicago plainclothes detective. And not a happy camper.

When Big had told me that Dewey had been a victim of a hit-and-run, I called Pork's room. He had said, "Jesus Christ with a fungo bat," when I told him about it. "The Cubs will freak if this hits the papers. But I got to call the cops. It's CYA time."

Forty-five minutes later, Podolak had arrived looking like a brown bear who had been caged up for a week, starved, poked and prodded with a sharp stick.

Pork and I had introduced ourselves.

Podolak had stared at Big for a good five seconds. Big had stared back. "Who are you?" Podolak had finally asked.

"Bellamy." Big had shot a warning look at me. "Clarence Bellamy."

Pork looked at me. *Clarence?*

Podolak smiled wearily. "Well, Clarence, tell me what happened."

"Me and dis cracker was. . . ," Big started to say.

"Clarence," Podolak said, "cut the shit."

Big nodded. ". . . were walking back on Michigan Avenue right at Ontario. The light turned just as we got to the crossing. Said 'Do Not Walk.'" He shook his head at the corruption of the big city. "Farmer didn't pay any attention. Walked right into the path of the car."

"Make?"

Big shrugged. "Not sure. Happened so quick. Sports car. Going like hell. I thought old Dewey was road kill. Have to give him this—he's got some kind of quick reflexes. He was more than a little smashed. He made a little half-spin— kinda like the Pearl in the lane . . ."

"'Pearl'?" Podolak said.

Big looked shocked. "Earl 'The Pearl' Monroe. Farmer only got grazed."

"License plate?"

Big shrugged again. "Illinois. Maybe."

Podolak sighed. "Driver?"

"Fox."

"Hair color?"

"Yellow."

"Any other description?"

"All them white foxes look alike to me."

Podolak took off his clear-rimmed glasses and used a napkin to wipe them off. "What we got here is basically nothing. Squat. I'm looking for a sports car with a blonde woman driver. Can't be too many of those in Cook County."

"You forgot the Illinois plate," I said.

Podolak turned his flat stare on me. "You are what?"

"Private detective."

"Marvelous. What's your interest in this?"

I told him I was part of the security team. I explained about the bar fight and the threats to Dewey. I showed him my license. He grunted. I told him about the doll and the incident in the parking lot.

He nodded. "Sounds like the North Side Sinners. Kinda

wimps. But you're lucky they weren't carrying. Florida coppers investigate these alleged threats?"

I shook my head.

"You seen the letters?"

"No. But I saw the doll."

"In *his* locker."

I nodded.

Big looked at me and nodded slightly. He and Podolak were on the same wavelength.

Podolak rubbed his eyes. "Send Farmer in tomorrow to make a statement. I got to tell you—I got three unsolved homicides, a shitload of paperwork and court appearances, and a drug bust going down."

"You're saying?" I asked.

"Minor traffic accident. This isn't a priority."

After Podolak left, Big said, "Red 1986 Nissan 300ZX Turbo. Illinois plate ay-en-tee-ee-kay-ee-one. Dinged up right fender. Blonde, about twenty-five years old. Didn't get the eye color."

I stared at him. "Why didn't you tell Podolak?"

He grinned. "Man, I've got my reputation to think about."

18

"Pork, can I use your phone?" It was the next morning in the Cub manager's office.

"Sure thing." Pork—in his blue sweat shirt and jock—waddled out to the locker room, making some gibe at the fat camper. I could hear his growl and the responding roar of laughter.

I sat behind his desk. I found the Yellow Pages in his desk and ran my finger down the row of law firms until I came to the number for Pomper & Duke. "Pomper and Duke, attorneys-at-law," a male voice with a crisp British accent said.

"Can I speak to Peter Duke?"

"He's in conference. May I say who is calling?"

I told him and said it was urgent. That I would be at this number for the next thirty minutes.

Then I called Springfield and got Fast Freddy. "What's wrong?" he said.

"Just checking in," I responded.

"Thoughtful of you, Miles, I hope you're keeping your eye on the ball."

"Trying to."

"Keep your priorities straight. Listen, we're coming up tomorrow. For a fund-raiser. I came up with a great gimmick. We're taking some high rollers out for a lake cruise and setting up a gaming room on the yacht. Everything they lose is a campaign contribution. Get it?"

"Casinos for contributors?"

"Right. This will be great pub. Anyway, the Man wants to see you at the Bismarck. Status report on the Duke deal. Afternoon okay?"

"Yeah. Fast, soon as I dot some i's and cross some t's, I want out of this Duke thing. It's going nowhere. I got this other case . . ."

"You're not talking about the fantasy camp?"

"Yeah."

"Well, the Speaker's not ready to toss in the towel on Duke, so toughski shitski."

"Fast?"

"Yeah?"

"Can you trace a plate number through the Secretary of State's office for me?"

"Sure. Why should I?"

"It could be important on the hit-and-run," I said. I just didn't say which one.

"What is it?"

I gave it to him.

He hung up. The phone rang. It was the firm's English secretary. "Hold for Mr. Duke," he said.

"Mr. Miles, what can I do for you?"

"First, I need to talk to Kevin again. I . . ."

He cut me off. "Impossible."

"How's that?"

"He's enrolled in a substance abuse treatment center."

"Where?"

"Minneapolis. Tell you what. If you make some written interrogatories, I'll see that . . ."

"No. Maybe you can help on the second thing."

"Anything I can do."

"I need to know how to get ahold of Kris, his sister."

There was a pause that stretched into an awkward silence.

"Mr. Duke?"

His voice became harsh. Authoritative. Demanding. "Her name is Kristin, not Kris. Under no conditions will you speak with her. Do I make myself absolutely clear? Stay the hell away from her."

"I don't understand. She was with Kevin prior to the accident. She may have valuable . . ."

"This is not a matter for debate. *Read my lips.*"

A little difficult over the phone.

"Leave her the hell alone." He hung up. I stared at the phone and then moved my head back and forth. I had touched a nerve and I had no idea why.

Pork came back in. A stub of a cigarette hung loosely from his lips. I gave him his chair. He sat down with a sigh. "Thought I should warn you. There'll be a reporter from the *Herald-Star* around the camp today and the rest of the week. Chet Hagan."

"'The Toy Department.'"

He nodded. "He's doing a feature on the camp and the game. Plus we're talking with him about doing the script for the project."

"Project?"

"We call it the baseball 'Dream-a-mentary.' Based on the game and the tapes we're shooting during the rest of the week." He shook his head. "Bright idea of my partners. At the very worst, it'll be a great advertising short for the camps. At the best, a TV movie."

"Won't Hagan write about Dewey?"

Pork shook his head. "Hagan's agreed not to print anything on Dewey until just before the game. He gave me his word. Actually, he talked to Dewey on the phone when Asshole was still in Florida. In fact, I think he may have some kind of a book deal going with Asshole. Assuming jerk-off makes it back to the bigs. Which I'm beginning to doubt."

"What do I tell Hagan?"

He stabbed out his butt in a coffee cup on the desk, pulled open his desk drawer, and fumbled around inside. He pulled out a pouch of tobacco and felt around in it. "Tell him the truth." He wedged a plug in his jaw.

"What's that?"

He spit into the wastebasket. "We hire the handicapped."

"Differently abled," I said.

Chet Hagan was a chunky guy of about thirty, bald, with a full beard and clear-rimmed glasses. I had seen him talking extensively to Dewey throughout the morning. Now he had come over to chat with me.

"You are who?" he asked, holding a mike close to me.

I stroked a hard grounder toward Pat. "Miles," I said. "Roberto Miles."

Pat scooped it up and lobbed it back in.

"Roberto? You don't look Hispanic. Camper?"

"Way to go, Pat!" I yelled. She didn't acknowledge me. "Coach," I said. I held up the bat. Pointed to my blue shirt.

"Right." He laughed. "You coaches all wear blue." Then he frowned. "Roberto? You play in sixty-nine?"

"Yeah."

In Midland, I thought.

He scratched his head with his free hand. "I went over the sixty-nine Cub roster just the other day. I don't remember . . . what position?"

"Utility. I didn't get in many games."

Take away the M and make that *any,* I thought.

He nodded. "I'll look it up. What you doing these days?"

"As little as possible."

He forced a chuckle. "Nah, I need it for the story. You're not in baseball?"

"No." I smacked a hard grounder to the left of the fat camper, who waved it as it rolled into right field. "Way to move!" I yelled.

"I don't give good *field*," he yelled back. "I paid three thousand to watch this, and I'm getting my money's worth."

I stroked a grounder to Pat. "Public service. I work for the Illinois General Assembly. Research consultant."

"I see." He looked and sounded bored. "You know anything about that big black guy in the running suit?" He pointed down the right-field line. "Kind of looks like Willie McCovey?"

"Peter Duke is royally pissed off at you," Fast said, as he greeted me at the door of the Speaker's suite at the Bismarck.

I looked around the empty room. "Where's the Man?"

"Meeting with the mayor. On the city's budget deficit." He shook his slick head. He started pacing like a caged wolverine. "The SOB's been in office only a few months, and he's got his hand out. The only thing surer than death and taxes is city mayors asking for more money."

"That's the name of the game," I said. I flopped down on the bed. "What's Duke's problem?"

"You want to talk to some girl who knows nothing about the case."

"Not *some* girl. Kevin's sister. Kristin."

Fast paused to light one of his ultrathin cigars. "Pay attention, Miles. She's Harold Pomper's granddaughter and she's strictly off limits."

I shook my head. "The Speaker thinks it's important that I talk to her. Now you say no. Why?"

"Because Pomper and Duke say so. They carry a lot of weight."

"Fast—listen up—she was with Kevin just before the accident. She might know something about a second person in the car. She might help the case."

He waved that away. "That doesn't matter. Since you've been out of the loop, the game plan has changed."

"How?"

"Nate Wood and I decided we need to get control of the program. Change the terms of the debate. We're going after the liquor manufacturer."

I shook my head. "You really lost me. Run that by me again."

Fast Freddy touched the ends of his 'stash. Then he resumed pacing, using the cigar as a baton. He talked as he did. "It's ingenious. We see it as a landslide civil rights case."

"I'll bet. Whose civil rights are we talking about?"

"Kevin Duke's."

I put my hands behind my head. "The veg is the one whose fundamental rights were—shall we say—negated."

"True. But Kevin was only the proximate cause. We're going after the root cause."

Proximate?

Root?

"Fast, you've been consorting with social scientists again."

He ignored me. He's had a lot of practice and he's good at it. "You remember when they put one of the auto manufacturers on trial for vehicles that turned you into toast if you got rear-ended?"

I nodded.

"Remember the *Twinky* defense?"

"The *product* made him do it?"

He nodded. "Duke's kid is an alcoholic. He's at a treatment center in Minneapolis."

That item of national security had been leaked.

"On scholarship?"

"Not funny. We are going right after the liquor manufacturer."

"On what possible grounds?"

"No warning label."

"They should have informed the kid that if he mixed booze with drugs, and then ran a light, he might hurt somebody? Why not go after the bartender? Or the bar? Dram shop negligence."

Fast gave me a withering look. He went to the window and stood with his back to me. "Not enough bucks there. We're looking for deep pockets."

I just shook my head. "I can't believe the Speaker would buy into such a scheme."

Fast turned around and said, "He will."

"This *Twinky* defense is just a smoke screen. It'll never fly."

"Yes, it will. First of all, it pushes the legal envelope. Second, there are precedents."

"Fast, you can't have it both ways. Whose bright idea was this?"

"Mine. And Wood's."

"Figures. Look. There may be a better way."

He came alert. "What's that?"

"An explanation, if not an excuse. He had a traumatic experience that probably contributed to his dependency problem."

Fast took a deep breath. "Fax me the facts on that," he demanded.

"He witnessed the shooting suicide of his best friend. At age thirteen. That would be enough to knock anyone off the rails. Maybe we can get his psychiatrist to testify. But Peter Duke may not want us to raise old memories."

Fast Freddy shook his head. "Tough-o shit-o. He's got to decide whether he wants to win this election or not. Whether he wants to be gov . . ." He stopped talking.

"What?"

"Nothing."

*   *   *

Mitch and I sat in the Easton bar with Dewey, listening to him rant about how he had been screwed over by major league baseball. We were giving Big a needed break. Dewey had put away at least four G-and-Ts.

Pork strode over from the bar with a beer and pulled up a chair and nodded at us. Dewey gave him a nasty look. "Have you seen enough, Pork-ass?" he asked.

Pork stared at him calmly. "Enough what?" He put down his lighter, cigarettes, and four quarters.

"My stuff." He took a drink. "My yakker. I can help the Cubs. You know it."

Pork shook out a cigarette and took his time lighting it. He blew a smoke ring. "I don't know that. We've been hitting you pretty hard in b.p."

Farmer flushed. "Never was a practice player. Plus, I've been dogging it. Don't want to show you old farts up. Get a bat, gramps. I'll show you." He started to get up. "Now."

Pork shook his head. "Where? In the middle of Michigan Avenue? Asshole, you had the arm. No doubt." He tapped his head, then his heart, and then his belly. "It's what's here, here, and here that I worry about."

Dewey stiffened. "You sayin' I choke?"

Pork shook his head again. "I'm saying," he said wearily, "that I don't know if you still have it. And I'm also saying that even if you do, I plain don't trust you. I remember eighty-four too well."

"Thirteen and one," Farmer said. "Runner-up for the Cy Young. Should of won if some writers hadn't fucked me over."

"I remember the one," Pork responded.

Farmer got still. "What do you mean?"

"You know what I mean."

"Spit it out."

"That was an awfully fat pitch to Garvey."

Farmer reached over and grabbed the front of Pork's shirt. "You son of a bitch."

Pork broke the grip with a quick sweep of his powerful arms. Farmer pushed his chair away and got up, cocking his right hand. But Barelli's left hook was quicker. Farmer's head snapped back. He was suspended for a second. He clutched at the table, knocking his empty glass to the floor where it bounced. Then he dropped to his knees and threw up all over his pants.

The background bar noise died. Everyone stared.

"So that's how a cracker crumbles," Mitch said.

20

"Asshole must be a lover, not a fighter," I said.

Mitch nodded. "Pathetic. One punch knockdown. TKO." He reached for a menu. We were grabbing breakfast in the Easton coffee shop before going to Wrigley for the last workout before the big game. "Bound to happen. Dewey's been baiting the Porker since he got here."

I had brought down a *Herald-Star* that had been slipped under our door. I glanced at "Wink" on the inside of the front page. An item in the middle of the column caught my eye: "'Wink' hears that downstate Democrat Tom Hobbs (D–Urbana/Champaign) is the ringleader in a rumored palace coup in the Illinois House. Dissatisfaction is growing with the Speaker's increasingly autocratic—some say, dictatorial—rule. Hobbs refused to confirm the rumor but did say, 'the members want more decentralization.'"

I read the item to Mitch. He took a sip of ice water. "They also want megabucks from the Speaker's campaign war chest come reelection time. Democracy may be sweeping Eastern Europe," he said, "but the Illinois General Assembly ain't ready for reform."

"Tom Hobbs is part of the Speaker's leadership team," I said.

Mitch nodded. "Hell, the Speaker probably organized the coup against himself. Fast Freddy's already worked out the terms of the treaty."

I grinned. "To give the foot soldiers the illusion of change."

Mitch nodded. I turned to Chet Hagan's "Toy Department" column on the back page of the sports section. As I started to read, the waitress hustled over. Mitch ordered ham and eggs. Whole wheat toast. Black coffee. I selected French toast with bacon. "Large fresh orange juice."

"You fall into an inheritance?" Mitch asked.

"Just a Democratic Majority VISA card," I said.

As we waited for our food, I read selections from Hagan's column aloud to Mitch:

On Saturday evening, a group of Fantasy Campers and former Cub and Met stars from 1969 will tangle in a replay of the infamous black cat game of 1969 when a black cat took a stroll in front of the Cub dugout at Shea. From that ill-fated '69 club, the Cub lineup will feature Joe "Pork" Barelli, Jess "The Mule" Farmer, Al Spangler, Nate "Peewee" Oliver, Paul Popovich, and Hank Aguirre. In addition, Mitch "the Professor" Norris, former backup catcher with the Cards and Cubs, will handle the receiving chores. Norris was best known for his intellectual bent and cannon arm. Filling in for the Cubs will be little-known utility man, Roberto "Nappy" Miles.

The Cub campers have worked out in the morning and the Met campers in the afternoon. The only woman camper, Pat Anderson, has become a favorite in the Cub ranks. "I like her sweet swing," Barelli said. "She's a player."

To add drama to the event, Dewey Farmer, the gifted but troubled right-hander, suspended for life from baseball in 1984 for gambling, has been working out in the Cub camp. Dewey is the brother of Cub camp coach, Jess Farmer. It is rumored that the Chicago Cubs are using Dewey's camp appearance to check his arm for a possible comeback. "He might fill a gap in our starting rotation," said a camp coach with ties to the Cubs.

Mitch chuckled. "That's not a gap, that's a hole you could drive a semi through," he said. He reached over and tapped the paper. "*Little*-known?" he said. I'd say, *UN.*"
"I'll buy the *bent* part."

Mitch and I hailed a cab. From the mad gleam in his eye, our driver was on a weekend pass from a psycho ward. I rode with my arm, as usual, braced against the back seat and a prayer on my agnostic lips. Mitch practiced his form of Zen fatalism. He leaned back and kept his eyes half shut, puffing on a stogie. As we careened along Lake Shore Drive, he calmly filled me in on his half of the investigation. "I checked all the applications and made the rounds last night. Talked to all of the campers except Pat."
"She's all mine," I said.
"I noticed. Keep your hands off her . . . sweet spot."
"And?"
He shook his head. "No leads. Not one camper put on his application that he came here to waste the Dewster."
Our driver was trying to muscle into the inside lane for the Belmont exit. A CTA bus would not yield. Our driver chuckled like Vincent Price and turned his wheels sharply to the right. At the last instant, the bus dropped back. Our cab raced through the intersection a full second after the yellow had turned to red.
"You think Dewey's in any real danger?" I asked.
Mitch gazed out the window placidly. "Not nearly as much as we are."

After I dressed out, I headed for the manager's office to talk to Pork about the security arrangements for the game. I heard voices, so I paused in the doorway. I caught Pork's rasp and a second voice, somehow familiar. Male, very Chicago.

I peeked around the corner.

A husky man with dark, slicked-back hair, wearing gold slacks, an olive polo shirt, and ivory-colored shoes, stood with his back to me. Smoke drifted around his head. "I warned you this was a bad idea," he said.

He turned slightly so I saw him in profile.

He was smoking a filter-tipped cigar.

Art "White Shoes" Kennedy.

21

White Shoes and Pork?

I sleepwalked through the practice. I felt as if I had accidentally stepped into a play where I didn't know my lines and I didn't have a prompter.

I kept stealing glances up at White Shoes in the stands. He calmly puffed on a cigar as he watched the practice intently from a box seat behind the third base dugout. He was sitting with a good-looking blonde in a big straw hat, red blouse, indigo skirt, and dark green sunglasses. She was chain smoking. I pegged her as at least twenty years younger than White Shoes. She and Kennedy didn't seem to have much to say to each other. Every now and then, Pork went over to the wall and talked to him. She ignored them. After a while, she got up and headed for the exit.

At the end of regular practice, Pork said, "A little extra b.p. for those who need it. Which is everyone. Coaches first." He took off his cap, wiped his thinning gray hair, and said, "Live pitching. Now's your chance, Dewey."

"All-fuckin'-right," Dewey said. He sauntered out to the mound. "I need someone to throw to."

Pork looked at Mitch, who groaned and started to put on the tools of ignorance, as the catching gear is called.

As Dewey took his warm-up pitches, he was popping Mitch's glove. I looked at the flags. The wind was blowing briskly out toward left field.

Pork grabbed a bat. "I own you," he called out to Dewey. "I could hit you with a broom handle." He stepped in and swung the bat rhythmically over the plate. Farmer went into his submarine motion and whipped a cross fire right under Pork's chin. Pork merely turned his head away. Disdainfully. "Bring that stuff in here," he muttered. He took about ten cuts making solid contact on most of the pitches. Then he stepped back and said, "Nappy."

I stepped into the cage. Believe me, I did not dig in. "Fast ball," Mitch whispered.

Farmer went into his motion and released the ball with his fingers almost scraping the ground. It was a white dart at my head. I hit the dirt.

I got up, knees shaky. I heard Mitch growl. I turned. He had taken off his mask and stepped toward the mound. I stepped in front of him. "Forget it," I said. "Not even close."

He shrugged. He looked out at Dewey. "One more tight pitch, Asshole, and your so-called career will be over."

Dewey grinned. "Got away from me."

I dusted myself and got back in. "Curve," Mitch said, out of the corner of his mouth. Dewey wheeled and delivered again. A slow yakker. Rising. I was out on my front foot, and I missed it by a foot.

"I can't hit when I know what's coming," I complained to Mitch.

He grinned up at me through the bars. "Want me to lie to you?"

"Just don't say anything."

"Okay."

Then Dewey fed me b.p. fast balls. I didn't hit one ball hard.

"Miles, we may have to DH my kid for you," Pork said, disgustedly. He turned to Pat. "Player, get in there for the feeb."

Pat stepped in. Mitch walked half way to the mound. I

couldn't catch what Mitch said, but Dewey kept the ball away from her. She hit weak grounders and popups and came out of the cage red-faced and muttering to herself. Dewey then toyed with the other campers, mixing in his slow curves with heat away.

"That's enough," Pork said.

Dewey pouted but left the mound. Jess Farmer took a turn pitching. The fat camper caught. Mitch put three balls in a row into the left-field bleachers. He came back behind the cage where I was standing with Pat.

"How do you do that?" Pat asked.

Mitch grinned. "It starts up here," he said, touching his cap. "Imagine what you want to do. Visualize the parabola of the ball as it arcs into the seats. Then actualize it." He spat. "In other words, knock the shit out of it."

I cocked the bat over my shoulder. I took a practice swing. "Visualize. Actualize. Knock the shit out of it. I got it. Why don't you write a book, Professor? Call it *The Power of Positive Hitting*."

"Nappy," Pork said.

I stepped in again. Took a deep breath. Relaxed my arms. Jess delivered great batting practice pitches. I stung the ball pretty good. Then Pork said, "One more." The Mule gave me a chest-high, room-service fast ball. I took an easy swing. The ball jumped off my bat on a line toward the ivy in left. Hot dog, off the wall, I thought. But it just kept carrying until it slammed into the basket just to the left of the 368 mark.

I hadn't felt the ball hit the bat at all. I was so elated I took a slow boat around the bases. When I got back to the cage, I said to Mitch, "How's that for visualizing and actualizing?"

"You knocked the shit out of it," he said.

As we finished up, I saw Pat—head down—walking slowly toward the dugout. Dewey Farmer approached her from behind and grabbed her arm. A little roughly, I thought. She turned. I could see her shaking her head vigorously and pulling away.

"Your loss, babe," I heard him say. He turned back toward the field and walked by me with burning brown eyes. "Fuckin' wool," he muttered.

I jogged to catch up with Pat and fell in beside her as she stepped into the dugout. She had a tight-lipped expression.

"Hi, Stats," I said, hoping to break the ice that had formed between us two nights before when I had asked her about Dewey.

She stopped and smiled. A real dazzler. The freeze was over. Women, I thought. "Hi, yourself," she said.

"Ready for the big game?"

She touched her trim middle. "Nervous."

"Natural. I got the butterflies myself."

"You're kidding. Nice tater."

"It's all luck. And knocking the shit out of the ball."

"I couldn't buy a hit," she said.

I shook my head. "Don't worry about it. Just do the job in the field." I felt like a junior high kid asking for a first date. "Hey, want to take in a flick tonight?"

She took off her cap and shook her glossy head. The sun glinted off her rich brown hair. My heart fell. But she said. "I'd love to. What's playing?"

"Baseball movie."

"Field of Dreams?"

I shook my head.

"Major League?"

"Nah. *Great Balls of Fire.*"

She grinned. "That's not a baseball movie. Dennis Quaid as Jerry Lee Lewis?"

I nodded.

She did a little shake and bake thing with her hips and sang, "'You shake my nerves and you rattle my brain.'"

I answered. "'Too much love drives a man insane.'"

* * *

Big came to my room about 5:30 that afternoon. He was wearing a fuschia-colored running suit and gold sunglasses and was chewing sunflower seeds. "Got the idea from Jess Farmer," he said. "Nice dude." He grinned. "For a honky redneck. Not an asshole like his brother."

"Where is asshole?"

"Sawing some z's." He paused to toss some seeds into his mouth. "Fucker never sleeps when normal folk do. I'm plumb worn out. When's this gig over?"

"As far as I'm concerned, our contract ends when the third out is made in the fantasy game. Tomorrow night."

He nodded. "Ump makes the out sign—bang—I'm out of here. You and Norris want a ride?"

I shook my head. "I still got business here."

He frowned. "Expecting trouble at the game?"

I shrugged and sighed. "I don't know. Maybe. Probably not."

We talked about security arrangements. Pork had told me the Cubs would have a couple of off-duty cops on hand.

"Think I should give Max a buzz?" Big said.

The aforementioned Maximum Security Face Johnson. One-man wrecking crew. I thought about it. Could I get the expenses by the Cubs? Would one more body make Dewey any safer? Yes and no. I shook my head. "Nah."

"Let me lay something on you."

I nodded.

"We got four incidents."

"Four?"

He nodded. "The bar, the doll, the parking lot, the hit-and-run."

I thought about it. "The parking lot? You think they're connected?"

Big shrugged. "That's the question. Know what I think?"

"What's that?"

He placed his hands about six inches apart as if holding a

book. "This is like a script, but we don't know the plot or the lines."

"Great minds," I said.

Pat and I decided to have an early dinner at DB Kaplan's Deli in Water Tower Place. It was crowded, so we had to wait ten minutes to be seated. I had a Brown's cream soda and a BLT. Carrot cake for dessert. She had a light beer, a pasta salad, and chocolate mousse cake. We talked about the camp.

"You know what I liked best?" she said.

I shook my head.

"Stepping out on the field the first morning. The sun. The sky. The ivy. The grass. It was like I died and went to heaven."

I nodded. "There's nothing like it. Not even . . ."

"Sex?" she said with a saucy grin.

"I was going to say hitting for the cycle. Single, double, triple, home run."

"Same thing," she said. "I guess."

When we came out of the movie, she said, "That might be the worst *baseball* movie I've ever seen."

I nodded. "They never get the action scenes right."

We window-shopped along Michigan Avenue for a while. Bloomingdale's, Saks Fifth Avenue, I. Magnin. Pretended we could buy anything we wanted. Then she got very quiet. But the silence was easy.

I pretended to hold a microphone. "Player, what are your thoughts going into the big game?"

She grinned. "I'm just happy to be here . . . I want to stay within myself . . . not try to hit a five-run homer . . . take it one play at a time."

When we got back to the Easton lobby, I nodded at the taproom and said, "Want a drink?"

She shook her head. "Not in the bar. Can't take the

smoke tonight. Hey, come up to my room—have a beer? I've got one of those refreshment centers."

"I'd love a Coke," I said.

There was just one chair in her small room. She nodded at it. I sat. She knelt, opened the refreshment center, and got out two cans. Her pert rear end was outlined by her cream-colored jeans. "I'll get some ice," I said, swallowing hard.

When I got back, I put ice in a glass and poured myself a Coke. Pat sat on the bed holding a can of beer. She leaned forward, her expression serious. "What kind of a ballplayer doesn't drink?"

"Not much of one." I pretended that a light bulb went on. "Maybe that explains it. If I had just been a drunk, I might have made the Show." I pointed to my head. "Any alcohol triggers my migraines," I said.

She nodded sympathetically. "Oh. My mom and sis had those. Sis couldn't eat chocolate." She paused and her thoughts drifted away for a few seconds. Then she snapped back. "I hope I don't screw up tomorrow."

"You'll be fine," I said. "Just let your natural ability carry you."

"That's what I'm afraid of. I know I won't hit. As you said, I have to contribute in the field." She paused to take a sip of beer. "Roberto, can you arrange to play short when I'm in there?"

I shrugged. "Probably. I'll talk to Pork."

"You've taught me a lot. You're my personal coach. My *tutor*. And good luck charm. It would help me relax."

"Glad to be of service. Can I ask you a question?"

"Sure."

"Personal."

She looked wary but nodded.

"What's with you and Dewey Farmer?"

She stared at me. "What do you mean?"

"I saw him hitting on you again today."

She sighed. "You won't let that alone, will you? Jealous?"
"Maybe."

"You shouldn't be. I hate that cocky bastard." She rested her beer on the bed. "Actually, hate is mild for what I feel."
"Why?"

She started to gesture with her right hand. She knocked her beer can onto the floor. Foam dribbled out on the rug. "Damn," she said. "Damn, damn, damn." She kicked the can on the floor.

"I'll clean it up," I said.

She shook her head. She went into the bathroom and emerged with two towels that she used to soak up the beer. Then she started to pace around the small room.

I decided to take a shot in the dark. "Did you know him before the camp?"

She paused. "No. I didn't."

I thought about that for a second. "You knew someone who did?"

She nodded. She took a deep breath. She gulped and rubbed her eyes. "I have to tell somebody."

She finished her story. "He didn't even come to the funeral," she said.

Stupidly, I said, "Your sister killed herself over Dewey Farmer?"

Pat shook her head. "*Because*. Not over." There were tears in her gray eyes. She stopped pacing and sat on the bed. I got up and sat beside her and put my arm around her. She nestled against me. "As I said, he got her pregnant. He made her get an abortion. At least he paid for it. It tore her up. She couldn't get it out of her mind. She took an overdose of sleeping pills a year later." She looked up at me. "Do you know what was the worst?"

I shook my head.

"After the abortion, that scumbag never spoke to her again. Never even called her once."

"Why'd you come to the camp?"

She reached over to the dresser for her small blue purse, opened it and showed me a small .22 automatic. "To use this. I'm a good shot," she said confidently. She shook her head. "Knowing what I know about him, I figured he would ask me out. And I would kill him. But I couldn't do it. When he touched me, I almost . . . It made me gag."

"How'd you know he'd be here?"

"I didn't for sure. I read some rumors in one of the Chicago papers and took a chance."

"You ever threaten him?"

"No."

"You heard about the voodoo doll?"

She nodded. "Sure."

"That your work?"

She stiffened and moved away from me slightly. "You know I dress in the ladies' room. I've never even been in the Cubs' locker room. Not once. Not even to look around." She shook her head. "I'm not into playing mind games. I was going to get him alone. For sex, he would think. Pull out my pistol, tell him who I was, and shoot him. In the groin. I couldn't pull it off. After half an hour with him, I pretended to be sick. Told him I might vomit. That was no lie. He made me want to puke. It grossed him out. I didn't have the guts."

"On the contrary," I said.

She looked at me. "Would you stay a while and just hold me?"

"Yes."

Half an hour later, she said, "Isn't this breaking training?"

"Yes," I said.

And a little later she said, "I believe you just hit for the cycle."

22

I was up at 6:00 for a run north along the lakefront. The Easton is about two blocks south of the Oak Street Beach. I took the pedestrian underpass below Lake Shore Drive. The walls were lined with graffiti, and the concrete underfoot was damp. As I emerged from the tunnel, I climbed a set of stairs and headed north, an empty beach to my right. Nets were set on the sand for volleyball. I could see the yellow caps of several swimmers doggedly paddling south. I jogged slowly about half a mile to a beach house, went past an overpass to Lincoln Park, and by an enclosed area where folks gathered to play chess during the day. At intervals, chessboards were laid out on the concrete tables. Even at this early hour, there were lots of runners out. To my right, the sky was dull gray and the lake was choppy.

I thought about Pat. She was a bright, positive, witty gal. And a heck of a player, even if she couldn't hit her weight. I liked her a lot. I didn't think she had the capacity to kill anyone—even Dewey—in a premeditated way.

I knew that if I said that to Mitch, he would give me his skeptical look and say, "And you, of course, are objective."

Since I had not returned to our room until early morning, Mitch might figure that last night had stripped away my last vestige of neutrality about Pat. And he would, as usual, be right.

I reached the gun club, where later in the day trapshooters would blast targets over the lake, and circled back. I turned my thoughts to Art Kennedy's unexpected appearance in Pork Barelli's office. Well, I thought to myself, Pork enjoys the Chicago nightlife. If Harry Caray was the "mayor" of Rush Street, Pork was at least on the city council. Ditto for Kennedy, according to what I had picked up in Springfield. Pork could have run into White Shoes on the town and they could have become friends. Sure. But then what was "the bad idea" Kennedy had referred to?

And who was the striking blonde with Kennedy?

When I reached our room, Mitch was already gone. I called the Speaker at the Bismarck.

"Robert, I just got back from my morning walk," he said. "You have something to report on Kevin Duke?"

"Not really. A question."

"Yes?"

"Why didn't you object when I said I wanted to attend the fantasy camp at the same time I was working on Kevin Duke? You usually want single-mindedness."

Silence. Then, in a formal voice, he said, "From your tone, I gather you have an idea why."

"Not really. Just another question. What is Art Kennedy's relationship with Peter Duke and Harold Pomper?"

"That's complicated. Personal or professional?"

"Both."

"Professionally, Arthur represents the firm's interests in the General Assembly."

"I would have thought Peter could do that."

"No. That would present an appearance of a conflict of interest. Peter recuses himself on a lot of votes."

"Anything else?"

"I believe Arthur's an investor in P&D Productions. As I understand it, it's a spin-off from the law practice. For several years, they have specialized in contract negotiations for Chicago-based entertainers and athletes."

"They are agents?"

"In effect, yes. P&D has begun sports promotions."

"And personally?"

"Arthur is married to Harold's daughter. Anne. Who happens to be Peter's ex-wife."

"Hold on a sec," I said.

There was a copy of the Dream Game Camp, Inc. brochure on my nightstand. I picked it up. There, in the left-hand corner below the blue logo, it said: "P&D Productions."

It *is* a small world. The Speaker had said something. "Pardon," I said.

"Have you talked to this girl, Kristin?"

"No," I said. "Peter Duke ordered me not to."

"I see. Odd. Did you know that Kevin Duke is in a treatment center?"

"Yes. In Minneapolis."

"Perhaps he should be re-interviewed."

"Perhaps."

"And I still think you should talk to Kristin. After all, she was the last person to see Kevin before the accident."

"Okay."

"Robert?"

"Yes?"

"Have you seen the morning paper?"

"No."

"There are a couple of items you might find interesting."

It was only after I hung up that I realized that the Speaker had never answered my first question: Why had he not objected?

Inference: He knew the two cases intertwined in some way.

I shook my head and called Pork in his room, asked him some questions, and he gave me some answers.

*   *   *

I read the *Herald-Star* in the coffee shop, waiting for Mitch. The front-page headline said: "Guv Decides Not to Seek Re-election." The Speaker had understated the case, as usual. The whole kaleidoscope of Illinois politics had just rotated. The Guv had been the cork in the bottle. Pent-up political ambitions would now be unleashed. On the inside of the front page, "Wink" said: "The reason for the Guv's surprise decision—surprise—*bucks*. He figures to make more than a million a year in private law practice. He is said to be considering offers from several LaSalle Street firms, including Pomper & Duke."

The next item said: "Lt. Governor Martha Williams of Naperville is considered the front runner for the GOP gubernatorial nomination in 1990. Maverick Republican Representative Peter Duke is considered a long shot."

At the bottom of the column was this item: "P&D Productions—the new venture of Peter Duke and Harold Pomper—is planning a 'dream-a-mentary' on the baseball fantasy camp and the Dream Game currently being held at Wrigley Field. The big game is tonight—'69 Cubs vs. '69 Mets—and admission is free."

Was "Wink" a wholly owned subsidiary of Pomper & Duke?

Mitch joined me. After we ordered, I told him about my conversations with the Speaker and Pork.

He lit a cigar. "Peter Duke was Pork's agent?"

I nodded. "And guess who else's?"

"Asshole?"

I nodded.

Mitch blew a smoke ring. "And now Pomper and Duke have invested in the camp? I'll bet the Speaker knew all along that Peter Duke was connected to the camp."

I nodded. "If I had to guess, I figure the Speaker thought we might turn up something useful on Duke. For his files."

Mitch frowned. "Only one problem with that, Bobby."

"I know. The Speaker's on Duke's side."

Mitch shook his head. "But why?"

"Loyalty?"

"When was the last time the Speaker did something solely out of loyalty?" He tapped the headline. "The Guv's stepping aside?"

"That's what they say."

"And give up room service?"

23

I called Big's room.

"Yo," he said.

"I want you to stick with Dewey like Krazy Glue tonight. I've arranged with Pork for you to be on the field. In the dugout."

"Really? That's great. Maybe I can get some autographs."

Mitch came back to the room about 3:30 in the afternoon. "Let's go to the ball yard."

"Haul ass," I agreed. We grabbed a cab and had a relatively sane ride to Wrigley. I overtipped the driver by a couple of bucks. We went directly to the locker room and found Pork there, already dressed in his Cub pants and the dark blue undershirt. "We don't win this game," he said puffing nervously on a cigarette, "I'll never down another brewski."

"Right," Mitch said.

"And I'll walk to St. Louis. Backwards. On my hands."

"Sure," I said.

Mitch and I changed into our uniforms. Mitch grabbed his old black catcher's glove that he called his "gamer," and we walked down the tunnel and out to the field. The scoreboard clock said 4:15. The game was scheduled to begin at 7:00. I looked out over the gray-green scoreboard with the National League games on the left and the American on the right. The Cub pennant second from the top—in July.

Zim is doing it with mirrors, I thought.

Ryne Sandberg was heating up. So was Mark Grace. The boys of Zimmer.

The sky beyond was a pale blue. No clouds. I flipped some grass into the air. The wind was blowing out. "Hitter's night," Mitch said.

"That's what I was afraid of," I said.

Mitch grinned. He pantomimed being hit by a pitch. "Nothing to lose. Give it your best shot."

I rubbed my left elbow. "Take one for the team?"

"Right." We started jogging slowly toward the left-field corner. Mitch ran with hands on hips. "Hope I don't have to face Cardwell. I never got a hit off that sucker."

At 4:30, we took batting practice. I was tight and hit only one ball out of the infield. I grinned at Pat as I left the cage. "Don't want to shoot my wad," I said.

"Oh?" she replied.

Pat sat fidgeting next to me in the dugout as the Mets took batting practice. Ed Kranepool, Ron Swoboda, and Don Clendenon hit ball after ball high into the seats. The small crowd reacted to each shot.

"Why do they look so much bigger than us?" she asked.

"Mutants," I said. "Clawed their way out of New York sewers."

"They're huge."

"Remember Hack Wilson. He was only five six. It's not the size of the dog in the fight . . ."

". . . tell that to the dead Pekingese," she said.

Pork rocked back and forth on his heels in front of the Cub dugout. "This is what we've been waiting for," he said. "Strap it on tight. I'm not going to give you one of those bullshit 'win one for the Porker' pep talks. I'm just telling you, if we lose . . . you all die." He shrugged. "Just remember this—a life without brewski is not worth living."

He went through a simple set of signs with us. Then he said, "I'll post the lineups in a few minutes."

"When am I going to pitch?" Dewey Farmer asked, petulantly.

"We'll see," Pork responded.

"Bullshit" Dewey muttered. "If I don't pitch . . ."

Sitting next to him, Jess nudged him hard. "Shut up, little brother," he said. "Cut the crap."

"Where you going?" I said to Pat, as she started up the runway.

She waved her blue glove at me. "Ladies' room. Got to put on my game face."

Pork posted the lineups in the dugout at 6:15. Campers and coaches gathered around to look at the starting lineups and rosters for the two teams. Rules stipulated that no more than five ex–big leaguers could be on the field at any one time. Neither Pat nor I was in the starting lineup. The Mule was pitching with Mitch behind the plate. Cal Koonce was starting for the Mets.

"Ex-Cub," Pat said.

"Gives us hope," I replied.

There was a lot of nervous kidding going on. I sat back on the bench, holding an aluminum bat between my legs. Pat sat down next to me, hitting her right fist into her blue glove. "I'm kind of glad I'm not starting," she said. "I'd be too nervous. Does this mean we'll be playing together?"

"It means we'll be on the field at the same time," I said. "Whether we're together or not remains to be seen."

24

As game time approached, the lights were turned on. But there was still plenty of daylight left, so the effect of the lights was minimal. Many in the small crowd came over to the dugouts to talk with various campers. I noticed Art Kennedy behind the Cub dugout seated next to the blonde who had been with him the day before. Again she wore oversized sunglasses and a large hat and smoked one cigarette after another. Peter Duke and Harold Pomper sat one row behind them. I nudged Pork and asked, "Who's the gal sitting with Art Kennedy?"

He glanced over. "Mrs. Kennedy," he said.

I did a double take. This woman wore her light blonde hair long, loose, and flowing. "Can't be," I said with conviction, remembering the mouse in the brown paper wrapper.

He gave me a funny look. "Hell it can't."

Unless Art Kennedy had gotten a quickie divorce, the blonde next to him was the same Anne P. Kennedy who had been in my office in June. At this distance, she looked as if she had dropped a good ten years and a lot of inhibitions. "She looks . . ."

He shrugged. "Yeah," he said. "She sure does."

As expected, a couple of security men in blue patrolled the stands. No one was allowed in the upper deck, the grandstand, or the bleachers.

Behind the plate and down each foul line, TV cameras were set up. In addition, there was a camera in each dugout to get player reactions to the game.

Chet Hagan roamed the field with his tape recorder. I saw him talking to Dewey several times.

The announcer sat behind a table next to the well-worn brick wall to the right of home plate. At 7:05, he began the player introductions with the Mets. They loped out of the dugout and stood along the first base line. Then he introduced us. After the introductions, he asked the crowd to rise for the national anthem, a scratchy recording, it turned out. Then our first unit took the field.

At that moment, a black kitten scampered past our dugout. "Where the fuck did that come from?" Pork screamed. He grabbed a bat. Mitch had to restrain him from going after the kitten.

I looked down the length of the dugout. Big was doubled over with laughter.

"What'll happen to the poor thing?" Pat said.

The game started badly for us. After the Mets' lead-off batter grounded out, Ron Swoboda drove the Mule's second pitch up in the wind into the left center-field alley. The camper in center field took a step in, and the ball carried over his head to the ivy and died there. The left fielder had trouble picking up the ball. "Should have never put three campers in the outfield," Dewey said loudly. "Lard butt doesn't know his ass from a hole in the ground."

Big was sitting next to him. "Button it up, cracker," he said.

Swoboda lumbered to third standing up. He had his hands on his knees, gasping, when the relay throw sailed over Popovich's head into the third base dugout. Swoboda walked home.

The Met dugout went nuts. Behind their dugout, a fan held up a hand lettered sign: "Deja View—'69 All Over Again."

Pork—standing at first—put his big first baseman's glove over his eyes.

"Jesus Christ," Dewey said. "This team is a bunch of fuck-ups."

But the Mule settled down and retired the next two hitters on a popup and a strikeout by Clendenon, who waved at a submarine knuckleball.

Mitch dropped the pitch and tagged Clendenon, a little hard, maybe.

"Get that horse shit out of here," Clendenon yelled at the Mule, as he flung his bat away and stalked back to the dugout. "Throw me some heat."

Mitch took off his mask and grinned at him. The Mule loped off the mound and pumped his right arm. "Let's get it back," he said.

"I've never seen the Mule show any emotion before," Pat said. "That fires me up."

Pork sat down next to me. "Nobody hurt," he said. He lit a cigarette.

"Like hell," Dewey groused.

Cal Koonce was on the mound for the Mets, taking his warm-up pitches. "This guy's a piece of cake," Pork said. "He throws base hits like Hollywood turns out slasher movies."

"He's an ex-Cub, isn't he?" Mitch said, as he took off his chest protector.

A camper led off. Koonce painted the outside corner, and the ump—a short, stocky guy—barked a strike. He had an exaggerated move with his right hand, punching the call, like Frank Pulli. The camper backed out and glared at the ump, who stood impassively.

Pork shook his head. "This bum umped in Double A. Thinks he's hot shit." Then he yelled, "Be consistent! Give the Mule the same pitch!"

The ump turned to our dugout and stared at Pork. Then he dusted off the plate and said, "Get in and hit," to the batter.

The next pitch was a slow curve, and the camper drilled it on one hop to Al Weis, who threw him out easily.

"Good metal," Pork yelled.

Weis was a slight utility man who had killed the Cubs (and the Orioles in the World Series) with unexpected home runs in '69.

The next two hitters hit soft rollers to the infield.

One to zip, Mets, after one.

"Let's hold 'em," Pork yelled as he walked back to first base, pausing to put his cigarette on the ground next to the bag.

For three innings, the score stayed that way. Mitch batted in the bottom of the second and hit a high fly to the warning track at the bend of the wall in left center. "Get outta here!" Pork yelled. The Met camper stumbled but made the catch with his back brushing the ivy. The ball passed just below the wire basket.

Mitch jogged back to the dugout. "Track power," I said to him as he put on the catching gear.

"Pulled that sucker a little less, it would have been out of here," he growled.

"If ifs and butts . . ."

He glared at me.

Pork had our only hit in the first three innings, a double that bit the chalk down the right-field line. As he hunched over at second base, panting, Al Weis yelled, "Anybody know emergency CPR?"

In the top of the fifth, our second unit took the field. It was fully dark now. I had opposed lights in Wrigley, but I had to stop at the top step of the dugout to admire the sheer beauty of the park at night. It looked like a billiard table under bright lights. The infield dirt was as smooth as a royal coachway.

I hustled out to short. Pat ran behind second. The new first baseman—the fat camper—tossed us the infield ball. I even had some zip on the first throw I fired to first. I felt an adrenaline rush. Marvelous what game conditions can do.

Pat bobbled the first practice roller tossed to her and threw stiffly. Then the ump motioned to Hank Aguirre—in relief of the Mule—that he had thrown enough pitches. Mitch gunned the throw to second. Pat dropped it, picked it up, dropped it again, and tossed it to me. Her face was taut, grim.

"Lighten up," I said. "Have some fun." She grinned, but it was forced. "Take it one play at a time."

The first hitter, a camper, swung hard and topped the first pitch—a slow roller right at me. A twenty bouncer. Take your time, I thought. Guy can't run. I anticipated a charity hop, but the ball stayed down and rolled between my legs into short center, where Pat ran it down.

I wanted to tunnel a hole to the dugout. Dewey Farmer was on his feet—red faced—screaming something—doubtless about my fuck-up and giving the Mets four outs—to the guys in the dugout. I saw Big grab him and set him back down. Hard.

I scuffed the dirt in front of me and used one of my dad's favorite expressions. "Shit fire," I said.

"Save the matches," Pat finished, as she underhanded the ball to Aguirre. "Lighten up," she said. "Nobody hurt."

I looked in at Mitch. He gave me a thumbs-up sign.

I didn't have any time to brood. Jerry Grote was up. Aguirre was not throwing very hard, so I shaded Grote toward the hole. He took a pitch up and in. A ball. I took a deep breath and relaxed my arms. Aguirre delivered a breaking ball over the middle of the plate. I leaned to my right. Grote swung and slashed a hard ground ball that way. I made the crossover step, extended my left arm as far as I could, and snagged the ball on a low hop. I planted and threw a strike to Pat. She pivoted, phantom-touched the bag, and short-armed the relay to first. The fat first baseman dug the throw out of the dirt. The play was close, but Grote wasn't exactly breaking the world record for sixty meters.

"Out!" the first-base ump yelled.

Grote spun around, a crimson flush on his neck. "I beat it."

"He was safe!" the Met coach yelled. "And she missed the bag."

The ump shook his head.

"As safe as a glass of beer around the Porker," Pat said.

"Atta boy, Nappy," Pork yelled from the dugout. "Nice relay, Pat. *Player* can *Play!*" he bellowed.

Pat winked at me.

"Good hose," I said to her.

"Never any doubt," she said.

Suddenly, I was in "the zone." I had been there once or twice before in basketball in high school. The feeling is unreal. I had a sure sense of where I was on the field. Time slowed for me. The grass in the infield was greener. The sky above blacker. The lights brighter. The ball a whiter shade of pale. The crowd faded into the distance. I looked down a narrow field of vision to the plate, anticipating. I *knew* where every ball was going to be hit even as the batter swung. As if it had already happened.

The next hitter singled cleanly to center. The ball went over me in slow motion. I didn't jump for it—no chance. I took the throw back to the infield. "Make 'em hit to me, Aggie," I said. Weis stepped in batting right-handed. He had a compact swing. I read him as a straightaway hitter. A contact hitter. Like me. I cheated up the middle and leaned in that direction. Mitch put down one finger. Aguirre pitched. The fast ball was down and in. Weis backed out and took a practice cut. Aguirre took the sign. Mitch wiggled his fingers. Change up. Mitch set up low and away. The pitch was a low screwball breaking away from Weis. I was moving as he swung. He drove a bullet by Aguirre's head. One hop. I dove for the ball, thrust the glove as far as I could, and smothered it. I rolled over and flipped it backhanded to Pat at the bag. Force out.

"A great play by Roberto 'the Napkin' Miles!" the announcer said.

The front of my uniform was covered with grass and red dirt. I dusted myself off and ran into the dugout banging my glove. On my way in, I noticed that Art Kennedy had moved down to sit with Duke and Pomper. The blonde—Anne Kennedy—was gone.

Pat ran next to me, grinning. "My hero."

"Aw, shucks."

I sat down, breathing hard.

Dewey walked over to me. "Nice play on the first ball," he said.

"How about the last two?" Pat responded heatedly.

"Showboating," Dewey said out of the side of his mouth. "Did you have to dive or was that just for the," he paused and leered at Pat, ". . . squeeze?"

"One more word and I break your face," Big said to him. We didn't score.

In the top of the sixth inning, I ranged into short center for an over-the-shoulder catch of a Met camper's Texas Leaguer. Then with two outs and a runner in scoring position, I leaped high—well, as high as I can—to grab a liner off Clendenon's bat.

As I trotted to the dugout, I heard someone in the Mets' dugout say, "Who is that guy?"

I got high fives all around. Mitch gave me a big grin. Pat patted my backside. Pork lit a cigarette. Dewey said, "Now make an offensive contribution. Get on base."

"Guy who makes routine play to end an inning always leads off the next," Pat said.

I put on my batting gloves and carried two metal bats to the plate. I flipped one to the batboy and stepped in. Grote said, "What else did you get for Christmas?"

Ron Taylor, a right-hander, was on the mound. Sinker, slider, I told myself. His first pitch was a slider away. I checked my swing and bounced right back to Taylor. I felt

silly running like mad down to first as he held the ball for
several seconds and then tossed it underhand to Clendenon.
He deliberately dropped the ball and picked it up just before
I reached the bag. He grinned at me and said, "Bang, bang
play. You're dead."

When I got back to the dugout, Dewey said, "Nice cut."

Pat followed me in the order. Taylor humped it up a little—actually a lot—and fired smoke over the outside corner. She was frozen. Our dugout gave him a scalding.
"Chicken shit!" Pork screamed. "Throw that chicken shit to
me."

"I hope I pitch against you!" Dewey yelled. "In your
fuckin' ear!"

Taylor looked at our dugout and grinned. Then he fired a
nasty slider. Her knees buckled. "Strike two!" Then he
backed her off the plate. Finally, she was called out on
strikes on a breaking pitch low and away.

Her face was red as she came back to the dugout. "God-
damn ump," she muttered. "That pitch was a foot outside."
She grinned. "At least six inches. I didn't even pull the trigger."

"You'll get another shot," I said. "Lighten up. Remember
the wiggle."

We went back into the field and retired the Mets in order.
I had no chances in the field, but Pat made a nice play to
her left to end the inning and our dugout exploded. "Player,
player," they chanted as she ran off the field, head down.

My next time up, I grounded weakly to third. Pat went
down swinging at a pitch that was cap high.

"Shit fire," she said.

"Hey," I said, "we throw some leather at them." I nodded at Pork and Mitch. "It's these guys' job to get us some
runs."

She grinned.

I looked up in the stands. Now Peter Duke was gone. Art

Kennedy was alone, smoking a cigar. He saw me and gave me a thumbs-up sign.

I glanced down the line and noticed that Dewey had left the dugout and was getting loose in the pen. I could hear the smack as his pitches hit the glove. Big sat sprawled on the bull pen bench, his shades down. Dewey finished his warmups and put on a blue jacket.

In the dugout, everybody was saying what a great game it was. "Bullshit," Pork said. "We're losing, ain't we?"

At the seventh-inning stretch, they played a recording of Harry Caray singing "Take Me Out to the Ball Game."

The fans and many campers sang along. I sang along with Pat and Mitch. Big, who had strolled down from the bullpen with Dewey, rolled his eyes back in his head.

At the last note, the wind shifted and started to blow in from left field. The temperature seemed to drop about ten degrees.

"No dingers now," Mitch said.

"Let's scratch out a run," Pork said. "Line drives. No one's going deep with that wind." He led off. He grounded a hard single into right field off Don Cardwell. He pulled up at first and called time.

Free substitution was the rule. "Nappy, run for me," Pork said.

"Run?"

"Whatever."

I trotted down to first. The next hitter popped up on the first pitch.

Cardwell stared over his left shoulder at me. I led off about a step. Mitch was the hitter. Cardwell threw over. I was standing on the bag.

"Is that your best move, Cards?" I taunted. I took a long lead, leaning back to the bag. "You couldn't pick your nose with that one."

He pivoted and fired over. I dove back. Clendenon tagged me on the neck. Firmly. Grinned nastily.

"Safe!"

Cardwell delivered a pitch out. Grote fired to first. I dove back in again. "Safe!"

I got up and dusted myself off. My uniform was flat dirty. Pork, now coaching first, touched the tip of his cap and winked at me. Cardwell went into his stretch again. Glanced over. Then looked home. I gambled and took off early.

I heard a sharp crack as I neared second. I saw the back of Swoboda's number seven in left. He was sprinting toward the green doors. Mitch had roped one over his head. A sure double and the tying run, I thought. Maybe in the basket. I nearly stumbled on the second base bag. I picked up the third base coach—Popovich. He was motioning frantically. "Back, back!"

What? Automatically, I kept running for a few steps. Then I stole a quick look toward left. Swoboda was scrambling to his feet and getting ready to throw. Light dawned. He must have caught the ball. I reversed course, but the relay got me by about ten yards.

I trotted off the field. Head down.

Where was that tunnel?

"Tough break, Bobby," Mitch said.

"How'd he catch it?" I asked.

"Wind knocked it down. Made a shoestring catch. Told you I never hit Cardwell."

"Some pinch runner. Terrible base running," Dewey fumed. "Play was right in front of you."

Pork shook his head. "Play second," he snapped to me. "Got to hold 'em. We'll get our shot."

And we did. Bottom of the eighth. A hit, a walk, and an error. Bases loaded. One out. Score still one to nothing, Mets. I walked to the plate and glanced down at Pork, who was leading off third.

He touched his cap twice. Then touched the red C on his chest. Squeeze play. The suicide squeeze. That means the runner takes off from third with the pitch. If you miss the bunt, he's DOA.

You're SOL. Shit out of luck.

Most times on the suicide squeeze, all you have to do is get the bunt down. The break the runner gets means that he will cross the plate about the time the ball hits the ground. No play. But with the bags loaded, there's a force-out at the plate. Mean Gene Garland—a relief pitcher with a real nasty streak—was taking his stretch, looking right at the Porker, who would not want to tip the play by breaking too soon. A bunt back to the mound won't get the job done, I thought. It has to be perfect or Pork—who you could time with a sun dial—will be forced out at home.

"Take him deep, Bobby," Mitch yelled from the dugout. Sowing confusion among our enemies. Right. I gripped the bat right down at the end. I touched my cap to indicate the play was on. Garland took his stretch, checked Pork, and fired sidearm, not as low as Jess or Dewey. Pork broke for home, timing the play just right.

Bunting is like catching the ball with your bat. The pitch was a fast ball, down the middle. I half-squared, held the bat loosely, and dropped the ball down the third base-line. Dead solid perfect, I thought. It rolled slowly up the line.

A Met camper charged the ball. I raced for first. Base hit, I thought. Game tied.

The Napkin cleans up.

"Let it roll!" Grote screamed.

I was past the bag. I turned just in time to see the camper kick the ball as it trickled into foul territory about a foot short of the bag.

Garland screamed at me all the way back to the mound. "Don't bunt on me, you son of a bitch! I'll put the next one up the side of your head!"

Grote went out to talk to Garland.

Pork called time and came down to me. He had a small glob of spit on his lips. He put his hands on my shoulders. "Tough break, Nappy." He winked at me. "Tell you what. If you get two strikes, try it again," he said. "They'll never expect it."

I nodded. Bunt foul with two strikes and you're out. That's pressure.

Grote came back and adjusted his face mask. "Thought I should tell you. The mean man has a bum knee. He's had a hard life since he left the Show. Don't even think about bunting on him again. He ain't got a job and his wife's a bitch."

And then I die, I thought.

I settled back in, choking up on the bat. Garland went into the stretch. He threw a slider that dipped outside. I checked my swing.

"Ball."

Grote growled at the call.

"Come on, Roberto," I heard Pat yell.

Garland stared me down. I could see his lips moving. He brought his hands to his chest and delivered. Right at my cap. I spun away and almost stumbled to the ground.

"Pitch got away, twinkletoes," Grote said.

"Fuck you," I muttered.

"Walk's as good as a hit," someone in our dugout said. That was not a ringing endorsement of my bat. In Little League, that's what you tell your ninth-place hitter, who's never gotten a hit in three years, I thought. But I settled in, willing myself to hit only a good pitch. Garland backed off the mound, rubbing the ball.

He missed with a fast ball, in.

Three and one. The cripple pitch. I thought about my batting practice homer. Forget that, I told myself. I choked the bat. He *has* to throw a strike. Maybe I could slap one into right field. I crowded the plate. His pitch started at the middle of the plate but dipped sharply away. I hacked at the slider and popped it up near the first base dugout. Clendenon glided over and settled under it. "Got it," he called.

I slammed the bat down. But the gale blew the ball onto the roof of the dugout. Clendenon almost stumbled in.

"Damned lucky there," Grote said. "You're history, bush." Full count. I glanced at Pork. He gave me a minute nod.

Garland stretched. Pork broke a beat early. I squared a tad too soon. But our actions confused Garland. He reacted instinctively. Knock me down. The pitch was a white blur at my head. I threw up my left hand. Pain ripped at my fingers. I felt something give a sickening snap. The ball caromed off my helmet.

I was on my back as Pork crossed the plate with the tying run.

Garland was swearing a blue streak.

Mitch helped me up. I walked to first, holding my hand. Garland glared at me all the way. He turned to the ump. "He didn't try to get out of the way."

The ump shook his head. "Ball four, anyway."

Pat came in to run for me. I gimped to the dugout. The trainer put some ice on my fingers. He was standing right in front of me. "Think something's broken," he said. I pushed him aside.

The next hitter fanned, bringing Mitch up. Blue five on his back. Slow, lazy practice swing. I could see red cords on Garland's neck. He was determined to strike Mitch out. He tried to throw one by him—up and in at the letters. Mitch's hole—the weakness that had kept him from being a big league star. But Garland got too much off the plate. Mitch's bat whipped around, and he drilled the pitch over the bag at third and down the line. The base ump signaled fair ball. The ball rattled around in the bullpen while blue Cubbies cavorted around the bases. Three runs scored. Four to one, good guys.

Pat trotted to the dugout, flushed with pride. Pork patted her on the butt.

Garland got the next hitter, stranding Mitch.

"Player, take second," Pork said. "Dewey." He nodded at the mound.

Dewey Farmer strutted to the mound. The ump walked over to our dugout. "No retaliation," he said to Pork. "I'll run him if he comes close to a hitter. I mean it, Pork."

Pork nodded and started out to talk to Dewey, who disdainfully waved him off. Dewey retired the first two hitters easily. Excitement was wearing off, and my left hand was starting to hurt.

"It's all over," I said to Pork.

He glared at me. "It's never over . . ."

Just as he spoke, a Met camper looped a single to right. "Nobody hurt," I said.

Pork turned away, muttering.

Clendenon doubled into the right-field corner, scoring the camper from first. Four to two. The next hitter, another Met camper, hit a fly ball down the left-field line that dropped in front of Spangler. Dewey glared out at him for a good ten seconds.

I was getting a sinking feeling that I had seen this game twenty years before.

On Dewey's next pitch, he tried to really hump it up, slipped, and appeared to strain his arm.

Mitch called time. Pork stepped from the dugout. He trudged slowly out to the mound and talked to Dewey, who nodded impatiently that he was okay, while trying to work some kinks out of his right arm. Pork looked down to the pen. The Mule was warming up, pitching with the same submarine motion as his brother. The bullpen catcher made a sign that the Mule was ready.

Pork nodded, gave the ball to Dewey, and returned to the dugout. Dewey stared at the hitter—Grote—and then buggy-whipped the ball to the plate, a called strike on the outside corner. The next pitch was a change-up curve strike that froze the hitter. Two strikes. One more pitch and it would be over. Our dugout was quiet. Dewey walked behind the mound and went to his mouth.

"Close him out!" Pork yelled. "Even if you are an asshole," he muttered.

Dewey toed the mound, rocked, and wheeled his crossfire delivery clear behind the Grote's head. It ticked his helmet. He bounced up and started for the mound. Mitch grabbed and held him in place.

"You're out of here!" the ump ordered Dewey.

Dewey threw up his arms. "It just got away," he pleaded.

Pork ran to the plate. The argument lasted only a couple of minutes. "I warned you," the ump said. Pork shrugged. Dewey swaggered back to the dugout and threw down his glove. "One more pitch," he said. "Just one more." He grabbed a white towel and wiped his face. Then he sat down at the end of the dugout, away from everyone else.

Big slid down the bench toward him.

"Get the fuck away from me," Dewey ordered.

Big knotted his fists, then shrugged and went to the water cooler.

Pork looked at Mitch, who nodded in the direction of the pen. "We got no choice."

"The Mule," Pork said.

Jess Farmer loped back to the mound. He took several warm-ups and said, "Ready."

"No more brush backs," the ump said.

The Mule looked at him without expression. A wide-eyed camper stepped in for the Mets. Jess went into his windup and delivered a ball, just outside.

Dewey stepped out of the far side of the dugout, twirled a towel over his head several times, and screamed, "Give us a break, ump!" He fired the towel in the direction of home plate.

The ump turned toward Dewey. He held up his hands for time. "I told you to get out of here," he said.

Dewey turned and walked toward the runway.

Mitch gunned the ball back to Jess, who went behind the mound to rub up the ball. The small crowd grew very quiet.

The silence was shattered by a sharp *Boom-crack!*

25

"This here's the private copper," Al Podolak said. He nodded at me like I was a piece of gum stuck to his shoe. No pun intended.

Then he started fiddling with a box of paper clips he had found on the desk. He took one out, bent it back and forth until it broke. "From Springfield," he elaborated.

"Springfield," Detective Isaac Jackson said softly, as if pronouncing the name of some obscure Third World country. He picked a baseball up off the desk and rolled it around in his left hand. In his palm, it looked liked a golf ball—everything's relative. "What you doing here, Springfield?"

"Coaching," I said. I shrugged. "Playing in the dream game."

"He was security for Dewey Farmer," Podolak said.

I started to shake my head.

"Really?" Detective Jackson spoke in the bone-weary tone of one who routinely expected to be lied to. He was large and loomed larger in the close confines of the Cub manager's office, now a temporary interrogation room. His expression was resigned, even stoic. His skin was the color of charcoal briquets. He had a well-trimmed mustache, and his intense eyes were dark brown. The whites were moist with a lot of red in them. His dark gray suit and spit-polished shoes must have set him back $750. He sparkled. He could have passed inspection in a West Point color guard dress parade. But what I noticed most were his huge hands. They were larger than Mitch's. The nails were closely trimmed, the palms a light pink. He sported a gold ring with a large diamond on his left hand.

Al Podolak, on the other hand, looked as though he was wearing the same rumpled brown suit he had on the night at the Easton. His face definitely displayed the same chronically hacked-off expression. He slouched down in the canvas chair behind the desk.

Jackson stood to Podolak's left with his back against the wall, playing with the ball. "Nice work," Jackson said to me. "Don't know about the coaching or the playing, but you did a piss-poor job of securing."

I refrained from pointing out that Dewey Farmer was hale and hearty. It had been the Mule who had been gunned down. Somehow, the point seemed beside the point.

Jackson flipped ball into the air and then snatched it quickly with his left hand. "Why don't you take it from the top, Springfield?"

I nodded. "Sure."

"Assume we don't know shit," Podolak said. "'Cause we don't."

"I will," I said.

I told them almost everything about the job of protecting Dewey. I neglected to mention anyone nicknamed "Player." I also omitted the Speaker, Art Kennedy, Peter Duke, Harold Pomper, and P&D Productions.

While I talked, Podolak closed his eyes and fiddled with another paper clip, again twisting it until it snapped. Jackson tossed the ball lazily back and forth between his right and left hands. When I finished, Jackson laid the ball on the desk, pulled a pack of Lifesavers out of his pants pocket, and popped three into his mouth. "Quitting smoking," he said. "Now I'm addicted to sugar." He rolled them around in his mouth. "Dewey Farmer got the threats. His brother got shot." He widened his eyes. "Can you explain that?"

I shook my head. "No."

"They both wore number thirteen?"

I nodded.

"Strange." He rubbed his moustache. "I never heard of that before. Must of been confusing. Why?"

Podolak leaned back in his chair, his eyes still closed. His breathing was audible. Jackson shot him a glance I couldn't read.

I spread my hands. "A lot of rules are relaxed for these camps. Both brothers wore thirteen when they played." I shrugged. "Players get attached to their numbers. The game was just an exhibition. So . . . no big deal."

Jackson sucked on the Lifesavers. "They both wore thirteen and they pitched with similar styles?" He picked up the ball again and made a sweeping underhand motion with it.

I nodded. "Virtually identical. Dewey copied his older brother." I rolled my head back and forth. "At least, that's what the Mule told me. Dewey probably tells it the other way around."

"Jess Farmer had pitched earlier in the game?"

I nodded.

"Why'd he come back in?" Jackson licked his lips with his pink tongue. There was a lime Lifesaver stuck on the end. "Thought that was against the rules." He paused and swallowed the Lifesaver. Snapped his fingers as if he had forgotten something. "Oh, yeah. Another exception?"

I nodded. "Dewey got himself tossed out of the game. For hitting a batter. The ump had warned him against retaliation."

"Retaliation?"

I held up the splint on my left hand. "'Mean Gene' Garland had decked me the inning before. Pork didn't have anybody left. Like I said, they relaxed the rules."

Without opening his eyes, Podolak said, "'Got himself'?"

I waved that off. "Just an expression."

Jackson drew a deep breath. "So you think Jess Farmer was gunned down by mistake? That the shooter was the someone who had been threatening Dewey Farmer and trying to extort fifty thousand dollars from him?"

I shook my head. "I didn't say that. One problem with that theory—Dewey is a lot slimmer than his brother. And a little taller. They're not identical twins."

Jackson nodded. "Who had a motive to shoot Jess Farmer?"

I frowned. "No one I can think of. Everyone liked the Mule."

Podolak grunted, opened his eyes, and leaned forward. "Where'd the shots come from?"

I shrugged again. I was starting to feel like a teenager. "I don't know. I was in the dugout. Getting treatment on my hand. I think . . . I have the impression they came from the direction of the outfield."

"The bleachers?" Jackson asked.

This interview was taking place at 12:45 A.M., more than three hours after the shooting. I had the feeling Jackson had a pretty good idea where the shot had come from by now. I shook my head. "They were empty. Blocked off. Unless . . ." I paused.

Podolak sighed audibly, stood, took off his jacket and put it on the back of the chair. Then he removed his glasses and started wiping them on his shirt sleeve. "Unless what?"

I closed my eyes trying to recreate the scene. "There's a TV camera box in left center. Would make a perfect sniper's nest."

"First thing we thought of," Podolak said. "It's clean." He slumped back down in the chair and picked up the box of paper clips.

"The scoreboard?" I said. "You could shoot through the holes for the line scores."

Jackson shook his head. "We checked that, too."

"One of the buildings across the street?"

Jackson nodded. "Bingo. There's an abandoned building across Sheffield Avenue. Condemned. With a fire escape. You can waltz right up to the roof. We found three shell casings. Cigarette butts, too." He popped another three Lifesavers. "The sniper went up the fire escape, set up the shot. Took out Jess Farmer. One in the head, two in the body. Got on the el. Grabbed a cab. Jumped into a waiting car. Whatever."

"Carrying a rifle?"

Jackson shook his head. "Probably a package. If he didn't ditch it somewhere. What does it sound like to you?"

"Pro," I said.

"Except for one thing," Podolak said. He sat up and leaned over the desk. He belched softly. "A pro wouldn't leave any evidence."

Jackson gave his partner a disgusted look. "And pros make certain of the target," he said. "It's an amateur trying to look like a pro. Which means we'll get him because he'll have made some other dumb mistakes."

"You come up with any suspects in your investigation?" Podolak asked.

It was the question I had known was coming, as surely as a three-and-two fastball with the bases loaded. "No," I said firmly, looking first directly at Jackson, and then, after several seconds, Podolak. "Actually, we haven't done much of an investigation . . . what with the camp and all. We were just trying to keep track of Dewey. Not any easy job."

"This Bellamy character," Jackson said in a flat voice.

"Clarence 'Big House' Bellamy," Podolak said slowly. "Also from Springfield."

I nodded. Oh, oh, I thought. Here it comes.

"Spring . . . field," Jackson said again, savoring the exotic name. "What was he doing here?"

"Attending the camp?" I tried.

He shook his head. "Not as a baseball player."

I said, "Fan?"

"He's a street player," Jackson said.

"What do you mean?" I said, stupidly.

Podolak shut his eyes again. For a second. Sighed heavily. "Give us a break," he said. "According to the Springfield coppers, he's into a little pimping, a lot of loan sharking. Maybe drugs."

"No drugs," I said. I dipped my head. "No hard drugs."

Podolak grinned coldly. "Whatever."

"There are no soft drugs," Jackson said.

"He was giving me a hand," I said.

"He licensed to do security work?" Jackson asked.

I said nothing.

"He's not. He was armed."

I nodded. "He frequently carries large sums of money."

"I'll bet," Podolak said. "A semiautomatic. Fourteen-shot clip. Ready for war."

I rolled my head back and forth. "He has a permit." Then I made the mistake of getting cute. "He's NRA. And he votes."

Jackson's expression hardened. "Springfield smart ass," he said. "I hate a smart ass. Especially a downstate smart ass. Most especially, I hate downstate private coppers who are smart asses. And you're not funny. I despise the gun-fuckers and the NRA. I've seen dead coppers because street punks had more firepower than we do." He stepped toward me and poked me in the chest with a big finger. "You had a run-in with some street punks the other day? Farmer was along?"

I nodded.

"And Podolak took a hit-and-run complaint on Farmer?"

I nodded again.

"Are we dealing one attempt or three?"

"I don't know."

"You don't know much, Springfield." He popped three

more Lifesavers into his mouth. "Dewey Farmer was suspended from baseball? For gambling?" he asked.

I nodded.

"Yeah, I lost a bundle on that asshole in eighty-four," Podolak said. "All he hadda do—"

Jackson cleared his throat. He glared at Podolak. "Stow that, Podolak. Nobody cares."

Podolak grinned at him.

"Dewey Farmer," Jackson said, "was here to try a comeback?"

I nodded.

"Joseph Barelli scouts for the Cubs?"

I nodded.

"Barelli get along with Dewey?"

What to say? I shook my head. "No." I shrugged. "Tell you the truth, Dewey gets along with nobody. He's a prize jerk. But Barelli was on the field at the time of the shot."

"We know that," Podolak snapped. "You know Peter Duke? Harold Pomper? Arthur Kennedy?"

I nodded.

"What were such heavy hitters doing at this fantasy game?" Jackson asked.

"They invested in the camp," I said. "That's my understanding."

"How do you know them?"

"From Springfield," I said. "Duke's a legislator, Kennedy's a lobbyist. Pomper's a . . . public-spirited citizen. I don't know them well."

Podolak yawned. "I talked to a copper named Kimball in Springfield about you. Interrupted his poker game. Says you're good for the funeral business. Says you're messy." He glanced at my stained uniform. "Says you like to try to clean things up." He paused. "Says Norris is okay, and Bellamy is essentially legit these days."

Jackson widened his eyes. "I'll bet." He poked me again. "Listen up, Springfield. This is my turf. Stay out of this investigation. Do I make myself clear?"

I nodded.
And meant it.
And I would have.
If the coppers hadn't solved the case so quickly.
Twice.

When I got back to the Easton, Big House was waiting for me in the lobby, still in his running outfit. He stood up and we slapped hands the way basketball players do after missing a free throw. "I'm splitting, man," he said. "Sorry."

I nodded. "Not your fault."

"Know that. Somebody had to die, sorry that it was the Mule, not the cracker. Listen."

"Yeah?"

"Did you see the cracker's reaction to the gunplay?"

I shook my head.

"Cold, man. Real cold. After the shots, I was picking myself up off the floor of the dugout with everybody else and he was halfway to the mound. I've seen it twice now. The hit-and-run and now this. That cracker is one chill dude under fire. Or . . ."

"What?"

"He's a hell of an actor."

26

Mitch had ridden to the hospital in the ambulance with Jess Farmer. He was still in his uniform. There was a faint spray of blood across the front of it when he walked wearily into the hotel lobby about 1:30 in the morning.

I had been way too keyed up to sleep. I had waited in an easy chair in the lobby reading yesterday's paper, but having to reread the paragraphs because I couldn't maintain concentration.

I looked a question at him, already knowing the answer.

He lit a stogie, shook his head slowly, and said, "He's gone. The docs were amazed that he was still alive—barely—when he got there. He *was* a Mule. If it hadn't been for that head shot . . . he was basically . . . very healthy."

"Big if."

Mitch nodded. "I need a brew." We went into the bar. Sat at a table by the window looking out on a quiet Michigan Avenue. Mitch ordered a Coors. I had a ginger ale. One lonely guy sat at the bar nursing a drink. Outside, there were still some strollers and light traffic on the street. "Speaking of Big, where's the House?" Mitch asked.

I made a circular motion with my right hand. "About Pontiac, I estimate," I said. "On cruise control. Doing about eighty-five in his hot-rod Lincoln. Breezing back to Springtown. Said he had business to take care of."

"What do the cops think about that?"

"Don't know. Probably don't care. They know he didn't shoot the Mule. He was sitting next to Dewey."

Then I told him about the Sheffield apartment building sniper.

Mitch nodded. "I thought it might be the scoreboard."

"Me, too." I drove my right fist into my left hand. "Three of us and we couldn't prevent it."

"Bobby," Mitch said patiently, "you'd have to have had the Secret Service, FBI, CIA, the KGB, and ungodly luck to prevent something like this. If somebody's out to kill somebody from long distance," he shrugged, "not much you can do. Nobody's fault."

"Oh, it's *someone's* fault," I said.

He nodded. "Who do you think was the target?"

"Depends," I said.

"On what?"

"If the shooter knew Dewey and the Mule, I don't think he could have made a mistake. Really knew them."

"He?"

"Whoever. At first glance, in uniform . . . same number . . . similar motion . . . yeah, you could be confused, but the truth is, they didn't look that much alike for someone who'd seen them together. Not enough to make a mistake like that. But if it was a hired kill, it could have gone down that way." I paused to collect my thoughts. "Sniper waits until Dewey gets into the game."

"Why wait?"

"Two reasons. One, the pitcher is isolated on the mound. A bulls-eye target. Two, by then it was dark enough for the sniper to conceal himself—or herself—for a clear shot. Now Dewey's in the game. The shooter sets up his—"

"Or her."

". . . equipment. That takes a few minutes and he—or she—is distracted. Misses the fact that Dewey is tossed out of the game. When the shooter is all set, he or she sees number thirteen out there with that same submarine motion and does his—or her—thing."

"Complicated," Mitch said.

"No more so than your average nuclear fission experiment."

"What do we do now?"

"Talk to Pork."

He yawned. "In the morning."

"It is morning."

The morning's *Herald-Star* was on the carpet outside our room when I opened the door at 8:15. The headline screamed: "Sheffield Sniper Slays Senior Slinger." I showed it to Mitch, who was tying his shoes. He grunted. "Anything for alliteration."

The story recounted the basic facts as Jackson and Podolak had given them to me. On the inside of the front page, "Wink" speculated that "Dewey Farmer may have been the real target of the sniper."

Chet Hagan had interviewed Dewey. That story ran on page three. I read one of his quotes to Mitch: "'I will not be intimidated.'"

"Not a damned word about his brother?" Mitch asked.

I shook my head. Then I glanced at the rest of the story. "Listen to this," I said. "A little editorial from Chet Hagan: 'The Cubs should immediately sign Dewey Farmer.'" I paused and tapped the paper. "Hagan doesn't inform the reader, but Pork told me he was planning a book with Dewey."

Mitch shook his head. "Another blow in the fight against illiteracy. It'll make a hell of a book now," he said.

I nodded and continued reading. "'First, Dewey Farmer can help right now in the position where the Cubs are hurting—pitching. Second, to show that the Cubs will not give in to domestic terrorism.'" I paused. "Third," I said, "to sell more books."

"Now who's editorializing? 'Domestic terrorism?'" Mitch looked at me in wonder. "What does he mean—the Mule was shot by the Weathermen?"

"If that damned triggerman had waited one more out, we had that sucker won," Pork said. His face was the color of a ripe tomato, and his forehead was blotchy. He puffed furiously on a cigarette. We were in the Easton coffee shop for breakfast, looking over menus. He paused, got a chagrined look on his face, slapped himself on the side of the head. "Scratch that last remark. I'm all fucked up—don't know what I'm saying. Jesus."

"Forget it," Mitch said.

"Pork," I said, "we need more information."

"Fire away," he said. Then he shook his head. "There I go again."

I waved that off. "You were with the Cubs in eighty-four?"

"As a coach," he said. He let smoke dribble out of his mouth. "Bull pen. What a year. Remember that game in June when Ryno lit Bruce Sutter up twice in extra innings? Every break went our way. Until it went in the toilet in San Diego." He studied the menu. "It's funny," he said. "I'm about the only guy to be with the sixty-nine and eighty-four Cubs. On the field. One man should not have to endure so much pain."

"Dewey joined the team in June?"

He nodded. "Yeah. Traded from the Angels. Asshole went thirteen and one with the Cubs. Mostly short relief but a couple of key starts. He was all but unhittable. I never saw anyone with his control. Hold the mitt on the outside corner—never have to move it. Until the seventh inning of the last game of the play-offs. Then he grooves one. To fuckin' Super Dad."

"Huh?" I said.

"Garvey. You introduced Dewey to Peter Duke?"

Pork frowned. "Yeah. Talk about pulling a major rock. When Asshole joined the team in June, he had just busted up with his agent and was looking for a new one. Duke and

Pomper represented me in the last stages of my so-called career."

"Duke and Harold Pomper became his agents?"

He nodded. "Yeah." He shook his head. "Pomper—what a blowhard. Everything was going along fine. The club was winning. It was a blast. Play hard . . . party hard. . . . Pomper and Duke threw a lot of bashes for politicians and their other friends. Sometimes up in Wisconsin. Near Lake Geneva. Often, they invited the players. Then . . ."

"Then what?" Mitch said.

Pork sighed. "I'll never forget it. I get this call from Pomper. Farmer's screwing up the whole deal. Seems Asshole is poking Duke's fourteen-year-old daughter."

A shock went through me. My fingers tingled. "Kristin?"

Pork nodded. "Yeah. She was one *mature* fourteen. But can you believe it? And he's getting high with Duke's son. Can you fuckin' imagine? The only control Asshole shows is on the mound. Seems Asshole met her at one of these parties. Got in the habit of seeing her at this cottage Duke owned up in Wisconsin. Somehow, Duke gets suspicious, hires a private detective who bugs the cottage. Got it all on tape. Busts in and takes pictures. Now Duke wants to call the cops."

"Why didn't he?" Mitch asked.

"Pomper talks him out of it." Pork shook his head. "She's his granddaughter, but all he's worried about is his investment. Man could talk Big House into buying suntan lotion. Points out that if Dewey gets arrested, the Cubs' chances are slim and none, and they lose a very wealthy client 'cause Dewey is about to renegotiate his contract. Also points out that the publicity would be nasty and hurt the kids. They'd have to use the tape and pics with the girl in them, which are pretty steamy. So Art Kennedy and me sit down with Dewey, explain to him the facts of life. Try to scare the shit out of him. He promises to stay away from the daughter. And the son." Pork shrugged. "Far as I know, he did."

I wondered about that.

"Then what?" Mitch asked.

"We win the division. Take the first two games of the play-off. Blow the Padres off the field. Then we go out to hot-tub heaven and piss it away. Dewey gives up the tater to Garvey. Word around is that Dewey has been seen with some glitter types from Vegas. The National League investigates. Evidently, some guys rolled over on Dewey. Baseball suspends him."

"Pomper and Duke lose a client anyway?" I said.

Pork nodded.

"And Dewey gets off scot-free on the rape," I added.

"Sounds to me," Mitch said, "as if Peter Duke had a pretty good motive to kill Dewey Farmer."

"You're crazy," Pork said. "Why would he do that?"

"Bobby just gave us the motive," Mitch said. "Revenge."

I called Pat's room. She answered. Her tone was lifeless. "Yes?"

"Hey, Player, Roberto here. Want to take a walk?"

"I was just packing. But sure. Meet you in the lobby. Ten minutes?"

We walked south along the beach toward the Navy Pier, which stretches out into the lake. The sky was dull gray, blending with the lake at the horizon. Just west of the pier loomed a large glass apartment building. We walked silently for about five minutes. Then we reached a park that extended out into the lake, and we turned onto a sidewalk.

"It was awful," Pat said. She leaned against me. "I didn't know what was happening. One second, Mule is rubbing up the ball. The next, he's on the ground. I heard . . . it must have been the first bullet . . . hit. Sounded like . . . an ax slicing into a side of beef. Then the head shot . . . I saw red mist. Then I saw the body jerk again. I tried CPR . . ." She drew a deep breath. "Who would want to shoot the Mule? He was a quiet guy—totally unlike his brother."

"No one," I said. I motioned for us to sit on a park bench.

She frowned. "Oh. I see." A gust of wind blew some trash by us.

"Pat," I said slowly, "was there anyone else your sister was close to? A man?"

There wasn't. She was adamant. She had said, "Somehow, I feel responsible. I wanted Dewey dead. Instead, it's the Mule."

"That's nuts," I had said.

"I know."

"When something bad happens, we all want to find reasons why we're at fault. I don't know why."

I had walked her back to her room. At the door, we had kissed without passion. "I have to pack," she had said.

"Sorry it ended this way."

She nodded.

"I'll call you."

She nodded.

We both knew I probably wouldn't.

Mitch was in the room, stretched out on the bed, reading *The New York Review of Books*. He threw it on the floor. "Left-wing garbage," he said. "Did you know *we* invaded Afghanistan? This stuff is almost enough to make me a neoconservative." He put it aside and glanced at me. "Any reason to stick around?"

I shook my head. "Let's take the train home tomorrow morning."

He nodded.

I spent most of the day walking up and down the lakeshore. Looking for answers and lucky pennies.

Finding neither.

But the next morning, the *Herald-Star* banner shouted: "State Rep Arrested in Wrigley Field Sniper Slaying."

27

"Miles," Fast Freddy said, "you're some kind of typhoon Mary. Every time we give you a simple assignment, the body count . . ."

The Speaker reached over and tugged lightly on Fast's left arm. Fast looked at the Speaker, caught his steely expression, slammed the brakes on his lips, and they skidded to a sputtering stop. I felt a fine spray on my right hand.

"Alfred," the Speaker said softly, "recriminations waste valuable time." He glanced at the splint on my finger. "Accident, Robert?"

I shook my head. "Not really."

He widened his eyes like William F. Buckley. "Purpose pitch?" he asked. "'Mean Gene' Garland?"

I nodded. The Speaker knows baseball?

"Give us a report, Robert."

"It's broken. Take about six weeks . . ."

He shook his head. "I'm sorry about that, but . . ."

"We're talking about the Duke outrage," Fast snapped. "How could he be charged with murder? Unbelievable."

"You know almost as much as I do," I said, nodding at the *Herald-Star* on the table.

We were in the Speaker's no-frills suite at the Bismarck, sitting at a small oval table. The window looked out on the el. A room-service waiter had just delivered drinks.

I had had to do a double take when I arrived. The Speaker could have placed in a North Shore yuppie-off. He was decked out in a white polo shirt with blue stripes, jeans faded almost to blue gray, and blue and white Adidas running shoes. He sat at one end of the table with a glass of untouched milk in front of him.

To his right, Fast Freddy, dressed in all black, was sucking an orange soda from a can. "Almost?" he said. "What's not in there?"

"Motive," I said. I took a hit off my glass of Coke.

The story in the *Herald-Star* had explained that, acting on an anonymous tip, the police had found the target rifle that had fired the shots that killed the Mule hidden in the fireplace in Peter Duke's Lake County home. The shell casings matched those found at the scene. The story also said that Duke had left the game in the bottom of the seventh inning, telling Art Kennedy and Harold Pomper that he had an upset stomach. The unnamed police spokesman had no comment on Peter Duke's motive for the alleged sniper attack. The story noted that Duke had been awarded medals for his marksmanship in Vietnam. Duke was refusing to answer police questions on the advice of his attorney, Nathan Wood.

"Wink" quoted "usually reliable sources" within the department: "The police believe that the real target was ex-Cub pitcher Dewey Farmer, who was suspended from baseball following the 1984 season, and that the motive for the attempted slaying has something to do with the 1984 baseball season and Duke's stormy relationship with his client at that time, Dewey Farmer."

The Speaker held up the paper. "I don't trust news accounts of anything. Especially in the *Herald-Star*. They couldn't get a three-car funeral right. But forget that. What I want, Robert," he said, "is your best professional judgment. Did Peter Duke shoot Jess Farmer?" He took a dainty sip from his glass of milk.

I spread my hands. "I don't know. He had motive and opportunity, and the police found the weapon in his home."

The Speaker shut his eyes for a few seconds. "I consider," he said deliberately, "that latter point to be in his favor. What was his motive?"

"Dewey Farmer raped his daughter."

The Speaker raised his eyebrows again.

"Five years ago," Fast said. "That's a long time to wait for revenge. And the way I heard it, it wasn't exactly rape."

I narrowed my eyes at him. "How do. . . ?"

"She practically asked for it," Fast said.

"Kristin Kennedy?" the Speaker asked. I nodded. "How old was she?" he said.

"Fourteen," I said.

"It was rape," the Speaker said with total conviction.

"Not necessarily," Fast responded. "You should get a look at her . . ."

The Speaker turned his pale blue eyes on Fast. "Legally, Robert is correct. And more importantly, morally." He picked up a napkin and wiped a trace of milk off his upper lip. "Is Peter an idiot?" he asked.

"You know him much better than I do. But, no."

The Speaker nodded with conviction. "Peter is *not* an idiot. For one thing, he's a firearms expert. To leave the shell casings behind! Impossible. To hide the gun in such an amateurish spot! Incredible. I conclude that he didn't do it." He nodded to himself. "If he didn't do it, he was framed."

"Couldn't his emotions have clouded his judgment?" I ventured.

The Speaker shook his head. "Peter never loses his cool on the floor. He's almost too controlled."

I blinked at that. Talk about the pot and the kettle.

"And he was," the Speaker continued, "under fire in Vietnam. I don't say he couldn't kill someone. He has. Any of us could, given the right circumstances. But, as Alfred says, why wait five years? Robert, the probabilities are overwhelming that he's innocent."

"All right," I said. "So what?"

"I want you to prove it."

I took a very deep breath. "To do that, I'll probably have to find out who did do it. And why."

"Oh?" the Speaker said.

"The Chicago police have to have a fall guy."

He nodded. "At the minimum, a plausible alternative."

"They told me to butt out and it wasn't a hint."

He nodded. "Let me worry about that. I'll talk to Richard."

He meant the mayor. I sighed. I could guess how Isaac Jackson might react to political pressure, and I didn't want his hands around my neck. But I would have to trust the Speaker's clout. "Okay. Now I will have to talk to the daughter."

"Duke's daughter?" Fast asked. "Why?"

"Duke's. And Anne Kennedy's. In a curious way," I paused, shaking my head, "she may be the key to this whole mess."

The Speaker trained his laser-like eyes on me. "I don't want to say I told you so, Robert, but . . ." He shrugged.

The Speaker wasn't gloating. He was just stating a fact. I nodded. "At that time, the issue was Kevin Duke."

The Speaker narrowed his eyes a fraction and said, "I'm aware of that. Robert, have you considered that Kevin Duke may still be the issue?"

Fast Freddy looked at me and then the Speaker. His mouth hung open.

I leaned toward the Speaker. "Sure," I lied.

Fast shook his head. "I'm not tracking," he said.

The Speaker looked at his watch. Then he turned to Fast. "We have about ten more minutes." He turned to me. "I have an important meeting with Daniel."

"Rosty," Fast mouthed at me.

The Speaker turned back to Fast. "Alfred, I'm suggesting that somebody is framing Peter. Who? We have to think about the unthinkable." He turned back to me. "Do you follow me?"

I nodded. He meant someone in the family, including Kevin.

Fast still looked baffled.

"On the interview with Kristin," I said, "I was told 'no way' by Duke."

"That's unacceptable," the Speaker said.

"Can you arrange it?"

He nodded. "Yes. Alfred, make a note of that. If need be, I'll speak to Peter personally. Now where do we stand on the Kevin Duke hit-and-run?"

"Innocent," Fast said.

"Guilty," I said.

Fast Freddy muttered, "Defeatism."

The Speaker allowed himself a quick grin. "Depends on your perspective," he said. "Absolute guilt or absolute innocence is no longer the issue if it ever was. Can the facts be arranged in such a way as to make it appear that he is innocent?" He wiggled his right hand. "For example, what about the second person?"

"What second person?" Fast said. He narrowed his dark eyes in concentration. "Oh—in Kevin's car. *Well?* What about it?"

I shook my head. "Nothing new."

"Have you considered the sister, Kristin?" the Speaker said.

"Of course," I said. But not a lot, I thought.

The Speaker frowned. He took another sip of milk and wiped his lips. "Check with the witnesses again. Talk to Kristin. And to Kevin again. You may have to go to Minneapolis." The Speaker turned to Fast Freddy. "Assuming the worst-case scenario—and I am—what is our fall-back position?"

"Kevin Duke wasn't responsible."

"Who was?"

"Society."

The Speaker's eyes iced over like a Colorado mountain

lake in late December. "Copout. *Society* is never responsible for anything. We can't peddle that."

Fast shook his head. "Just shorthand. I meant the medical profession and the liquor industry."

The Speaker shook his head. "Too general."

"Okay. Kevin's doctor and the liquor manufacturer . . ."

"How is the doctor responsible?"

"He prescribed the Valium to someone with an alcohol problem."

The Speaker's expression soured. "I see. And the manufacturer? Don't tell me. No warning label?"

Fast nodded. "And then there's his childhood drama . . ."

"Trauma," I said.

"Whatever. His best friend committed suicide right in front of him. Probably triggered his chemical dependency."

The Speaker sighed. "Malarkey. By that reasoning, no one is ever responsible for anything. Hasn't Nathan come up with anything better than that?"

"You work with what you've got," Fast said.

"I guess."

"You're committed to helping Peter win."

Which prompted me to say, "One thing I've never understood—"

"*One?*" Fast interjected.

The Speaker frowned at him.

". . . is your interest in Duke's senate election. After all, he is the enemy. At least, he wears their uniform."

The Speaker nodded. "Philosophically, I could quote Pogo—'I've met the enemy and he is us.' Practically, the differences between parties in Illinois are small and inconsistent. True, we are in different parties, but Peter and I are in tune." He paused. "It's complex. Partly personal. I owe Peter. Partly political." He shut his eyes. "That's all I care to say at the moment."

I pressed the point. "Wouldn't it make sense just to support the Democrat—LeRoy Dumbrowski—for the Senate?"

The Speaker nodded again. "Of course. And in public, I am and I will."

"That SOB," Fast said.

"Oh?" I said. "It's that way."

The Speaker nodded. "Yes." He started to get up.

"Dumbo," Fast said, "screwed us over on 'Casinos for Kids.'"

The Speaker checked his watch. "Got to go," he said. "If Peter gets elected to the Senate, I could work with him." He sighed. "And down the road," he shrugged, "but now . . ."

"Now Duke's whole political career is in the dumper," Fast said.

The Speaker nodded. "And Leroy will be the senator. But sometime, he will pay a price."

"Don't get mad, get even?" I said.

Fast shook his head.

"Right," I said. "Even is a tie. Get ahead."

The Speaker headed for the door. He paused. "Wrong," he said.

Fast grinned. "Get a *head*," he said.

28

The next morning, Peter Duke was formally charged in a drab Cook County courtroom for the murder of Jesse "the Mule" Farmer. Nate Wood represented Duke. Wood was decked out in his downstate legislator best: a green sports coat, blue shirt, green tie, yellow slacks, and black and white shoes.

"Hicksville," Fast said to me as he brushed an imaginary speck of dust off a suit the color of French vanilla ice cream.

The room was filled with reporters. I sat in the back with Fast Freddy, who gave me a running critique of Wood's performance.

"Guy's out of his league up here," he said. "Should have gotten Maury Champion, Creed Champion's son."

Creed Champion was the head of the legislative Black Caucus and a power in Cook County politics. His son was an up-and-coming Chicago defense attorney.

Over the strenuous objections of the state's attorney, bail was set at $50,000.

Then Fast and I went to lunch at the Italian Village, where we discovered to nobody's surprise that we had absolutely nothing in common. For example, he ordered vegetable lasagna.

As we left, I said, "Did you find out about that license plate?"

He snapped his fingers. "Slipped my mind."
I frowned, then said, "Probably not important."
"Want me to forget it?"
Mentally, I flipped a coin. I shook my head. "No. Get it."

After lunch, Fast and I met with Peter Duke, Harold Pomper, and Art Kennedy in the offices of Pomper & Duke, Attorneys-at-Law.

It was my introduction to LaSalle Street law.

The law firm occupied numerous floors in the National Bank of Illinois Building on LaSalle. An elevator not quite large enough for a chamber orchestra whisked us from the lobby of the bank to the fiftieth floor. The elevator door opened silently into the entryway of a classy outer office decorated in muted shades of brown. A severe-looking man with a clipped British accent, dressed in a maroon blazer and gray slacks, met Fast and me and escorted us briskly to a large, empty conference room.

The room was modeled after a jury room—but not of my peers. It was as cool and hushed as an art gallery. The carpet was oriental and deep as Linda Lovelace's throat. The lighting from red and orange shaded lamps in the four corners of the room was low-key. Dominating the room was a long oak table. Twelve chairs were arranged around the table. At the back of the room was a large window that afforded yet another high-rent view of the lake. At the other end was a wet bar complete with enough booze for a cocktail party with Hemingway, Faulkner, and Hammett as honored guests. And an ebony refrigerator. Along the walls, dark-stained walnut bookshelves stocked with legal tomes with rich red covers alternated with stunning color aerial photographs of the Chicago skyline and lake. Standing next to the wall across from me was a large antique grandfather clock. As we entered, the tick-tock was the only sound in the room.

In a few minutes, the others joined us. We all sat around

the table, Peter Duke at one end and Harold Pomper at the other. For someone charged with murder, Duke looked as calm as John Wooden in an NCAA championship huddle. Pomper looked as if he were working up to a stroke. Fast Freddy tapped a pen restlessly on the table. Kennedy slouched in his chair and chain-smoked his filter-tipped cigars.

In opposite corners of the room there sat one paralegal of each sex, with yellow legal pad on lap and pen at the ready. Both were dressed in light maroon blazers and gray slacks. The firm's uniform? At some invisible signal, the door opened and coffee was served by a brisk black woman dressed in a black skirt and white blouse. She served from two silver pots—one containing decaf—carried on a silver tray and poured into delicate china cups.

I shook my head when she approached me. "You wouldn't have a Dr. Pepper?" I said.

Next to me, Fast Freddy winced.

She frowned. "Ginger ale?"

"Terrific."

She got me a green can of Vernor's from the refrigerator and a spotless glass with small cubes of ice. She poured just enough so that the foam reached the top of the glass. She put the can and the glass on coasters.

"Thanks," I said.

She smiled slightly.

Peter Duke nodded at Fast Freddy. "Your show," he said.

Fast took a deep breath. "Right. I believe we've all met," he said. "Nathan Wood had to return to Springfield for a court date."

Pomper opened his mouth and then shook his head.

"He asked me to brief you. Peter, the first thing I want to do is affirm the belief of all of us—I'm sure—in your innocence and ultimate vindication."

"Well said," Pomper said.

"Thank you," Duke said to Fast. He smiled ruefully. "All

clients are presumed innocent. As lawyers, we know that's bullshit, but thank you, anyway." His face got grave. "As it happens, I am innocent."

"Such courage," Pomper muttered.

Art Kennedy covered his mouth and coughed.

"We're here," Fast said, "to talk basic strategy. Before we begin, I thought I'd lay out the responsibilities. Nate . . ."

"Excuse me," Pomper said.

Fast paused. "Yes?"

"I can get the best criminal attorney on either coast . . ."

"That won't be necessary," Peter Duke said sharply. "Please continue."

"Nathan is well regarded downstate . . .," Fast went on.

Pomper sighed. Downstate was nowhere to him.

"Miles," Fast paused to nod at me, "will handle the routine legwork on the investigation. Nate Wood, of course, will lead the defense team. The basic strat—"

Harold Pomper cleared his throat. Loudly. "Pardon me." Fast glanced the length of the table at him, clearly annoyed. Pomper made a temple of his fingers. He looked up at the ceiling. "I have something I feel a need to say. To get it out on the table, so to speak."

I looked at Art Kennedy. He blew a cloud of smoke. Then he winked at me.

Fast leaned to me. "Jesus," he stage-whispered, "Pomper's impersonating himself."

I nodded. I knew what Fast was trying to say.

"This bogus murder charge," Pomper said, "is clearly part of a vendetta against Peter. An undeniable pattern of harassment against his person, his family, and reputation has been established. First, the trumped up and blown out of proportion charges against Kevin for a traffic *accident*. Now, *this*. We all know what's at stake here. Peter is destined to be the next governor of Illinois."

I glanced again at Kennedy. He had shut his eyes. A small smile played on his lips.

"Powerful interests," Pomper paused to gather himself, "will stop at nothing to prevent that. Peter is a victim of a systematic and coordinated campaign of fear, loathing, and intimidation. A political conspiracy of immense proportions." He paused again and looked dramatically at each of us. "And, if I may seem immodest for a moment. . . ,"

Fast rolled his eyes at me.

". . . I may be a target myself. Not for nothing did the *Herald-Star* call me the 'fiscal conscience of Illinois.' I, too, have the same powerful enemies who may see the golden opportunity to kill two birds with one stone, as it were. My commission on waste, mismanagement, and inefficiency in government has stepped on a lot of big toes in Cook County and downstate. In both parties." He glanced at Fast and then pointedly at me. "I don't want to appear critical, but . . ." he paused again and looked up again at the ceiling as if for inspiration and then nodded at me, ". . . this Springfield fellow may be well-intentioned, even competent in his own limited way, but he didn't do too well on the previous matter. As I said, a routine traffic accident. He didn't follow through despite the fact that I gave him some very provocative leads. We still have no report on the alleged victim who, for all we know, might be an alcoholic, a drug dealer, or a serial killer. This is just one man's view— no offense. I'd be inclined to look for a Chicago-area investigator. One who has a large staff and political contacts. We have to counter the resources of the police. I think we need to show prejudice on the part of the media, the police, and the prosecutor."

"Harold," Peter Duke said in measured tones. "I'm the one at risk. I'm satisfied that . . ."

"That's not totally true, Peter," Pomper responded. He pointed around the room. "We have to think of the reputation of the firm."

"Why don't you just put a lid on it, Harold," Kennedy said out of the corner of his mouth. "Let's get on with it."

Pomper flushed a deep red. "Really . . ."

"This 'Springfield fellow' is not even sure he wants the job," I said.

"Just a minute," Fast said.

I shook my head. "If it means that I have to put up with much more of his" I paused and nodded at Pomper, "line of crapola."

Kennedy grinned.

Duke nodded.

Pomper started to sputter something.

"Miles," Fast Freddy said. "The Speaker . . ."

I held up my right hand. "I won't take this job unless I can talk to Kristin Kennedy. Today. *Now*."

"Impossible," Harold Pomper said. "I won't permit . . . it's irrelevant . . . immaterial. I absolutely . . ."

"This ain't a courtroom, Harold," Kennedy said. "Do us a huge favor. Shut the fuck up."

Pomper sat back. Florid faced, speechless.

The room was silent except for the tick of the clock.

Peter Duke gave me an appraising look. "Why?"

"I think you all know why," I said. "She's your motive. As far as the cops are concerned."

"You'd better spell that out," Duke said.

"Okay. Farmer raped your daughter and got away clean."

"He did not," Pomper said, "get away clean. We got him suspended. For life."

"Which means he could be back pitching tomorrow," I said. "All the commissioner has to do is say the word and 'heeee-s back.'"

Duke stared at Pomper, who looked down and studied his hands.

"The Speaker thinks this is important, too," Fast said.

Duke nodded. "Okay. Only if Art sits in."

"Why?" I said.

"She needs someone to counsel her."

"Absolutely not," I said. "That's just what I don't want,

some legal eagle objecting to my questions. I'm out of here." I pushed back my chair and started to get up.

"Let's stand at ease for five minutes," Fast said.

"Good idea," Kennedy said.

It ended up in a family conference. We had to wait an hour for Anne Kennedy to arrive. Fast Freddy left, and Harold Pomper was excluded by consensus. He went away talking to himself.

Anne Kennedy swept into the room. Her hair was back in the severe bun. She was dressed in a conservative dark blue suit and white blouse—halfway between mouse and femme fatale. She gave Peter Duke a look of pure malice. She nodded coolly at me. "Mr. Miles," she said. "We meet again." She turned to her ex-husband. Her tone was irritation just short of anger. "I don't see why you had to drag me into this. You pulled me away from an important engagement."

"Antiquing?" Duke said.

She flushed. "That's none of your business. You know my position. It's adamant."

Duke pointed to me. "Listen to the man," he said.

She sighed.

I made my pitch to talk to Kristin. I ended up saying, "I can't do an investigation if I can't talk to the people involved. It's that simple."

Peter Duke looked at his ex-wife. "I'm inclined to let him talk to her," he said.

"Why?" she asked.

"If he's going to be our investigator, we have to cut him the slack to do the job."

She gave him a withering look. "'OUR investigator?' Frankly, Peter, you are the one who's been accused."

"Okay. Mine."

She reached into her purse, took out a cigarette and lit it. Blew smoke. "Peter, you are many things, most of them bad. Believe me, I know from painful personal experience.

But even I don't believe you are a cold-blooded killer." She adjusted her glasses. "Still, I don't like it."

"Why?"

"I think that Kristin has finally put that sordid episode behind her. This will reopen the wound." She tapped some ash into an ashtray. "Isn't there some other way?" She looked at me as if to plead.

"No," I said.

Art Kennedy cleared his throat. "Anne," he said, "I think we have to do whatever we can to help Peter."

She stared at him. "Even if it hurts Kristin?" She crushed out her cigarette in the ashtray.

He nodded. "Even if it does."

She shrugged. "I guess. Why break his perfect record?"

"I finally found you," I said.

She sat across the square table from me, about a first baseman's stretch away. We were in a smaller private conference room on the forty-eighth floor. The room was a rectangle. A large, ornate mirror decorated one wall. No windows. A small washroom in the back.

Space for the drones who had not made partner.

She looked even better than her picture. And older—maybe midtwenties. She had straw blonde—now tightly curled—hair. Her eyes were aquamarine. As she moved her head slightly from side to side, they seemed to shift from green to blue like Lake Michigan on a partly sunny day. She was lightly tanned, and her skin looked as smooth as Dwight Gooden's delivery. Her lips were a pale pink. She wore a simple, ivory-colored silk dress with a tan belt, a multi-colored scarf, and hose and shoes the color of the dress. Her light-colored purse lay on the table.

She smelled like an invitation to a summer party in a rose garden.

She hit me like a stun gun.

I could see a resemblance to Anne Kennedy in the shape of the eyes, nose, and lips.

I was having problems trying not to pant. She was a real mankiller. Goldie Hawn's innocence with a touch of Madonna's decadence. Drop-dead sexy.

She gave me a cool look. "That's not even a good line at a singles bar. I didn't know you were looking." She raised her eyebrows. "But . . ." She shrugged as if to say, I don't like your chances, but take your best shot.

"You are Peter Duke's daughter?"

She frowned and licked her lower lip. "Yes." She smirked. "As far as we know."

"Anne Kennedy is your mother?"

She nodded. "Aren't I the lucky one? A couple of real winners in the parenting department."

"Art Kennedy is your stepfather."

She nodded. "Art's not so bad. What's with the family history?"

"I just want to make sure I have it all straight. Kevin Duke is your half brother?"

She nodded. "Of course."

"Your name is Kristin?"

She frowned and nibbled that lip. She started to say something.

"But you prefer Kris."

She nodded. "It's such a phony name."

I decided to go for a shock effect, trying to knock the complacency off her face. "What do you think, Kris—did your father take Jess Farmer down?"

"Take down?"

"Kill."

Her eyes changed from blue to green. "Who?"

I shut my eyes. "As far as I know, Jess Farmer's the only one your father has been accused of shooting."

"Oh?" she said, innocently. "The ex-ballplayer. I'm sure I don't know." She paused to give me a devil-may-care look with those eyes. They shifted back from light green to light blue. "My father's capable of anything." She reached back and touched the ends of her hair. "I'm sure that sounds callous." She raised her shoulders. "That's how I feel."

"I see. I hope Nate Wood doesn't call you as a character witness."

"Don't worry," she said. She leaned forward and touched my right arm. "Who are you?"

"Robert Miles. I'm a private investigator working to try to clear your father."

"Good luck. You'll need it from what I see on the TV news. What do you want from me?"

"I have some questions to ask you about what happened in nineteen eighty-four."

She frowned and licked her lower lip. "So long ago. I was a mere child."

I doubted if she ever had been a *mere* child. "I'm sorry," I said, "to have to raise painful . . ."

She tossed her head. "Painful? I'm sure I don't know what you are talking about. Unless it's what daddy did."

"Dewey Farmer," I said. "Jess's brother."

She widened her eyes. "What about him?"

"I don't have time to pussyfoot around. I understand that he raped you."

She got a half smile on her face. "Really?"

I nodded. "I understand there are tapes. And pictures."

"Were. I made sure *Daddy* destroyed them. You know what they say about rape?"

I raised my eyebrows.

"If it's inevitable, you might as well relax and enjoy it. Do I shock you?"

"Yes."

"It was hardly rape." She shrugged. "I seduced him." She gave me that look again. "It wasn't hard. *He* certainly was. So we had an affair." She smiled. "It was quite . . . passionate." She looked around the room and then put her right hand to her right ear. "Bugged," she mouthed.

Of course. That's why Duke and Kennedy had given in so easily. Hell, they probably had a one-way mirror, too. I resisted the temptation to give them the finger.

I nodded my understanding.

"I have to go to the bathroom," she said, gesturing with her head at the small washroom in the corner. She motioned for me to follow. I did. There were a sink and a john. She stood with her back to the sink, reached around and turned on the water.

She was so close I could feel her body heat. If I moved my leg forward, I would be touching the inside of her thigh. Her eyes were sea green. She put a hand on my shoulder and nestled her head against my chest for a second. "Shall we dance?" she said, grinning up at me. She wiggled her hips. "I love dirty dancing."

I stepped back, bumped into the wall, and removed her arm. "Passionate affair?" I whispered. "At fourteen?"

"Almost fifteen."

"You said you were a child. A mere child."

She shrugged and grinned. "In some ways."

"Children don't have affairs."

"Don't they?" She put the little finger of her right hand in her mouth and licked it. She reminded me of Melanie Griffith in the Gene Hackman movie, *Night Moves*. A seductive child. I was beginning to get Fast Freddy's point. "Don't be too sure."

"Your father . . ."

She flushed. "My father—the moral paragon—is no one to preach."

"What do you mean?"

"He's not the goody-goody he tries to appear. Why do you think my mother divorced him?"

"I don't know. Why?"

"I believe," she said, "that the term since Gary Hart is

womanizing. Peter Duke gives it new meaning. And speaking of mommy-dearest . . ."

"I think we're getting away from the subject."

"Hardly." She giggled. "Mommy thought old Dewey was kind of cute, too. I wouldn't be surprised . . ."

I cut in. "The subject is how Dewey Farmer took advantage . . ."

She laughed and poked me in the stomach. "'Took advantage?' Come on. You don't look like a senior citizen."

I stared at her.

"'Took advantage.' How quaint. I told you—I seduced him. And Dewey wasn't my first. And I'll tell you something else. I think Peter was jealous."

I let that sink in for a moment. "You mean . . ."

She nodded.

Jesus. "Did he ever. . . ?"

She shrugged. "That's for me to know and you to find out. But his more than fatherly interest in me was one of the reasons mother tried to keep Peter from seeing me. Peter is *not* a nice man. He killed lots of people in 'Nam. So you see, I really don't know if Peter shot Dewey's brother or not, but he was capable of it."

I decided to change directions. "How close are you to Kevin?"

She shrugged. "Average, considering we mostly lived in different homes. And different worlds. His is chemically induced. I prefer a natural high."

"You were with him the day of the hit-and-run accident?"

She nodded. "Briefly."

"In a bar?"

She nodded.

"How was he?"

"No different from usual."

"Which means?"

"Stoned. He was always stoned. It was just a matter of time."

"You let him drive off alone?"

"Who's to stop him?"

"He *was* alone?"

"Sure."

"You didn't go along?"

"Who told—no, I didn't."

"What did you do?"

"I don't remember. Probably went off with some friends. Tell the truth, I got a little blasted myself."

"Can you shoot?"

She frowned, then tossed her hair back and said, "Depends on the target."

"In May, you left school, didn't tell your parents where you were going, and went to Florida."

She bit her lower lip. "Yes. So what?"

"Why?"

"To blow off school. Work on my tan." She moved a fraction closer to me. "I don't want to talk about that."

"Who was the man?"

She shook her head. "I don't know what you're talking about." She leaned forward again.

"The man in Florida."

"There was no *man* in Florida. Just boys. I just went down to Sarasota. Laid around on the beach."

"I'll bet. What about Tampa? The Red Lobster."

"Red Lobster?" She inched forward. "Can you see me in a Red Lobster?"

"You lit up in the nonsmoking section."

She got a look of revulsion on her face. "I don't smoke. Filthy habit."

"The drink-throwing incident?"

"What drink-throwing incident?" She inched forward.

I tried to retreat and bumped up against the wall again. She put her arms around me and tried to pull my face down. I resisted, but she was very determined. Our lips were about three inches apart when Harold Pomper burst into the room.

"Caught you red-handed," he huffed.

"Wrong appendage," I said.

29

Pomper stood in the middle of the small room, hands on ample hips, staring accusingly at Kristin and me. She leaned in even closer to me, half turned and batted her eyes at him. He huffed and puffed some more. "What do you think you're doing?" he demanded.

I shrugged. "Gentlemen do not bust in on other people's conversations," I said.

"Some conversation. Kristin, I'm shocked."

"Harold, you're such a prude," she said.

"Such impertinence." He pointed to me. "This 'interview' is terminated."

"I was just leaving."

I figured I had learned all I was likely to from her. For now. I walked to the door.

"Mr. Miles," Pomper said.

I paused and turned.

"I shall report this incident to Peter. And the Speaker."

"Man's got to do what a man's got to do."

Kristin laughed and gave me a saucy wink. "Come back and see me some time. The conversation was just getting interesting."

I took the elevator to the ground floor and walked from LaSalle Street to Michigan and then headed north along the Magnificent Mile. To cool off. I window-shopped at a Cubs souvenir store, and then I stopped in at a Kroch's & Brentano's bookstore and bought David Halberstam's *The Summer of '49.*

I didn't care for his politics, but his pro basketball book, *The Breaks of the Game,* was a good read.

I still had the smell of Kristin in my nose. I felt a mix of lust and disgust.

To tell the truth, I was sick of the Duke children and this case. I wanted to get back to Springfield. Short of that, I wanted to lose myself in the purity of the pennant duel between the Red Sox and Yankees, Ted Williams and Joe Di-Maggio.

But when I got back to my room at the Easton, there was a message to call Fast Freddy.

Urgent.

Natch.

I called his room at the Bismarck. "We've got another problem," he said.

"We seem to be cornering the market. What is it?"

"Kevin Duke. He's missing from the Minneapolis treatment center."

"Marvelous. For how long?"

"A few days."

"Be more precise."

"Saturday morning."

The day of the dream game. "And we just found out?"

"Well, it seems he was involved in some sort of weekend furlough arrangement, and they weren't sure . . ."

"Furlough?" I said. "Hell, he just got there."

"Hey, it's not like a prison. I understand that personal responsibility is part of their holistic wellness philosophy. Hey, they made a wrong mistake. What can I tell you? Anyway, they've been trying to reach Peter all day. But he's been in conference, unavailable. As we know."

"Any idea where Kevin might have gone?"

"No. Here's the deal. He was visiting a host family in St.

Paul. Seems some girl picked him up in a sports car early in the morning, and off they went. They thought he was going back to the center. He never returned."

"Did he have any money?"

"Credit cards. Art Kennedy just called me about it. I suggested that you look for Kevin. We need to find him before he gets in any more trouble. Kennedy agreed."

"I thought I was supposed to clear the old man."

"That's true, but this is a more immediate priority. We can't stand any more negative publicity for Peter. Imagine if Kevin gets arrested for some fool stunt."

I sat down on the bed. "Have you considered the possibility that these events are related?" I was playing with the Speaker's suggestion that Kevin was the key.

"I don't know what you mean."

"Well, Kevin took a powder and *then* Jess Farmer got shot and *then* Kevin's old man was—to quote our leader—'framed.'"

There was a long silence. "I see. You think Kevin might have . . . No, no way. Hell, maybe you got something there. But why?"

I told him what Kristin had hinted at.

"Peter Duke had an incelestial . . ."

"Incestuous," I said absently.

". . . whatever . . . relationship with his own daughter?" he said. "I don't believe it."

"Neither do I. Necessarily. But Kevin might."

"What do you think we should do?"

"I think I should talk to Peter Duke again. Alone. How about I use Mitch to try to find Kevin?"

"Okay."

"Get me the name and address of that family in St. Paul. And, Fast?"

"Yeah?"

"Get me the registration on that license plate. It's important now."

*   *   *

I was lying on the bed, *The Summer of '49* on my chest. Resting my eyes.

"How's the book?"

I snapped awake, stretched and yawned. "Great preface."

"Had dinner?" Mitch asked.

I shook my head.

"Berghof?"

The old German restaurant on Adams just off State. My favorite next to White Castle. "Let's do it."

We took a cab back down Michigan. I had adjusted to Chicago cab drivers and therefore covered my eyes only once on the trip.

There was a small line just inside the entrance. We talked pennant race. "Cards are hanging back in a good spot," Mitch said. "Lulling the opposition."

"Dreamer."

"If you think the Cubs are going to win, you're the one who's a space cadet. Come September, the boys of slumber."

"Not this year. Oh, I know they can't win it all. This is a dry run. Wait till next year."

"Cub fans have been saying that since William Howard Taft."

"This is different. I love Dwight Smith," I said. "Jerome Walton. Co-rookies of the year."

"Bobby," he said patiently, "never judge a rookie on part of a season."

"Mitch 'Wild Thing' Williams. Lloyd McClendon. Mike Bielecki. Sandberg is starting to smoke. The Hawk . . ."

Mitch lit a cigar. The woman behind us frowned. "In a pennant race in September," he said, "it all comes down to pitching."

"Granted. Which the Cards don't have either. Expos added Mark Langston, and the Mets got Frank Viola."

He nodded. "And the Cubs?"

I shrugged. "Dewey Farmer?"

Mitch laughed.

"Hey, you dance with them what brung you."

"'Nuff said."

After we were seated, I studied the black and white photographs of turn-of-the-century Chicago that covered the walls. A time of innocence when the Cubs won pennants and World Series. A non-Germanic-looking-and-sounding waiter in a black tie and white shirt came to take our order. Mitch ordered sauerbraten and beer; I asked for chopped sirloin and root beer. We both got the creamed spinach, which is the best in the world.

"Chopped sirloin? What would you order in a Chinese restaurant, pizza?"

The waiter brought our drinks and rye bread and butter. While we munched on the bread, I told Mitch everything I had learned. The political side—the assignment to prove Peter Duke innocent from the Speaker. The family side from Anne Kennedy and Peter Duke. The intimate side from Kristin Kennedy. The legal side from the meeting at the firm. And finally, about Kevin's disappearance.

"Jesus," he said. "What a mess. It really is 'all in the family.' What if the media get ahold of the incest bit?"

I shrugged. "The press has already mugged Peter Duke. His kid is a hit-and-run menace. Peter allegedly shot the Mule. If it gets about that he has a thing for his own daughter? That might be the last straw. They'll have to hold the trial on the Aleutian Islands to get an unbiased jury." I took a sip of that slightly bitter root beer. "I'm not sure that little blonde witch wasn't just pulling my chain." I blew on my finger to cool it off.

He nodded.

"Up close, and I'm talking groin to groin here, she could have told me she was Margaret Thatcher's illegitimate daughter and I would have bought it. Now that the ashes have cooled, I don't know."

"Let's assume," he said, "for argument's sake, that the Speaker is right."

"Usually a good assumption. About what?"

"Duke may be a bad guy in the family values department, but he is not a total idiot."

"Even the Speaker has his blind spots, but okay, where does that take us?"

"A non-idiot does not hide the murder weapon where it was found. In his own damned fireplace. With all the water around here."

I nodded. "So?"

"That points to someone with access to the Duke house."

"And someone who can shoot."

He nodded. "When did Kevin leave the treatment center?"

"The morning of the game."

"I suggest," he said, "that we check with the airlines flying from Minneapolis to Chicago."

"What's his motive?"

Mitch shrugged. "Avenging his sister's honor?"

"Honor is not in his vocabulary. He sure took his time. And the Mule was shot, not Dewey."

"He's a screw-up."

"Verdad."

"Here's another thought," he said. "Pork Barelli might have hired the shooter."

"Why?"

"He detests Dewey."

"So does Dewey's whole circle of acquaintances."

"Think of the publicity for his 'dream-a-mentary.' See 'live on tape'—a pitcher knocked clean out of the box."

"He would have had the shooter nail Dewey, not the Mule."

"Shit happens."

I nodded. "The Dan Quayle theorem," I said. I shook my head. "But think of it this way. Pork's new brochure says,

'Come to the Dream Camp, play with ex-big-leaguers, and get your ass shot off?'"

"Bobby, this made McNewspaper—*USA Today*—and McNews—'Headline News'! 'A Current Affair' is probably next. *Any* ink is good ink. The Porker can double the prices, and he will have to fight them off with a stick."

"So?"

Mitch rubbed his face. "I really don't think he was involved. But I think someone should go talk to him."

"Why?"

"All that tape that was shot the night of the game."

"So?"

"There might be something interesting on it."

I hadn't considered that possibility. "Me?"

"You. What about me?"

"Pack your bags."

"You want me to look for the kid?"

"You do speak Minnesotan?"

"You bet."

When I got back to the room, oddly enough, there was a message to call Pork. I did. "Just wanted to remind you and Mitch to get your expenses in," he said. "Unbelievable about Peter Duke. How's it going?"

"Funny you should ask."

I told him what I wanted.

"I can do better than that," he said. "Can you come out to our offices in Schaumburg tomorrow?"

I said I could. "I'll take out a small loan using my Democratic Majority VISA card and rent a cab."

30

"Show and tell," Pork said. "Let me show you something first."

It had been a half-hour cab ride to the office of Dream Game, Inc. The cabbie dropped me in the parking lot of a long, single-story cinder-block building. The small shopping center featured a beauty shop, a cut-rate shoe store, a discount clothing store, video rentals, a computer store, and a toy shop featuring "Nintendo."

At the far end, I found a plate glass window with a large facsimile of the camp brochure in the window.

I opened the plate glass door and entered a small room crowded with baseball and TV equipment. On one wall, there was a blown-up black and white photograph of Pork crossing home plate. Above, the headline read: "Cubs win opener on Pork blast."

Pork stood next to a table in the middle of the room in front of five television monitors. He had a VCR control in his right hand. Four more were arranged on the table.

The pictures on the first four monitors were frozen. Each showed the Mule on the ground behind the mound. From four different angles. The last screen was garbled gray and black lines.

"What's all this?" I said.

"We worked on these suckers most of the night," Pork

said rocking back and forth on his heels. "Can't sleep any-way—keep seeing it over and over. Might as well try to do something useful. I'm a part-time hitting instructor for the Cubs. I fool around with tape a lot. Looking at hitters from different angles. Tape 'em when they're hot and when they're slumping. See if I can figure out the difference. Use split screen stuff."

I nodded.

"Cops asked me to give them all the tape we had on the shooting."

I nodded.

"So before you told me what you wanted, I had screened all the raw tapes. We had five cameras rolling. Behind the plate. First base line. Third base line. Our dugout. Theirs. Want to take a look?"

"Yeah."

He hit the reverse button, and the machine on the left rewound. He picked up a second remote and hit rewind again. Then he did the same for the other two. The last screen remained garbled. "I had our technical guy edit the tapes so you can see what happened from four perspectives. I skipped their dugout."

"Kind of like four Zapruder films," I said.

He gave me a shrug. "Whatever." He started the first tape. "This sucker starts earlier than the others. It begins with the pitch before Asshole got himself ejected."

The angle was from behind the plate. Slow motion. No sound. Dewey Farmer's fast ball was right at Grote's head. Grote hit the dirt, his batting helmet flying off. The umpire stepped out in front of the plate and made a dramatic you're-out-of-here gesture. Mitch stepped between Grote, who had scrambled to his feet, and Dewey. Dewey stalked off the mound, mouthing obscenities—if you were a lip reader—at the ump.

Pork stopped the tape. "Whatta you think? Ump right? Deliberate?"

"Mitch said Dewey can paint the black with his pitches. He threw at Grote. Hell, behind him. No doubt about it."

"Got *himself* thrown out of the game."

"Why?"

"Think about it." Pork picked up a second control and hit the play button. "Dugout," he said. "Normal speed."

The action picked up. Dewey sauntered past the other players to the far end of the dugout, his lips moving. You could see spittle flying out of his mouth. Big followed him. Dewey turned and glared at him and motioned for him to get away. Big shrugged, went to the watercooler, and got a drink. The picture faded to gray, and then the tape began again as Dewey picked up a towel, stepped part way out of the dugout, twirled it over his head three times, and tossed it toward the umpire. Pork stopped that tape and started the third one. It was from the right-field line angle. This one in slow motion. He turned up the sound. Crowd noise. Close up of the pitcher's face—the Mule. He stepped off the rubber in slow motion and stood behind the mound, rubbing the ball, his back slightly to right field. The camera angle showed the shortstop and third baseman in the background. Then suddenly Farmer pitched forward. A second later, the two infielders turned their heads toward right field. Finally, I heard the *boom-crack!* Then in another second, both infielders flinched visibly. A second *boom-crack!* Then they both ducked, covering their faces with their gloves. A third *boom-crack!*

Pork stopped that tape and started the third machine. Normal speed. Left-field line, long shot. This shot showed Farmer, the second baseman, Pat, and the right fielder. The ivy-covered right-field wall, the empty bleachers, the TORCO sign and the buildings across the street. "Watch this," Pork said pointing to one of the buildings. A small puff of smoke appeared. Farmer pitched forward. Then in a few seconds, a second and then a third puff. The reactions of the players were the same, flinching, ducking, instinctively seeking cover, except that the right fielder actually hit the grass. Pork stopped that tape. He went back to the first control.

The next shot was from home plate, wide angle. This shot showed the umpire, the catcher, the Mule, the Met runner leading off second, and the center-fielder. The action was repeated.

Pork looked at me expectantly. I shook my head. "Except that you could actually see where the shots were fired from, I don't get it," I said. "The police know where the shots came from. They knew that night." I paused. "Any way to blow that one picture up to identify the shooter?"

"No. We tried that. Just showed part of what must be the head. Wearing some kind of dark cap. Lost all definition." He pointed the control at the monitors. "Here's the clincher. Back in our dugout," he said. He started the machine. I saw myself. The trainer stood to one side, working on my finger. Pork was kneeling on the top step, puffing on a cig, looking out at the mound. Big was slouched down on the bench, dark glasses down, looking terminally bored. Down at the far end, Dewey was walking toward the exit. Suddenly, he stopped and turned back toward the field. His face was distorted as he screamed at the field. Then the trainer flinched. I had a puzzled look on my face. Then I flinched and ducked to the side. The trainer hit the floor of the dugout. Pork ducked down below the wall. Even Big hit the deck. Pork froze the picture. Dewey was standing, staring out toward the mound. Pork hit play. Dewey started to run toward the field.

"Now look at this," Pork said. He turned on the fifth monitor. "Our technical guy's a whiz," he said. "This is a split screen—four ways—so you can kinda watch the shooting from four different angles. They are all set in the same time sequence."

I watched, fascinated and horrified, as the entire scene was repeated from four perspectives.

Pork hit the pause button.

"Did you see that SOB? What do you think?" he said.

"Pork, you ever want a job as a detective, see me." I nodded. "One, Dewey deliberately got thrown out of the game. Two, he may have given a signal to the shooter with that towel."

"May? *Did*."

"Three, he probably knew that the shooter was *not* targeting him."

"'Probably' my tired, red ass. He *did* know."

"So instead of ducking, he rushed to the 'aid' of his dying brother. Such concern. You showed this version to the coppers?"

He shook his head. "Gave them the raw tapes. What do you think?"

"Suggestive," I said. "Highly suggestive. But not conclusive."

"Conclusive enough for me," he said. "The bastard."

"Tell me one thing, Pork."

"Sure."

"Do you think baseball will lift his suspension?"

He shook his head. "No. But it won't matter."

"Why?"

"You saw it all week." Pork held his right arm with his left and let it drop to his side. "He just don't have it any more. In b.p., we lit him up like a Christmas tree."

We showed the whole dog and pony show to Jackson and Podolak late that afternoon. "Interesting," Jackson said, stifling a yawn. He opened a pack of Lifesavers and popped three into his mouth.

"That's all?" Pork said. "*Interesting?*"

Jackson said, "All that fancy shit proves to me is what I already knew. Dewey Farmer didn't shoot his brother."

"Peter Duke did," Podolak said. "We got the motive, we got the weapon, and he's got no alibi."

"What's his motive?"

Podolak said, "Hate."

I stared in disbelief. "Can you guys explain one thing?"

"What's that?" Podolak said.

"How come—out of all those people—only one reacted like Dewey?"

Podolak nodded. "You know him?"

"Yeah. Unfortunately."

"Well, he is seriously different."

Jackson stood. "Thought I told you to stay out of this," he said to me. His face was bleak. He clenched his ham-like fists.

I turned my palms up. "What can I say?"

He poked me in the chest. I hate that. "Springfield," he said, "I've gotten some calls about you. Telling me to look the other way. I don't like that, you know what I'm saying?"

I nodded. Better get off the Chicago force, I thought.

He turned to Pork. "Since you went to so much trouble, you might as well make us copies of that."

31

"When the police questioned you," I said, "did you get any sense of what *they* thought your motive was?"

Peter Duke leaned forward and trained his dark gray eyes on me. "Yes."

We were in his office at the law firm. Also on the fiftieth floor. The window was smaller than the one in the conference room, but he still had a terrific lake view. Today it was an almost ocean-like deep blue in the midmorning.

On his desk there was a large color photo of him, George Bush, and the Guv at some campaign event in the Palmer House. Duke was holding Bush's right arm up in a gesture of triumph. Next to that was a color photo of Duke alone with the Gipper. A third picture showed Duke in combat fatigues with his unit in Vietnam.

On one of the paneled walls were crossed hunting rifles. On another, the head and antlers of a deer.

"And?"

He turned his right hand back and forth. "From their line of questions, I gather I was supposed to be avenging my daughter's honor." He drew a deep breath. "They didn't bother to explain why I waited five years."

"About that," I said. I paused. How to say this? "Your daughter says you were jealous of Dewey Farmer. In more than just a fatherly way."

He leaned back in his chair, face impassive, and sighed. "I'm not surprised she'd say something like that." He tilted back in his blue leather chair. "It's my fault," he said.

"What is?"

"Everything. Kristin. And Kevin, for that matter." He looked at me as though I were a constituent and he was explaining a difficult vote. "I've given my life—first, to my country, then, to my law practice, and finally, to public service. In the process, I cheated on my family. Families. Literally and figuratively. And paid a price. Two divorces. Frankly, lots of other women." He shrugged. "I've rationalized that it was part of the life-style. I wasn't a good parent to either Kristin or Kevin. I came into their lives for fifteen minutes of photo ops and meaningless chatter once a week. They both resent the hell out of me, and I can't really blame them. Then in eighty-four, I brought that animal into our home. That was unforgivable. He was a bad influence on both my children."

"Dewey Farmer?"

He nodded. "Of course. It was so heady—to be around a so-called team of destiny. You had to be here. I got caught up in the hysteria. I hope I've learned my lesson. I've been biding my time, waiting to run for governor for a decade. Now I've got my chance, and I'm reaping the whirlwind." He smiled bitterly. "As they say, what goes around, comes around."

"I don't know quite how to ask this . . ."

He looked me squarely in the eye. "I never laid a glove on Kristin. I swear to you."

"Why would she make such a suggestion?"

He rocked back in his chair. "Spite. She was my kitten when she was young. Then it seemed I didn't see her until she was thirteen or so. I think she hates me for that." His eyes got remote. "She was a knockout even then. I won't say . . ." He stopped.

"Did she have any reason to suppose. . . ?"

He nodded. "Yeah, she did . . . does." He turned his hand over again. "Women have some sixth sense about stuff like that. She's damned sexy. I can't say I never—like Jimmy Carter—lusted in my heart for her. But it never happened. Never, ever."

"The Speaker believes you've been framed."

He nodded. "He's right." He turned and looked out the window. "The Speaker is loyal—even to the opposition."

"You go way back?"

He nodded. I leaned toward him. "Let's face it. If it's a frame, it must be someone close to you."

He swiveled to me, frowning. "Explain."

"The rifle in your fireplace. Who put it there?"

"I see what you mean."

"You must have thought about this."

He nodded, warily.

"Look, on the morning of the game, Kevin split from the family he was supposed to be spending the weekend with in St. Paul. A blonde girl picked him up. Could Kevin have been the sniper?"

He narrowed his eyes. His composure was unbelievable. He shook his head. "I can't believe Kevin would do such a thing. He's an addict—reckless, careless, impulsive—but he's not a cold-blooded killer."

"Did he have the ability to put three shots into someone at two hundred yards?"

"Easily. If he was sober. I trained him."

"Any idea where he might be now?"

A faint shadow crossed his face. He leaned forward and stared directly at me. "No."

"Could the girl who picked him up have been Kristin?"

He nodded. "Could have. She has a car of her own. She's also been a bad influence on him. But my children would never plot to frame me. That's too outrageous."

"What about Anne?"

He thought. "No." He paused and turned away again.

"Listen, don't worry too much about this bullshit murder charge."

I shook my head in wonder. "'Bullshit?' Don't 'WORRY'?".

He nodded. "You may have wondered why I wasn't more concerned the other day. Frankly, had I been concerned, I would have taken Harold's suggestion of replacing Nate. Don't get me wrong. It's not my faith in the system. I have an airtight alibi. I just don't want to have to use it."

I sighed. "A woman?"

He sat silent.

"Who?" I thought for a moment. "Anne Kennedy?"

He looked amused. "No chance. She hates my guts. You could see that." He turned his right hand over a couple of times. "Just a bimbo. But she is married. She'll testify if she has to."

I should have known. "You're taking a beating in the media."

"Yeah, but everything has its upside."

"Oh?"

"Think what it's doing for my name recognition downstate."

Mitch called from Minneapolis. "He didn't take a plane," he said. "I even checked charters."

"Try the trains and buses."

"Right."

"Any description of the girl who picked him up?"

"Yeah. Long blonde hair. Big sunglasses. Fancy car. Smoked like a chimney."

"Kristin Kennedy?"

"Possible."

"How long does it take to drive from Minneapolis to Chicago?"

"If you pushed it, eight hours. What do you want me to do after I finish here?"

"How'd you like to go to Florida?"
He sighed deeply. "If I must."
"With a stopover at O'Hare."

Late that afternoon, I met Mitch at an O'Hare cocktail lounge. I handed him several pictures. "Fly to Gainesville. Rent a car. Drive to Micanopy. It's the Payless gas station," I said. "Show the attendant—Billy Jack—these pictures."

"Mr. Mills?" The voice was familiar.
"Miles."
"The detective?"
"Yes?"
"This is Kevin Duke. Okay?"
He was whispering.
I had been lying on my bed at the Easton in the early evening, absorbed in *The Summer of '49*. I was finding out that Tommy Henrich and Ellis Kinder were the real heroes of the '49 pennant race when the phone had rung.
Now I sat up and took a deep breath and shifted the phone to my other ear. "Okay. What do you want?"
"I need to see you. Okay? I can clear my father. He had nothing to do with the shooting. I can prove it."
"Did you do it?"
"Oh, man . . ."
"Why are you whispering?"
"So *they* won't hear. Okay?"
"Who's 'they'?"
Silence.
Then he said, "There's something else."
"What?"
"The accident. I lied. I wasn't driving."
"Who was?"
More silence.
"Kristin?"
He didn't say anything.

I took that for assent. "Where are you?"

"Wisconsin."

"Lake Geneva?"

"Yes. Well, actually, Lake Como."

"Tell me how to get there."

"Take the Edens Expressway."

"Which one is that?"

He sighed. "Interstate ninety-four. North. Okay? Toward Milwaukee. Get off at Kenosha. Highway Fifty west to Lake Geneva. Drive through town. Stay on Fifty. About three miles, you'll see a sign for the French Country Inn. Okay? When you get to the inn, turn right. Go about one and a half miles. The cottage is on the lake. Redwood. Peter Duke on the mailbox. You can't miss it, okay? There's a large maple in front and a flag pole too."

I heard background noise through the phone.

"Got to go. Please hurry. Okay?"

In the Loop, I rented a Chevy Cavalier, using the Democratic Party's VISA card. I had a feeling I was approaching even the Speaker's credit limit. Big drops of rain hit my windshield as I pulled into the Loop traffic. I fought my escalating impatience as I inched my way through downtown to the expressway.

I immediately got caught in a major traffic jam. Repairs had closed the expressway to one lane. The single open lane continually had to merge with traffic from busy streets leading onto the expressway. As I drove, jagged bolts of lightning split the sky. Rain poured down.

Finally, the expressway widened to two lanes of traffic. Off on the other side of the expressway, I saw flashing red and blue lights. A state police car was stopped behind an old car, and a small drama was being played out. Two black men were up against the side of the old car. One of the cops was holding a huge handgun against the head of one of the blacks. The second was patting down the other black. More police cars were approaching.

Honk! Honk! A semi roared by me.

Gaping at the scene, I had drifted into the middle lane. When I finally cleared the construction, I had to stop to pay tolls. Naturally, I didn't have change for the exact change lane. By then, I was pounding the wheel in frustration.

When I reached I-94, I drove at a steady 75 miles an hour through a dense downpour. When I got off I-94 and onto 50, the road was hilly with lots of blind curves. I got caught behind a slow-moving van. Finally, I took a chance and passed, narrowly squeezing back into the right lane in front of an oncoming truck. I could hear the blat of his air horn as he receded in my rearview mirror.

I felt a migraine start.

Kevin's directions took me through Lake Geneva—a tourist town of about 5,000—sitting on the lake. The rain had diminished to a drizzle. Traffic was heavy and slow in the town. I crawled past a movie theater showing *When Harry Met Sally,* numerous antique stores, and other tourist shops. At a main intersection, I turned right. There was a small park along the lakeside to my left. The town seemed to sit in a small bowl with the lake at the bottom. After I got out of the bowl, I drove slowly until I came to the turnoff marked by a sign for the inn. I turned right and passed some condos as I wound down a hill to a two-level yellow structure with red roof and trim. The inn. Then I angled right along the Lake Como shoreline.

Numerous cottages sat on the lake side of the road. I glanced at the clock on the dashboard. It was close to 11:00. About three hours after Kevin had called.

As I checked the names on the mailboxes along the road, flashing lights ahead got my attention. I got a very bad feeling. Eventually, I came to a sawhorse roadblock and had to pull off to the side.

I got out and stepped around the sawhorse and took in the scene.

In the rotating red and blue lights, I could see the Duke cottage with the large maple in front. It was two-story constructed from stained wood. In the light from a dormered bay window, I could barely glimpse a deck facing the water. People in uniforms were milling around inside. In the flickering light from three patrol cars and an ambulance, I could see a neat flower bed with roses under the window. There was a garage across the road. A boat on a trailer was parked in the driveway. A weeping willow tree sat on the far corner of the lot; next to it, a flagpole. I noticed a sandstone chimney at the side of the house that was presumably for the fireplace. Through the damp air, I could hear the distorted sound of a police radio.

A young man in uniform and a yellow rain slicker stepped from one of the cars, approached me, and said politely but firmly, "I'm sorry, sir. This road is closed."

"Is something wrong?" I asked.

No, idiot, this a disaster drill, I thought.

He shook his head. "I'm afraid . . ."

"Is Kevin okay?" I asked.

He just stared at me.

32

Kevin was not okay.

The night before, I had simply turned around and driven back to Chicago. I got back to the hotel a little after 2:30 A.M. and went to bed with a crushing migraine.

When I staggered out of bed at 10:07 next morning, feeling hung over, the morning *Herald-Star* headline told the story: "Suicide Ends Bizarre Dream Game Murder Case."

I carried the paper over to the chair by the window. In part, the story said:

> County deputies discovered the body of Kevin Duke, son of Representative Peter Duke, dead of an apparently self-inflicted shotgun wound to the face in the Duke family lakeside cottage on Lake Como, just outside Lake Geneva, Wisconsin. Deputies had been called by neighbors who heard the blast. The apparent suicide climaxed a string of tragedies afflicting the Duke family, beginning with the suicide death several years before of Kevin's best friend, continuing with the hit-and-run accident in which Kevin was alleged to have run over and severely injured a pedestrian in early July, and, of course, the sniper killing of Jess "The Mule" Farmer—of which Peter Duke had been accused.

Beside Kevin's body was a typed note in which he allegedly confessed to the sniper slaying of the former Chicago Cub relief pitcher. Apparently, according to the note, Kevin intended to shoot Farmer's brother, Dewey. The note apparently exonerates Peter Duke. Duke has been cleared of all charges and has announced that he is taking a two-week sabbatical at an undisclosed location to "reassess the direction of my political career."

All tied up in a neat package.

But why had Kevin called me and then killed himself before I got there?

And who were "they"?

I turned to the inside page. "Wink" said:

Those close to the Duke family say that Peter Duke—now in seclusion at an undisclosed location—is distraught, may seek psychiatric counseling, and blames himself for the triple tragedy that has befallen his family. His partner, Harold Pomper, indicated he will relinquish all his public service activities and assume the full burden of the law practice. Pomper said: "When the going gets tough, the tough get going." "Wink" will present a special inside look at the Duke tragedy in our next edition.

"There are a lot of loose ends," I said.

"Always are," Podolak grunted. "Nature of the beast." He popped a stick of gum into his mouth and hitched up his baggy pants.

We were in a long room in the basement of police headquarters at 11th and State. It was called, ironically, the bull pen. The room was filled with cheap wood desks. All around us, plainclothesmen in shirtsleeves and shoulder holsters sat back in chairs and typed on manual typewriters or talked on phones, receivers tucked under their chins. "Look, it's simple," Podolak said. He popped some more gum into his mouth. "Kevin Duke shot Dewey Farmer by mistake and tried to pin it on his dad. As a perennial fuck-up, he wasted the wrong guy. He got an attack of the guilts and called you. Then he decided to end it all. Wrote a note, confessed, and ate that shotgun. We got our killer. End of story."

"Two days ago, you were convinced Peter Duke was the sniper."

He chomped the gum vigorously and shrugged. "Looked that way at the time. We're not perfect. But when a case is handed to you with a blue ribbon and a pretty pink bow on it . . . a *confession*, for god's sake."

"Typed."

"So what? His prints were on it."

"He couldn't type."

"How do you know that?"

"He told me."

He nodded at the rest of the bull pen. "Any clown can hunt and peck."

"What about Pork Barelli's tapes?"

"What about them?"

I sighed. "You saw them. Dewey gave a signal. He didn't flinch at the shots. He knew what was going down."

He chomped on the gum for a few seconds. "That's one interpretation."

"What does Jackson think?"

Podolak waved his left hand at me. "He don't think nothing. About this case . . . it's yesterday . . . ancient damned history. He plain ain't got the time. He's got three unsolveds and a multiple homicide on the West Side this morning. Tell the truth, I ain't got the time to jaw with you either."

"Okay. One thing."

"Yeah?"

"Who else was at the cottage?"

He shrugged. "No one so far as we know."

4

"Kevin said 'they' on the phone. He was whispering."

"Hey, the kid was not too tightly wound, according to what I hear."

"None of the neighbors saw anyone else around?"

"Not that I know of. You mighta misheard."

"No way."

"Look, the suicide's the jurisdiction of the Lake Geneva coppers."

"How'd he get from St. Paul to Chicago to shoot the Mule?"

Podolak shrugged. "That's two things. Plane?"

"No. My associate checked."

"Hitchhiked?"

"Hitchhiked?" I said.

"Sure. Kids do it all the time."

"Then who picked him up in St. Paul?"

"That's three questions. Who knows? Who cares? He killed himself in Lake Geneva."

"Como."

"Whatever."

"How'd he get to Lake Como?"

"Same way he got to Chicago."

"Why did he try to frame his dad?"

"You read the note. The kid hated his old man for neglecting him."

"I take it the investigation is closed?"

He dipped his head to the right. "Take it any way you want to."

Art Kennedy and I met in the lobby bar at the Drake Hotel. I had called him and told him I wanted to try to tie down some loose ends about the case. "Sure," he had said, "not that I think I can help. But I want to see you anyway. I may have a job for you. Meet me at the Drake."

The Drake was up on the north end of Michigan Avenue. It's Lisa's favorite hotel in Chicago. Mine is the Bismarck.

Which is one reason for the no-fault separation.

One measure of the class at the Drake is that the doorman didn't give me a second glance when I walked through the revolving doors and up the stairs to the lobby. White Shoes was waiting for me.

What did he want? Maybe the Kennedy family would like to sign me to a personal services contract, I thought.

We entered the Palm Court with its large fountain, mirrored columns, and small bar on the far side of the room. We sat on a low paisley couch. I saw my reflection in one of the mirrored columns. A woman was playing Gershwin and other standards softly on a piano in the background. Accompanied by a harpist.

Kennedy's red jacket and red and white checked pants definitely clashed with the decor. A Hispanic waiter came around to see about drinks. I ordered a Coke. White Shoes ordered a beer. I declined his offer of a cigar.

"Doesn't seem like your kind of place," I said to make conversation.

"Why I like it. What did you want to talk about?" he asked.

"Kevin Duke."

"Tragic. Really tragic." He rubbed his large hands together restlessly. "He had a lot of promise—all wasted. Perhaps it was inevitable."

"How so?"

"At least since the suicide. The first one, I mean. Of his friend—Donnie—I think the kid's name was." He paused to light a small filter-tipped cigar. He gave me a calculating look. "Not many people know this, but Kevin may have shot Donnie. Probably did shoot him."

My face must have registered shock.

He nodded. "By accident, of course. Once that happened," he shrugged, "one thing led to another."

"There was a cover-up?"

He shook his head slowly. "The problem was . . . managed. Wasn't going to change the fact the kid was dead. Let's just say Donnie's family received a handsome settlement from Peter Duke."

"You cut the deal?"

He nodded.

"You planned to do the same thing this time around?"

He shrugged.

White Shoes wasn't helping me. The fact that Kevin had shot his friend would just convince Podolak of Kevin's guilt more than ever, I thought. "Why did Kevin attempt to kill Dewey Farmer? Assuming that was his intent."

He nodded. "Good question." He stared at the thin plume of smoke drifting up from his cigar. "What I heard was that it was Dewey that really got him hooked on the juice. In eighty-four. So . . ." He spread his hands wide.

"Could Kevin have been responsible for the threats to Farmer?"

He looked surprised. "What threats?"

I explained.

"I don't know. Doesn't sound likely. But a shit like Farmer has more than one enemy. What you're telling me sounds like gambling debts."

I nodded. "Why would Kevin frame his dad?"

He puffed on his cigar for a few moments. "In his twisted way, I think Kevin blamed his dad for all his problems. His dad introduced him to guns. He kills his friend with the gun his dad taught him to use. His dad brings Dewey Farmer into his life. Dewey gets him hooked on the sauce. And he believed that the reason he was in so much trouble over the hit-and-run—I know this is bullshit, but he believed it—was that his dad was a public figure. The dad who always neglected him. So it was an accumulation of things. But he couldn't go through with it."

"You make it sound plausible." I paused. That's your job, I thought. "What is your relationship with Peter?"

The waiter brought our drinks. Kennedy paid the check. He leaned back. "What do you mean?"

"You married his ex-wife."

He grinned tightly. "Let's say our relationship was civil." He stabbed out the cigar in an ashtray. Took a gulp of beer.

"Peter and I are pros. Not that it was ever easy given the climate between the two of them."

"Not an amicable divorce?"

"That's putting it mildly."

"Tell me about Kristin."

He looked at me intently. "What about her?"

"She seems . . . I don't know quite how to say this."

"Hot to trot?"

"Precisely."

"Some of that's an act."

"Some? Somebody picked Kevin up in St. Paul. A blonde. Sunglasses. In a fancy sports car. Chain-smoking."

Kennedy narrowed his eyes. Then he shrugged. "Couldn't have been Kristin."

"Why?"

"Health freak. She wouldn't be caught dead with a cigarette in her mouth. Calls them cancer sticks. Always after me and Anne to quit."

"You sure?"

"Yes. Listen, I speak for Peter on this, too. He doesn't want any more prying into his kids' affairs. Enough's enough."

"Okay. But one more question."

He nodded.

"What exactly was Kristin's role in all this?"

He sighed. "I wish I knew."

"You said you wanted to talk to me? About a job."

He nodded. "Ironic. I've been impressed with how you've handled this mess. Especially when you stood up to Harold." He paused. "This is difficult. I want you to follow Anne."

"Why?"

"The traditional reason." He took a very deep breath. "I think . . . I'm almost positive she's fooling around, cheating on me."

33

The next morning, a sharp pain in the little finger on my left hand awoke me at 6:05. I took four aspirin and went for a last run along the lake, looking for lucky pennies and trying to fit the pieces of the Duke puzzle together.

I failed on both counts.

There didn't seem to be any reason to stay in Chicago. I had turned Art Kennedy's job down. "Not my kind of thing," I had said. "I don't know Chicago. She knows me. I don't do marital." I gave him the name of a Chicago p.i. whom I had met at a security convention.

"No hard feelings. See you at the zoo," he said, meaning the General Assembly.

I checked out of the Easton using the Speaker's VISA card and took a sentimental cab ride to the AMTRAK station. I just made the morning train back to Springfield.

In the station, I bought a *Herald-Star*. As the train jerked to a start, I turned to sports. The headline: "Three-Way Duel for Bears QB. McMahon to be Traded?"

I certainly hoped so.

By reading the fine print, you could learn that the Cubs had beaten Montreal to move within a game of first place.

Go, Cubs, go.

I reversed the tabloid to the front page. A western Illinois congressman had been killed in the crash of a private plane.

Terrorists in Lebanon were threatening to kill more hostages. On the editorial page, an Ivy League professor upchucked a column arguing that the hostage crisis was a golden opportunity to open a new dialogue with Iranian moderates.

Yeah, I thought, a new dialogue. Iranian moderates. Let's moderate Iran by making it a toxic waste dump, I thought.

I laughed at myself. I had the worldview of a Chicago cabbie.

There was a special insert section in the paper, jointly bylined to "Wink" and Chet Hagan. It purported to be a full account of the Peter Duke affair. It included some facts, a lot of gossip, speculation, innuendo, and near-libel. Carefully attributed to anonymous sources.

In other words, a typical *Herald-Star* hard-news story.

The spin of the piece sounded very much to me as if Art Kennedy had been one of the sources.

Hell, maybe Art was "Wink."

I put the paper aside and glanced out the dirty train window at the Joliet oil refineries. It made a juicy story.

And some of it might even have been true.

Back in Springfield, I dropped my bag at the apartment and walked to the office. When I got there, I found a postcard from Mitch and notes to call Ben Gerald, Lisa, Pork, and Fast Freddy. Mitch's tiny printing on the card was a mock telegram: "Went to Micanopy via Atlanta and Gainesville. STOP. Billy Jack could *not* definitely i.d. Dewey. STOP. Billy Jack's attention span is that of a little orange kitten. STOP. Sorry about that, Clockie. STOP. On my way to Tampa. Then home. STOP. Get a haircut. STOP. Mitch."

I called Lisa at home. Not home. At the university. In a meeting. Of course. That's what a public university is. An excuse to use tax money to subsidize faculty and administration meetings. Occasionally a class breaks out.

Then I called Ben Gerald.

He answered. "Must of been," he drawled, "a hell of an exciting game. Especially the fireworks in the ninth."

"Yeah. Late-damned-lightning."

"I'd like to do an interview with you on the camp and the Peter Duke connection," he said. "For a feature. 'Eyewitness to a Greek tragedy' . . . blah, blah, blah . . . you know."

"'Wink' has already done that."

"But 'Wink' didn't have an exclusive interview with Robert Miles."

"The Speaker doesn't like to see the names of staff in the papers," I said.

"True. Okay. On background?"

I owed Ben plenty.

"Make you a counteroffer."

"I knew it. What's that?"

"I'm not sure this thing is finished."

"Oh? Tell me more."

"Can't. When I can, I'll give you the exclusive."

"Such a deal."

He hung up. The phone rang immediately. "Miles, it's Martin here. Guess where I'm calling from?"

"If it's jail, you just blew your one phone call."

"Guess."

"A head shop?"

"Nah."

"I give up."

"My Mazda. On my new cellulite phone. Bet I'm coming in as clear as a bell."

"Huh? What'd you say, Fast?"

"Get your butt over to the capitol."

I called Pork at his Schaumburg office.

"The check's in the mail. Case you been wondering. I've been sitting here," he said, "sipping a brew or two and thinking about the Mule. His funeral was down in Wildwood, Florida. I went down, even though it meant I had to see Asshole. He showed up half looped. Pretending to be grief-stricken. We almost had round two. Is it over?" he asked.

"Yeah," I said. "When the fat Chicago copper says it's over, it's over."

I called Lisa. She was out of her meeting. "Just got a minute," she said. "Search committee meeting in five minutes."

I made arrangements to retrieve Clockie.

"Oh, Rob," she said, "it must have been sickening. Seeing him gunned down like that. The poor man."

"It was. As bad as Marvel Turner's fall."

Turner was the Lincoln Heritage basketball player whose death plunge in the capitol I had witnessed. "Change the subject?"

"Sure."

"The Wisconsin trip? The one we had to postpone."

"Rob, I can't go until the end of the summer session."

I went to the bank and got some cash for Big House which I dropped off at the Right Stuff.

He carefully counted it. "'Bout time," he said.

Then I walked over to the capitol to find out what the Speaker wanted.

I was manic-depressive.

Simultaneously.

The depression was caused by the nagging feeling that the Duke case had ended too neatly for somebody. Kevin Duke was conveniently dead and was conveniently responsible for everything. And what did I have to contradict that? Nothing but Pork's tapes and my suspicions.

But despite what I had said to Pork on the phone, I didn't really believe it was over. I just didn't know what I could do.

The up side was the Cubs. As I strolled east from the office toward the capitol on this clear July morning—eyeing the American flag flying high over the dome—I was savoring the twin facts that the Cubs were in striking distance of first place and Shawon Dunston had discovered the strike zone. Miracles still happen. I didn't think the two events were unrelated. In June, I had been willing to trade Dunston for a groundskeeper to be named later. Now I would send a letter bomb to Cub general manager Jim Frey if he even hinted that Dunston might be available.

What did I care what August and September would bring? My only nagging worry was that the little gnome, Don Zimmer, was starting to act as if he believed the papers that said he was a genius. Changing pitchers in the middle of counts. Walking hitters with runners on first and second to load the bases. You know, playing the percentages.

Sure, I knew that the pitching couldn't hold up. The three reliable starters—Maddux, Bielecki, and Sutcliffe—would collapse under the weight of the pitching load of a pennant chase. Without someone like Dewey in '84 to back them up. And like the center, the bull pen would not hold. But let's take it one day at a time, sweet Jesus, I thought.

As I walked up the steps of the capitol, I noticed that the cleaning of the statues of Lincoln and Douglas had been completed and they were now a dull bronze color. Like slightly worn pennies. I looked down and lying at my feet was a bright, new, shiny penny. I picked it up and went into the capitol.

Inside, a few tourists had gathered for one of the guided tours close to the statue of the woman with her arms outstretched. I trotted up the marble staircase to the third floor and entered the alcove to the Speaker's office. Just emerging were Nate Wood, who gave me a brusque nod.

Fast Freddy grabbed my arm and hustled me into the office.

The Speaker was standing over by the window, back to me. He turned. "Robert," he said. He glanced at my hand. "I trust your injury is healing."

I held up my splint. "Yeah." I made a sour face. "The Duke thing sure turned out to be a loser."

"Spilt milk," he said. "I was . . . ," he paused to take his chair, "too damned cagey for my own good." He picked up his silver gavel and held it up to the light. "A good lesson."

"Nonsense," Fast Freddy said.

The Speaker raised an eyebrow.

"What I meant," Fast Freddy said hastily, "is that no one could have factored in a Kevin Duke."

"All experience is useful," the Speaker said.

"There are," I said slowly, "a few points about the case that still trouble me."

The Speaker nodded. "Me, too. It's hard to believe that this kid acted alone."

"I agree. For example, how . . ."

"But," the Speaker said firmly, "it seems prudent to disengage at this point and let the Chicago police worry about the details."

"Tell me one thing."

The Speaker nodded.

"Why were you so interested in Peter Duke's election to the Senate?"

The Speaker rubbed his chin. "Insurance."

"Against what?"

"Ultimately losing control of the House."

I frowned. "I don't get it."

Fast Freddy answered. "Remap."

I shook my head. "I must be slow today."

"Today? The word was out," Fast Freddy said, "that the Guv was stepping down."

"What's that got to do with remap?"

"If the General Assembly passes a plan, the governor has a veto," Fast lectured. "We were angling for a cat fight in the Republican Party primary. A primary so divisive that a Democrat would be elected governor. We figured Duke was the man to make that fight. To build credibility, he needed to win the special Senate election."

The Speaker nodded. "And if the impossible happened

and Duke got elected governor, we still had a friend in the mansion." He shook his head. "That's not why I wanted to talk to you this morning."

"Oh."

"I need a favor."

"Of course."

"Lucas."

I frowned. U.S. Senator Lucas "Tree" Courtney. Former Speaker of the House. One of the current Speaker's closest political allies. "Yes?"

"He's coming to town in a couple of days. Staying at the Cap Centre."

"Where else?"

The Speaker smiled slightly. "Go talk to him."

"What about?"

"Better that he explain. He says it's personal."

As I turned to leave, Fast Freddy said, "Miles."

I paused.

"White Shoes."

I frowned. "Kennedy?"

"That plate number you gave me. ANTEKE 1."

I nodded.

"It's registered to Art Kennedy."

Of course it is, I thought.

The next morning, I got the five-minute special haircut at a nonunion barbershop on South Sixth. Cost me six bucks. Then I drove downtown and found a parking place on Capitol Street.

The office door was open and smoke trickled out. Mitch had his feet up on the desk, smoking a cigar and reading *Illinois Issues* when I got up to the office. I had a strong sense that I had played this scene before.

"Little old to be enlisting in the Marines," he said, nodding at me.

I reached over and rubbed his bald head. "You're still my

idol." I pointed to his flowered shirt. "Who picked out your outfit, Ray Charles? How was Florida?"

"Wet, hot, humid, boring."

"Paynes Prairie?"

"Seen one sink hole, seen 'em all."

"Historic Micanopy?"

"Don't ask."

"Such a romantic. I take it Billy Jack was a fizzle?"

"If it came to cross-examination, he would be a defense attorney's dream. Four months ago is like the Dark Ages to him. And I think his attention was more on Kristin's assets." He frowned. "Seemed to remember her as being . . . older. Said it was sexy seeing her suck that cigarette."

I nodded. "Even if he could identify Dewey, I'm not sure what it would prove. What about Tampa?"

He shook his head. "Washout. The waiter who served them is long gone. No forwarding. What now?" The ash from his cigar dropped on the floor.

"I don't know." I told him about my doubts about Kevin's guilt. "First, if he shot Jess, how did he get to Chicago? Second—and related—who picked him up in St. Paul? Third, how did he get to his dad's place to stash the gun and then to Lake Como after the shooting? Fourth, who was with him there? Fifth, why did he call me and then kill himself? And finally, why did Dewey Farmer act so differently from the rest of us when the shots were fired?" I paused. "You should see Pork's tapes."

Mitch nodded. "I'd like to see my bases loaded double again."

I stared at him.

"Just kidding." He lit another cigar from the butt. "I understand what you're saying, Bobby. You're trying to build a case that first, Peter Duke was framed. And then Kevin. By Dewey Farmer."

I nodded.

"And?" He held up his hand. "Don't tell me. Kristin?"

I nodded. "They probably hatched the plot in Florida. But there are some gaps in that theory."

He nodded, skeptically. "You got a lot of questions but damned few answers. Much less proof."

"I know. But . . ."

"*But*—the Chicago coppers say, 'drop it.' White Shoes says, 'drop it.' Peter Duke says, 'drop it.' Speaker says, 'drop it.'" He shrugged. "There's a cue in there somewhere."

I nodded. "Right. I don't see that there's anything I can do. The Speaker got us another job."

"Oh?"

"For Tree."

"What's the little solon's problem? Political?"

"The Speaker said it's personal."

"With Tree, the personal is political."

34

But Tree got tied up in D.C. and didn't get back to Springfield until early August. I met with him at the Cap Centre.

"Good to see you, Miles."

Tree was sprawled out on a couch in his suite on the seventh floor of the Cap Centre, the closest thing Springfield has to luxury accommodations. Kept alive by a federal loan guarantee that Tree had engineered.

Tree was as short as Wood but much more laid back. Along with Strom Thurmond and a few others, he was the last of a generation of non-media-genic senators.

He wore a purple and gold bathrobe with a CC monogram and black dress socks with garters. His thin legs were white and hairless. He was smoking a long cigar and occasionally sipping something amber from a shot glass.

"Good to see you, Tree. What's up?" I said.

"Let me tell you a story. You remember the Paul Powell shoebox affair?"

I nodded. Everyone in Illinois over forty remembered that one. "Powell died up at the Mayo Clinic," I said. "Banner headlines in the *J-R*. Cops sealed off his office. A little later, the maid at the St. Nick found three-quarters of a million dollars in a shoebox in his hotel room closet. Racetrack money, everybody thought."

Tree pointed the cigar at me. "Yeah. Paul was like a

godfather to me—politically. I got involved in the cleanup of that whole mess. That's a hell of a story. The inside scoop has never been told. The money was not the real issue."

"So I understood," I said. "Seems like an eternity ago. What. . . ?"

Tree reached for a folder next to him on the couch and waved it at me. "Something has come up that reminded me of that business. You heard that Congressman Virgil Fiske died in that plane crash?"

I nodded.

He took a sip of the amber drink. "Such a waste. He had a hell of a career in front of him. Mighta made Speaker."

"I didn't read the story. Did the plane go down in a storm?"

He shook his head again. "Nah. Clear, blue sky. They haven't established the cause of the crash yet." He paused. "Might be something to take a look at. Anyway, he represented western Illinois. I've been his attorney for years. I was named executor of his estate. In Quincy. So I went over there the other day. I started going through his stuff. To make a long story short, I found something very interesting." He waved the folder again.

"Money?"

He nodded. "Over two hundred grand. Old bills. Soft money. And a note. Sent me to his library. Must'a had a thousand books. Mostly history. Lincoln collection. I 'member he told me he wanted to donate some of his Lincoln collection to the state . . . I'm getting off the track. I found the book, a volume of Sandburg's biography of Lincoln, and . . . well, some documents, tucked in between the pages. And correspondence."

"What kind of correspondence?"

"Historical." Tree got up and walked over to the bar and poured himself another drink. "Want a drink?"

I shook my head.

"Documents?" I said.

Tree scratched the side of his neck. "Actually, what I found are mostly photocopies of documents. Just one original. I don't believe Virg ever had the other originals. From the correspondence, he was negotiating to purchase them. I'm no expert, but if these documents are what they seem to be—and if they become public—there's going to be a real media circus in this state. Hell, in the nation. I'm talking major scandal."

"Concerning Fiske?"

"Hell, no."

"Paul Powell?"

He shook his head.

"You?"

"No. Abe Lincoln."

Mitch spent his July scouting legion games and playing golf.

I watched Cub games and worked on my Esperanto.

The night before our trip to Madison, Lisa called. "Hey, the Chicago Symphony Orchestra is playing at the fair tonight. It's free. We grab a bite at the Ethnic Village. Turkish hamburgers. Greek salad. Then munch our way to the grandstand. Corn on the cob. Funnel cakes. Pork sandwiches. Lemon shakeups. Want to go?"

Actually, no, I thought. "Yeah, sure," I said.

"Such enthusiasm."

I attended the CSO concert with Lisa and about 5,000 other central Illinoisians, thirsty for beer and culture. In that order. The program included Scott Joplin for the rubes, which definitely included me. Mitch would have regarded it as condescending.

During the concert, we watched a lunar eclipse. On the way home, I turned on the radio to learn that the Cubs had won again. Lisa spent the night in my apartment and did no cleaning.

What an unlikely conjunction of events.

We left Springfield in Lisa's Honda Accord about 8:30 next morning, stopping at the vet's on Stevenson to drop off Clockie. He had given us both his most soulful look of betrayal. We took I-55 north to Bloomington-Normal where we picked up U.S. 51, the mostly two-lane road that cuts Illinois in half from Cairo to South Beloit. Always filled with heavy trucks. Traffic was slow, not only because of the trucks but because they were working on widening 51, a project that had been going on since Lincoln was a Whig. Just south of LaSalle-Peru, we had switched to I-39, which took us to Rockford and lunch at a restaurant in a mall just off the highway.

At the restaurant, we chatted about Lisa's upcoming sabbatical. "I have to get out of Springpatch," she had said. "I'm burned out at LHU. Teaching and administration are getting to be a job, not a vocation. I need to get back to some scholarship." She nibbled on her salad.

I nodded. "I understand."

Like hell, I did. Academic burnout was a world-class oxymoron.

Just out of Rockford, on I-90, the scenery changed from corn and soybeans to rolling hills and dairy farms. Just across the Wisconsin border, up on one of those green hills, we saw a large barn decorated with a yellow and blue cow.

Lisa popped Sinatra into the tape deck. We sang along with a whole set of standards from the '30s, '40s, and '50s.

Lisa winced at my duet with Frank on "That Old Black Magic."

When the tape had finished, I said, "He's a pretty fair country and western singer." Lisa made a face at me. We agreed that the theory of progressive evolution was not given much support by current developments in popular music.

Lisa had gotten her Ph.D. in American studies at the University of Wisconsin in the early '70s. She loved Mad City and took every opportunity to go back.

We checked into a fancy bed-and-breakfast on Pinckney, close to Lake Mendota. Lisa used her gold AMEX card to register both of us.

"Keep a record," I said.

She nodded. "Count on it."

Before the trip, I had insisted on paying my full third of the expenses prorated to our annual incomes.

The rooms were decorated out of the nineteenth century, but I was glad to see they had cable with remote. We caught the end of another Cub win. Sandberg hit two homers.

I take it back, Zim, baby. You are a genius.

Then we visited the bookstore near campus. I got a new Gaylord Dold paperback mystery.

We went for a run, ending up in an area of expensive homes along the east side of the lake. "I'd love to retire here," Lisa said.

"Not in January," I said.

After we cleaned up, we walked over to State Street to have dinner at the Ovens of Brittany, a small French restaurant.

Lisa's choice.

They had low-cal specials.

My preference would have been Ella's Deli for an egg salad plate and a pound cake sundae.

"Madison, Wisconsin," I said. "Key West with seasons."

Lisa grinned and licked her chocolate almond ice cream cone. Single dip. Regular cone.

I had strawberry. Triple dip. Waffle cone.

The crucial differences between us were summed up in Wisconsin butterfat ice cream.

It was slightly chilly in the early evening, so she had slipped a white cardigan sweater over her long, blue dress with a red floral design. I had on my tan jacket, a white short-sleeved shirt, and beige slacks.

We were strolling along State Street away from the UW Madison campus. Bookstores, record shops, delis, tee shirt shops. Ahead of us loomed the lighted state capitol. It has a rep a little different from the one I usually looked at. The difference between the upper Midwest progressive reformer like Bill Proxmire and the Illinois pol like Paul Powell or the Tree.

We had walked up to the Student Union after dinner and had sat outside watching the ducks on the Lake. Then we had bought the cones at the Union.

Now it was about 8:30. There was still a trace of light in the sky. The street was alive with students, former students, hangers-on and serious freaks. A jogger dressed as Uncle Sam ran by juggling three balls, red, white, and blue. To our immediate left, in a small park-like area, five street people were engaged in an intense game of hacky-sack, a game played by counterculture types with a bean bag. They were doing incredible things to the bag with their feet. In front of us, a seventy-year-old skateboarder wearing a bowling shirt and Bermuda shorts wove in and out of the crowd.

We could observe every kind of male haircut imaginable—from dreadlocks to skinheads to brush cuts to aging hippies in ponytails. There were enough earrings to outfit a pirate ship. There were dudes on racing bikes, in orange tops, racing caps, and skintight black pants, and lady joggers in mauve designer running gear. In one block, I heard three separate languages, none standard English.

I pointed to a black guy dressed like a pimp in an all-leather outfit across the street. We crossed and listened for a few minutes. He was a former philosophy prof who didn't get tenure. He was hectoring the small crowd about university racism, classism, and homophobia.

"He left out ageism," I said.

"Madison," Lisa said. "Where the truly weird turn pro.

Every night is Halloween. I just love it." She licked her cone and said, "You seem a little distracted."

"Sensory overload," I replied, gesturing at the street scene.

She stopped and touched my arm. "No. That's not it." She took a last bite of ice cream and dropped her cone in a trash container that had a flyer for a meeting of the Students for Creative Anarchy—no time or place given—on it.

"How can you *not* eat the cone?" I asked. "That's like *not* reading the last chapter of a mystery."

She shrugged. "I don't read mysteries. Speaking of the last chapter, you're not satisfied that Kevin Duke did it, are you?" she said.

I nodded. "At minimum, he didn't act alone."

"Want to talk it out?" She resumed walking.

"Sure."

I told her my reasons for doubt.

She listened intently. "You can't leave it like that, can you?"

"I don't see that I have much choice. If I mess around in Chicago, Detective Isaac Jackson will rearrange my internal organs."

Back at the B&B, Lisa said, "Do you have a pen? I want to write a postcard to my mom."

I reached into the pocket of my tan jacket. No pen. But I felt a penny and a piece of wadded-up paper. I pulled the wad out. Yellow message paper. I started to pitch it. Then, out of curiosity, I unwadded it. I recognized my scrawl. I had written a telephone number with a 904 area code. I pointed to the antique desk. "Don't have a pen on me. There's one." I stared at the number trying to remember the last time I had worn the jacket.

Florida.

In the rain.

She nodded. "What's that?" she asked, pointing to the piece of paper I held in my hand.

I shrugged. "Beats me. Phone number I jotted down for some reason." I tossed it in the wastebasket and turned on the TV to catch the Cub highlights on Channel 9.

Half an hour later, my curiosity got the better of me. I retrieved the scrap and punched out the number. It rang three times. Then a familiar voice came on. A recording. "Meat, Dewey the great ain't at home right now. In fact, he ain't even in the state or the region. Hopefully, if this is a general manager what got smart and decided he wanted to win the pennant by signing the Dewster, he can be reached at 414-233-7675. Otherwise, leave a message when you hear the little beep."

I shut my eyes. I conjured up the clerk at the Holiday Inn in Gainesville showing me Kristin's bill. So she had called Dewey Farmer in Ocala from the Holiday Inn in Gainesville.

I punched the number up again and took down the number Dewey had left on the message. I looked at it. Frowned. That area code seemed familiar. I looked it up. Southeast Wisconsin.

Lake Geneva country.

I punched out that number.

"Who you calling now?" Lisa asked.

"Kristin Kennedy," I said, as the phone rang.

35

Lisa and I took U.S. 12 to Lake Geneva. It was another winding Wisconsin road. When we reached the town, it was just about 10:00. A lot of folks were still on the streets. I dropped Lisa off at the Harbor Side Cafe at the foot of Broad Street, across from the pier on the lake. The circular sign over the restaurant said: "Cakes, Waffles, Fancy Burgers, Ice Cream Sodas & Sundaes, Brew."

And the last shall be first.

"What will you do if she's not alone?" she asked.

I held my palms up. "If I'm not back in two hours, send in the cavalry," I told her.

"One," she responded.

Then I followed the route I had previously taken to Peter Duke's cottage on Lake Como. I parked the Accord on the side of the road about three houses down from the cottage. I could see lights on. I stepped out of the car and paused. What to do? Just go up and ring the doorbell?

I had no weapon other than my version of the truth.

My pride told me I could handle Dewey. If he was there. But I wasn't so sure about the femme fatale.

Suddenly, I felt something cold and hard against my neck.

Powerful arms grabbed me and pulled me off to the side of the road. Spun me around to face two men in dark rain-coats. The shorter one was holding a large automatic pistol at his side. The larger one had his arms folded across his chest. Looking disgusted.

"Jesus Christ," the shorter one said.

That was Al Podolak.

"Springfield, what the hell are you doing here?" the taller one said.

That was Isaac Jackson.

"Little out of your bailiwick, aren't you guys?" I replied.

"We never were completely satisfied that Kevin Duke did it," Jackson said. "Or if he did, that he acted alone. The coppers up here were suspicious about the suicide. It's damned hard to fake a shooting suicide. The note was typed. No signature." He paused to put a large spoonful of sugar in his cup. He took a sip of coffee and winced. "Hot. That's good coffee." He glanced at Lisa. "We wanted to see what would happen if we appeared to accept the solution that was handed to us on a silver platter."

"What convinced you? Barelli's tapes?" I asked.

"Nah. They were interesting. But as Harold Washington used to say, that's just hocus pocus dominocus." Jackson blew into his cup and took another sip. "Nothing you can take before a jury."

Podolak tipped his glasses back on his forehead. He had a plastic toothpick in the corner of his mouth. "Just like we said, the amateur did something stupid and we got a break," he said.

"What was that?" Lisa asked.

Jackson shook his head. "In good time," he said. "Go on." He nodded at me. "How'd you get here?"

We were back at the Harbor Side Cafe. It was close to midnight. Lisa had an iced tea and I ordered a Coke.

"Dumb luck," I said.

"I'll buy half of that," Podolak responded.

Lisa frowned at him.

I grinned. "I swung the bat where the pitcher threw the

ball." I told them about my Florida adventures looking for Kris Kennedy. Then I described the scene at the Madison B&B. "Pulled that Florida phone number right out of my jacket pocket where it had been hiding since June. Got Asshole's answering machine and he gave me the number here." I shook my head. "Talk about dumb. I called. She answered. You could'a floored me." Then I said, "Your turn."

They both gave me cold stares. Looked at each other. Nodded. Jackson started the story. "Most of what we got, we can prove. It's a web of circumstantial evidence. She drove her car up to Minneapolis. We got credit card receipts. Witnesses. We figure she convinced Kevin to leave the treatment center. Ran him back down to Lake Geneva and out to the cottage on Lake Como on the way to Chicago. Told him to stay out of sight. Then she drove her car to Wrigley Field, parked in the player's lot, watched the game for a while, left, changed clothes, moved her car to a side street, went up on the roof of that building from where she shot Jess Farmer."

I nodded. "It's not chic to take the el to a sniping. She shot him on purpose?"

They both nodded.

Lisa frowned. "Could she shoot that well?"

"Peter taught all his family," I said.

"Right," Podolak said. "She waited for Dewey's signal. Got to admit, that's one point where the tapes may come in handy. We were *supposed* to think the sniper killed the wrong Farmer. Yeah. She pulled off the sniper attack perfectly. But she parked her car in a no-parking zone. The folks around Wrigley are pissed off about the street parking at the night games. Somebody called the coppers. It got towed. Now get this. She took a *cab* back to the North Shore. Carrying a long, brown package. She dumped a portable ladder in the trash in the alley. We found it. No prints—but we may be able to trace where she got it. Anyhow, here she is in the cab, dressed in black. With a partially smudged face."

"The cab driver i.d.'ed her?"

Podolak hesitated. "Sure did."

I glanced at Lisa. She nodded. Soft spot in their case.

"What about the car? Let me take a stab in the dark. Red Nissan 300ZX Turbo, license plate Illinois ANTEKE 1."

Podolak frowned. "How'd you know?"

"Just a lucky guess."

He gave me a skeptical look. "She claimed it a couple of days ago. Dumb, but probably figured she had to. Anyway, Kevin's stashed here, but learns of his dad's arrest somehow. Called her in a panic. She and Farmer came up to 'reason' with Kevin. He pretended to go along, I'm guessing. Then Kevin called you. They overheard. Set up the fake suicide along with the note."

"The old suicide ploy. How'd you tumble to it?"

Podolak nodded at Jackson. "I said we were not satisfied. His idea to check all the tickets and towing in the area that night. Came up with ANTEKE 1."

"What are you guys doing up here?" Lisa asked.

"Building the case," Podolak said. "We were surveilling her off and on. Spare-time stuff. Hoping to put her with him. Bingo. She picks him up at O'Hare and brings him up here. In the same car. Perfect." He nodded at me. "Then yo-yo wanders in and almost screws everything up."

"I'm not so sure," Jackson said.

I knocked on the cottage door. "Just a minute," a female voice said.

The door opened.

Anne Kennedy stood framed in the light in a short, pink bathrobe. Her blonde hair was tousled. She kept her right hand in the right pocket of her bathrobe. "Yes?" she said through blurry eyes. She stared at me for a few seconds. Frowned.

I was out of context.

"Gotcha," I said. "Anne with an e."

Her eyes widened. "Miles? The private snoop?" She nodded, comprehension showing on her face. "What the hell are *you* doing here? Was that you who called earlier? I hate it when people ring you up and then don't say anything. Don't you hate that?"

"Absolutely. Can I come in?"

She shook her head firmly. "I really don't think so." She faked fear. "I'm all alone."

"Are you?"

"Of course."

"I don't think so. I have something to tell you. And Dewey. Actually, quite a bit." I nodded. "I think you'll be interested."

She shrugged. "Dewey? Farmer? He's not here. You must be crazy. Go ahead."

"You and Dewey are finished."

She nodded. "Long ago," she said.

"You admit you had an affair?"

She shrugged. "In eighty-four. So what?"

"Same time as Kris?"

"Kristin. After, actually. I told Peter that I thought something might be going on between the two of them. So what?"

"The Chicago coppers have filled in most of the blanks. But I'm the final piece in the puzzle."

She nibbled her lower lip. "I don't know what you are talking about."

"First, let me give you some idea of your situation. You remember how they got 'Son of Sam'?"

She shook her head. "I don't even remember 'Sam,' much less his son."

"Parking tickets."

She looked puzzled.

"It must have been a real shock to you when you got back

from the sniping and found your 300ZX gone. You'd have been better off if someone stole it. And then to be dumb enough to take a cab back to Winnetka." I shook my head. "Carrying the rifle in a brown paper wrapper." I shook my head again. "Pathetic."

She bit her lip this time. "I think maybe you'd better come in."

I nodded. She stepped aside. I walked into a rustic living room with a fireplace at the end. Over the fireplace was the head of some four-footed critter with antlers. To my left, there was a large plate glass window and beyond, a deck leading out into the lake. Moonlight was reflected on the surface. To my right, a darkened hallway. "I thought this was Peter's place," I said.

When I turned, she had the automatic trained on me. "We share it," she said. "Every other month. Terms of the divorce. I'm going to ask this only once." Her gray-green eyes were as cold as the North Sea. "Why are you here?"

"The market economy."

She looked puzzled again.

"To sell my services."

"Oh?"

"My silence. The case against you is strong—especially *if* and *when* the taxi driver identifies you. But one critical link is missing."

"What's that?"

"The direct tie to Dewey Farmer. Your motive. And his."

She glanced involuntarily at the hallway.

Dewey stepped out, wearing nothing but black bikini briefs and three gold chains. "Meat," he said, "what brings you to America's dairyland?" Absently, he scratched his flat belly.

I spread my hands. "The cheese?"

"You were saying?" Dewey said.

"I can tie you two together. In Florida. In May." I looked at Anne. "Sending me down there to trace Kristin was just too cute. Way I figure it, you knew she was in Sarasota. At your condo. You must have lifted a couple of her credit cards. You played her part—that took a lot of nerve to pretend to be nineteen. But then you were an actress."

She tossed her hair self-consciously. "Yes, I was. A pretty good one."

"But you made some bad mistakes."

"Oh?" She turned to Dewey. "Light me a cigarette, will you?"

"That's one," I said. "Your habit. Kristin doesn't smoke." She nodded. "So what?"

"I can put you and Dewey together in Micanopy. You probably stopped there for antiques."

I saw Dewey nod, involuntarily.

"And Tampa," I continued. "The witnesses all say the girl smoked."

Dewey walked over to a small table, picked up a pack of cigarettes, lit one, and took a quick hit. Then he handed her the lighted cigarette.

She took a greedy puff. "You might prove it wasn't Kristin. But you can't prove it *was* me."

"You and Dewey," I said slowly, as if I were working it out now, "planned this whole thing from the beginning. I think the original idea was to pin the shooting on Kris. Excuse me, Kristin." I looked at Anne and rolled my head back and forth in mock admiration. "You played her part. With the sunglasses, the big hat, and the long hair. I think the story would have gone something like this. Unstable Kristin comes to Florida and looks up old boyfriend. They have a few laughs, but then Kristin wants to get serious. Maybe get married. Dewey tells her to get lost. They have a public fight in a restaurant. Liquid gets tossed in Dewey's face. She flips out, returns home, and tries to kill him but kills his brother instead."

"That's just too fantastic," Anne said. She blew smoke in my direction.

"I agree," I said, nodding. "You must have been eating mushrooms when you dreamed it up. I think Kristin—the scorned—was the one who was supposed to kill herself and leave the suicide note and the confession. But then you started to improvise." I looked at Dewey and then back at Anne. I shook my head. "The mistress of improv," I said. "I wonder when the old Dewster might get the suicide impulse."

Dewey laughed. "Like everyone says, I love myself too much for that."

I shook my head. "You better watch yourself around her, Dewey. I think Anne likes to keep her options open."

He frowned at me.

"You can put her in Florida."

Anne forced a chuckle. "Go on. This is . . . interesting. What was the point of this charade?"

"Kristin was the means. Peter Duke was the real target. You wanted to destroy him by using her. She was ticketed to be framed for shooting the Mule. Everyone would have assumed she meant to shoot Dewey for throwing her over and shot the Mule by mistake. The scandal would all but end his bid to be governor. But in mid-June, Kevin had that hit-and-run, which set him up to be an even better fall guy. After the accident, he had already killed once, maybe twice."

Dewey scratched his flat belly again. He was playing catch-up. "Why would I have my own brother shot? My own kin?"

"Dewey," I said, "I don't think you thought twice about it." I tried to edge a step toward Anne. She froze me with a small gesture with the automatic. "Two reasons," I said. "First, it would dramatize your comeback attempt, create sympathy for you in the media, and maybe force baseball to clear you and the Cubs to sign you."

He chuckled bitterly. "Didn't work, did it?"

"I didn't say you were smart. No, there were even better reasons."

"What's that?"

"You probably knew you didn't have it anymore."

"Like hell."

"I know you were talking to Chet Hagan about a book. We'll probably find out you got in touch with him in May. He must have expressed interest."

"A *book*? That's weak, Meat."

Anne laughed. "We did all this to write a book?"

I nodded. "As told to Chet Hagan. Not just a book, a bestseller, you hoped. Fueled by the shooting. At minimum, to grab a big advance. People like to read the confessions of crooks, grifters, and even killers."

Dewey laughed. "I was going to confess?"

"Posthumously."

He frowned. "Huh?"

"Anne might have been the only one left to tell the story."

"What's my motive?" Anne said.

"You hate Peter."

"At least you got that right," she said.

"But you kept changing the game plan. After the shooting, you evidently decided at the last minute to pin the Mule's murder on Peter. When Kevin got wind of that, he wouldn't play ball with you. So you changed course and selected Kevin as the fall guy again." I looked at Dewey. "How long before she turns on you to save herself? You know how it works? She pleads to a lesser charge and gives them you. How long before she breaks down and says you tricked her into it? Or how long before you decide to take your own life? And leave a confession? She works the suicide squeeze very well."

He grinned. "A long time, Meat."

She sat on the couch. "What do we do with him?" she said.

"Kick him out. He's got nothing."

I nodded and turned to leave.

"No," she said. Firmly. "Stop. I *will* shoot."

I believed her.

"He's got enough that this could unravel," she said to Dewey.

I nodded again. "I got a good hold on the end of the string. But I'll let loose for a share of that fat book contract."

"We could pay him off," she mused. She shook her head. "But that's a bottomless pit."

"Babe, he's got nothin'."

"If he's right about the Chicago police . . ."

"They got nothin'. To them, the case is closed."

She thought about it. "No. We can't take a chance."

He shrugged. "Fine. Then let's quit dicking around. I never liked him anyway. Say the word and I'll snuff his pilot light."

36

I was scared.

Make that terrified.

They bound me hand and foot with some rope and stuffed a white tennis sock in my mouth. At least it was clean. Then they sat around trying to figure out what to do with me. It would have been comic if I hadn't had that cotton mouth and if they hadn't talked about me as though I was a garbage disposal problem.

"I still say we turn him loose and take our chances," Dewey said. "He's got a great big zilch." He yawned and stretched. "Zippo. Those Chicago cops couldn't find their ass with a road map."

I nodded.

She shook her head. "No." She paced back and forth, puffing another cigarette.

He shrugged. "Okay, babe, I'll slice his feedback loop. I'll shoot the fucker and dump him in the lake."

She considered it. "What if the body is found?"

"We'll make sure it isn't. Weigh him down with something." He looked around the cottage.

She shook her head. "I'm not sure we can be certain he won't pop up again. I'd rather," she said slowly, "not have him found swimming off our dock."

He thought about that. "How about we drive him up

north, shoot him in the head, and dump him in the woods? We could even bury him."

She nodded. "Better." She turned to me, walked over, and yanked the sock out of my mouth. "Where's your car?"

I coughed. "Fuck you."

She looked at my left hand and smiled coldly. "Dewey, love, break another finger."

"Parked across the road," I said hastily. "The Honda Accord. Keys in my jacket pocket."

"Very cooperative," she said, as she fished out the keys and tossed them to Dewey.

"Hostage victim psychology," I said. "Start to feel affection for your captors."

My smart mouth was in part due to the fact that I expected the A-Team to crash the party at any moment.

And in part to cover my growing unease that the game plan had somehow gotten screwed up.

She cuffed me smartly across the face with her automatic. "Can't have that," she said.

My face stung. "It's amusing as hell," I babbled, "to sit here, all tied up, while you bozos try to figure out how to kill me and get rid of the body. Have you considered dismembering? You could scatter the pieces . . ."

I stopped when Anne narrowed her eyes. "Very bloody," I said, quickly. "Leaves a mess to clean up. Hard to do without the proper equipment. How about another suicide? Overdose of cheddar cheese?"

Where the hell were Jackson and Podolak? And Norm Tucker, the sheriff?

"Check his car," she said to Dewey. He started for the door. "First, put on some clothes," she snapped. She rolled her eyes at me.

Dewey went to the bedroom, slipped into his jeans and tennis shoes, and went out the back door.

Anne then went back to the bedroom. I tried to get to my feet and hobble toward the door. I fell over. I couldn't get back up. In just a minute, she came out wearing wheat-colored jeans and a light blue jacket. She glanced at me on the floor and smiled.

Again, I wondered just what the hell Podolak and Jackson and the county coppers were doing. Maybe they had decided to try to catch Dewey and Anne in the act.

I hoped they had their timing down.

They shoved me in the back seat of the Accord. Sock back in place. Dewey went around the back of the car and put something in the trunk. It clunked ominously.

"Nice wheels, Meat," Dewey said, as he got in on the passenger side. "But you should'a got a Prelude. Sportier."

She drove slowly up the road past the inn. Then out to U.S. 50. She turned west. I kept trying to twist my head around, hoping to see following headlights. Hey, this is kidnapping, I thought. Call in the resources of the FBI—it's a federal crime.

I didn't see any cars behind us.

"Keep it right at fifty," Dewey said.

She nodded impatiently.

In about ten minutes, we wove through a small town I later learned was Delavan. There was road construction and a detour, and Anne got lost for a few minutes while Dewey cursed.

"Shut up," she said.

We drove west for what seemed like an hour but was probably closer to twenty minutes. Finally, she slowed and turned left into an unmarked, unpaved side road. She pulled off to the side of the road and parked.

"What's up, babe?"

"Make sure no one is following us," she said.

Several cars passed. After five minutes, she started the car and continued down a steep hill. At the bottom of the hill, she pulled the car off to the side again. I still couldn't see any following lights.

"What's up, babe?"

She shrugged. "Let's get it done. I'll shoot him. You bury the body. And then let's get the hell out of here." Dewey stepped out. "Get the shovel," she said. He moved to the trunk.

She opened the door and gestured for me to get out. I didn't see that I had any choice. I hopped out. I energetically nodded my head toward the Accord and made mumbling noises. She pulled the sock out. "What do you want?"

"What you going to do with my car?" I said.

She frowned.

"You could set it on fire, but cars are remarkably hard to burn up and it might attract attention."

She thought about that. "Dewey could drive it somewhere and ditch it."

"How's he going to get back?"

"I'll follow him in my car."

"That's good. A caravan. Why not a parade?" I shrugged. "Someone might notice and remember. It's a risk. I've got a better idea . . ."

She nodded. "So do I."

Dewey loped around the side of the car, holding the shovel aloft. "Let's do it," he said. "Maybe I'll just clunk him in the head. Save bullets."

"Dewey," she said. "Put it away."

"Huh?"

"Let's go back to the cottage."

"Jesus Christ."

She motioned for me to get back in.

"What's happening, babe?"

"He has to go into the lake. In his car. It has to be an accident."

"Good plan, babe."

"About a quarter of a mile down the road from the cottage, there's a ramp for boats to be launched into Lake Como," she explained to Dewey. "We'll force him to drink a lot of booze, put him behind the wheel, and run him off into the lake."

I started to raise objections, but the sock was back in place.

"Great plan, babe."

They led me back inside the cottage.

Dewey pulled the sock out and headed for the liquor cabinet.

"I don't drink," I said hastily. "Everyone who knows me, knows that."

She frowned. She looked at Dewey.

"He's just shining us on," Dewey said. Then he probably remembered the cocktail lounge at O'Hare. "Wait. He *doesn't* drink. What do we do?"

She thought about it. "Knock him behind the head—unconscious—and then drive the car into the lake."

He hit his left palm with his right fist. "That's it. That'll play."

She motioned for me to get up. We moved outside again. As we moved back toward the car, I saw a red glow—head high—about fifteen feet in front of us. My eyes adjusted. It was a man smoking a cigar. I looked at his feet. Pale shoes in the moonlight. He said, "Anne. Dewey . . . Miles? Fancy meeting you all here."

Everybody in Chicago goes to Wisconsin on the weekends, I thought. When does Peter Duke show up?

"Bad timing, Art," Anne said. She showed him the automatic.

He took a reflective puff on the cigar. "So it seems."

Back inside again. Art Kennedy had joined me as a prisoner. They tied his hands with an electric cord.

Evidently he had decided to play private detective himself. I could see his sharp mind sizing up the situation. He looked at Anne in wonder. "*You* killed the ballplayer? And Kevin?"

She just nodded and walked over to me. She took my gag out.

"White Shoes," I said, nodding at him. "Doesn't pay to be your own lawyer or private detective."

He grinned ruefully.

"Your disposal problem just doubled," I said to her.

"What are we going to do, babe?" Dewey asked.

She thought for a few seconds. They came up together to spy on me. I, of course, just wanted to get away from the memories of the city. From there, same plan. Art drinks like a fish. We'll load him up with booze . . . put him behind the wheel. A terrible accident."

"Great plan, babe."

Suddenly, the cottage was framed in bright light.

"*Police!*" someone said on a loudspeaker. "Put down your weapons. Come out with your hands up."

About fucking time, I thought.

Dewey buried his head in his hands. "What are we going to do, babe?"

She seemed unfazed. "We still have a couple of cards to play," she said. She moved next to me and jammed the automatic against my head. "Now you are a hostage," she said. She pushed me to the door of the cottage and cautiously opened the door. "Out," she ordered. We stepped out into the blinding light onto the porch. She stood behind me, gun pressed into my back. "I have two hostages here. I'll shoot them if I have to," she said in a harsh voice. "I want . . ."

"*Put your gun down!*"

I moved slightly forward and pretended to lose my balance. I stumbled off the porch to my right. I felt her lean into me. I drove my right elbow into her side. She gasped and staggered back. She righted herself, held the automatic with two hands, and I found myself looking into a narrow tunnel of death.

I flinched.

An explosive shot rang out.

Her eyes went blank.

*   *   *

Podolak and Jackson stood over Anne's lifeless body. "That's," said Jackson, sucking on a Lifesaver, "what I call a real cardiac arrest."

They put us up in the French Inn for the night. The last thing I did before snuggling down next to Lisa was to call Ben Gerald.

Collect.

37

We spent a good portion of the early morning giving statements at the county sheriff's department. A deputy had actually fired the shot that killed Anne Kennedy. At the scene, neither Jackson nor Podolak had been permitted to draw their weapons.

Podolak and Jackson had played it by the book and had previously cleared their surveillance of the Duke cottage with the sheriff's office. After Podolak and Jackson had intercepted me at the cottage, and after we had talked at the Harbor Side Cafe, we had rousted Sheriff Tucker out of bed. He had reluctantly gone along with the scenario to use me as a staked goat.

Now, with the wife of a prominent Chicago attorney dead at the hands of one of his men I'm not too sure he wasn't regretting it. Lucky for him that Art Kennedy had been one of the hostages. He wasn't likely to complain.

We had been questioned together in the sheriff's office. The whole room was as neat as the Speaker's desk. A diploma from the University of Wisconsin—River Falls hung on the wall.

Sheriff Tucker was wiry, wore clear-rimmed glasses, and looked more like a community college teacher than a cop. Until you got a glimpse of his ashen eyes.

Podolak handled most of the talking for our side. "What

244

you got to understand," he now said to Tucker, "is that neither of these turkeys was playing with what you might call your full deck of fifty-two. They had a plan, but they kept ad libbing. They had *no* chance to get away with it in the end. But the very amateurish way they did it was confusing."

I nodded. "I can testify to that. Personally. They kept changing their minds about how to kill me. And then White Shoes dropped in." I paused and looked at Tucker. "How'd that happen? How'd he get by your men?"

He gave me a look of mild reproach and shrugged. "Damned if I know. My boys musta thought he was a resident." He leaned back in his swivel chair. "We didn't want to cause a ruckus. Good thing they brought you back from the scenic tour. We were hanging back—not wanting to get spotted—and lost you the first go around. At the detour in Delavan." He shook his head. "How I ever agreed to go along with . . ."

"Yeah," Lisa said. "I was about to spaz."

"Got results," Jackson said.

Tucker looked at him and nodded. "Saved us the cost of one trial." He took several seconds to light a corncob pipe and turned to Podolak. "Tell me how you see it."

Podolak took off his glasses. "Anne Kennedy and Dewey Farmer had an affair back in eighty-four. Dewey was set to try a comeback with the Cubs. He called his old flame, Anne, to let her know he might be back. But he soon realized he didn't have the right stuff. We'll probably find out some high school kids were tattooing him down in Ocala. He was out of shape and his arm was shot. He could throw hard for about six pitches. Dewey called Anne with the bad news. She despised her former husband. She cooked up the plan. Dewey and Anne got together in Florida in June. With Anne disguised as her daughter, Kristin. To make plans to ruin Peter Duke and create incidents that would make Dewey a good bet to get a fat book contract with a Chicago sportswriter named Chet Hagan. The voodoo doll. The car that almost hit Dewey."

Tucker frowned and asked, "Why did she pretend to be her daughter? That still doesn't make sense to me."

Podolak sighed. "To put the frame on her."

Lisa gasped. "Her own daughter? I don't buy that."

Podolak rubbed his face. "Lady," he said patiently, "I've seen fathers rape their three-year-old daughters. I've seen mothers smother their infant sons 'cause they weren't girls. The most brutal crimes I've ever seen have been family. Much worse than framing a daughter. Face it, Anne Kennedy was not a nice person."

"But those people were crazy," Lisa said.

"Do you think she was sane?" He glanced at me. "So they shifted to Kevin Duke, then to Peter Duke, and finally back to Kevin. Kevin had this hit-and-run and got put in the treatment center in Minneapolis. Anne probably goes— hey—maybe we can muddy the waters even more." He paused. "She was very into improv and options. She took the quick trip to the Twin Cities and brought Kevin down here as a backup. Then he heard about his dad's situation and called Miles. They overheard. Exit Kevin."

"She killed her own son?" Tucker had asked.

"He was not *her* son," I said. "Duke's second wife. But in Anne's eyes, he was worthless anyway."

"But she did so many stupid things," Tucker said. "Leaving the car where it might get towed. Taking a cab. Meeting up here with Dewey so soon."

"That's exactly our point," I interjected.

"You say she faked a try on Dewey in Chicago?" Tucker asked.

I nodded. "Hit-and-run."

"Any proof of that?"

I rolled my hand over and back.

"Would you like to explain all this to a jury?" Lisa said.

"No way," Podolak said.

Back in the bull pen at the Chicago police station, Lisa asked, "What will happen now?"

Podolak took off his glasses and wiped them on his shirt sleeve. "We'll fight over jurisdiction of Dewey. I think we'll lose. I'm not sure I care."

"You might go in the dumper?" I said.

"Never."

"But you don't look forward to trying Dewey as an accomplice in the sniping of his own brother?"

"Not when the Wisconsin coppers have a kidnapping beef and a potential murder charge up there. And all I got are videotapes."

On the drive back to Springfield, I said, "Sorry about the vacation."

Lisa nodded. "Doesn't matter. I have so much to do to get ready for Oxford." She was sitting without her seat belt on, reading a new bio of Faulkner, and taking copious notes.

I popped in one of my tapes. Fifties rock. Buddy Holly and the Crickets. "That'll be the da-ay-ay when I die," I sang. Took my hands off the wheel and played the air guitar. The car stayed right on course.

Lisa grinned at me. "Watch the road. You know, there's nothing more ridiculous," she said, "than a grown man singing kiddy rock from the fifties—out of tune. Out of time."

"Lisa," I said, "what are we going to do?"

"About what?"

"Us. This no-fault business."

She sighed. "There's nothing to be done."

I made my final report to the Speaker and Fast Freddy in the Speaker's office.

"Hard to believe," the Speaker said. "I've known Anne Kennedy for years. Never particularly liked her—or disliked her. I wouldn't have thought she had the capacity for this combination of murderousness, deviousness, and stupidity."

I nodded. "There was a lot of hate there. I think she saw Peter getting closer to the brass ring, and she couldn't stand it."

"Dewey Farmer?"

"Dumb and mean."

"What will happen to him?"

"My best guess is that he will serve some time but not enough. Might make a bundle off a book. *Inside Dewey Farmer.*"

"Frightening thought." He shook his head. "But life's never been fair."

"Did you ever learn anything about the second person in Kevin's car?" the Speaker asked.

"You don't want to know. Trust me."

He nodded.

"What about Peter Duke?" I asked.

"Don't ask," Fast Freddy said.

The Speaker sighed. "Retiring from politics. To spend more time with his surviving child, Kris."

Oh.

Oh, oh.

Fast Freddy looked up from his yellow legal pad. "Have you talked to Tree?"

"Yes."

"What's it about?" Fast asked.

The Speaker frowned. "Alfred, it's personal."

I said, "I don't know yet. Exactly."

Fast looked at me in disbelief. "I thought we gave this to you a month ago."

"Alfred . . ."

But Fast Freddy was not to be denied. "Miles, I can sum up your performance so far in two words."

I waited.

"Un-believable."

It was the last day of August. Chicago wasn't big enough for both of them. Ditka had traded McMahon to San Diego. The Cubs were in first, but their lead was slipping fast as the pitching fell apart. Zimmer was making more trips to the mound than an Indian archaeologist. Lisa was off in Oxford, Mississippi, studying Faulkner. Dewey Farmer was out on bail.

Mitch and I were driving west on 136 toward Nauvoo, the former Mormon settlement on the Mississippi. Tree had asked us to do a background check on a guy named Joe Smith, who had somehow run across this explosive material on Lincoln.

"Cubs can't hold on," Mitch said. "White Rat will outfox the Gerbil."

Translation: Whitey Herzog will outthink Don Zimmer in the big games.

I grinned. "Don't care. They've given me a great summer. I thought they'd lose a hundred games."

"You care." He held up a piece of paper. "Got a letter from Pork," he said.

"Oh?"

"He's starting a camp in Florida. Sixty-four Cardinals and Yankees. January. He's invited you and me to coach. Want to sign up?"

I held up my crooked left little finger. "Check this out. I drove in the tying run? At the sacrifice of my body?"

He nodded. "You're saying?"

"Call Harold Pomper. I want to renegotiate my contract."